The Putney Bridge Killer

ALSO BY BIBA PIERCE

DCI ROB MILLER MYSTERIES
Book 1: The Thames Path Killer
Book 2: The West London Murders
Book 3: The Bisley Wood Murders
Book 4: The Box Hill Killer
Book 5: The South Bank Murders
Book 6: The Soho Killer
Book 7: The Marlow Murders
Book 8: The Putney Bridge Killer

THE PUTNEY BRIDGE KILLER

BIBA PEARCE

JOFFE BOOKS

Joffe Books, London
www.joffebooks.com

First published in Great Britain in 2025

© Biba Pearce

This book is a work of fiction. Names, characters, businesses, organisations, places and events are either the product of the author's imagination or are used fictitiously. Any resemblance to actual persons, living or dead, events or locales is entirely coincidental. The spelling used is British English except where fidelity to the author's rendering of accent or dialect supersedes this. The right of Biba Pearce to be identified as author of this work has been asserted in accordance with the Copyright, Designs and Patents Act 1988.

No part of this book may be used or reproduced in any manner for the purpose of training artificial intelligence technologies or systems. In accordance with Article 4(3) of the Digital Single Market Directive 2019/790, Joffe Books expressly reserves this work from the text and data mining exception.

Cover art by Nebojša Zorić

ISBN: 978-1-80573-107-8

CHAPTER 1

Lucy Andrews stood under the awning on the pier at Chelsea Harbour, waiting for the ferry to dock. Rain pelted the worn, wooden boards, spray bouncing upwards like tiny glittering geysers. Fat droplets pockmarked the surface of the water, sending ripples flailing outwards, but despite this, it wasn't that cold. April showers never were — fleeting downpours that soaked you to the bone in moments if you were caught unawares, as so many people were, but tinged with a muggy hint of spring. Lucy had learned the hard way to always carry an umbrella with her. This was England, after all.

She heard a series of grunts and the distinctive sound of oars rattling against the catch as an eight boat of rowers came heaving past. Even in this weather they trained, but then the famous Oxford–Cambridge Boat Race was coming up. Was it this weekend or next? She couldn't remember. Large, colourful posters adorned the wharf area in Putney, but she hadn't looked closely enough at the date.

Finally, the ferry appeared and performed an elaborate docking manoeuvre as it slid into place against the pier. The engines chugged, coughing up river water as it ground to a halt, and then the security gate opened and a smattering of passengers disembarked. More were waiting to board. The ferry came from Canary Wharf via the City, stopping at Chelsea Harbour and then Wandsworth, before ending its journey at Putney.

It was an unusual way to commute to and from London, but one of the better ones in her opinion. Besides, it suited her down to the ground since she worked at the Design Centre, a stone's throw from the harbour.

The ferry took less than half an hour, and she disembarked at Putney Pier. From here, it was a short distance to the redeveloped wharf area where she was meeting Justin. She walked along Lower Richmond Road until she came to the bridge. Pausing at the busy intersection that marked the start of Putney High Street, she checked her phone.

Perfect timing. They'd agreed to meet at eight o'clock, and it was ten to eight now. She smiled as she thought about her fiancé. Who would have thought things would have worked out like this — for both of them. After everything that had happened . . .

The traffic lights changed and she crossed the street, then walked through the arches and past the centuries-old St Mary's Church, its ancient spire piercing the gloomy, grey sky, a comforting presence standing sentinel over the bustling high street.

Beyond the church, the wharf area opened up into a square lined with bars and restaurants, although it wasn't very busy this evening. The weather, and it being a Wednesday, meant the usual after-work drinkers were saving themselves until closer to the weekend, and apart from a waiter hurrying to his shift, she didn't see anyone else about.

Coppa, the bar she was meeting Justin at, was further down, on the far side of the wharf. She thought longingly of the crackling fireplace and his warm embrace, such a pleasure after a long day in the showroom.

Tugging her trench coat around her and angling her umbrella up against the incessant drizzle, she hurried past the dark slipway that led down to the pebbly foreshore. The steely grey waters of the Thames were receding rapidly, exposing the rocky but surprisingly clean underbelly. Still, in this light, it looked sinister and chilly.

Lucy was almost past it when quick footsteps made her glance over her shoulder. As she did so, an arm snaked around her neck, while a hand covered her mouth. She screamed but it came out as a muffled yell.

She dropped her umbrella as her assailant dragged her down the slipway into the shadows. Was this really happening? Here? In Putney?

Twisting her body, she tried to escape his grip, but he was too strong, and he kept pulling her with him. Her heels dug into the cobblestoned slipway, and she felt one shoe come off. Then they were on the pebbly foreshore, where it was colder, the breeze stiffer. Rain pricked her face, stinging her skin. She closed her eyes, still wriggling. If she could only get away for long enough to cry for help, someone would hear her. They had to.

They were under the bridge when he removed his hand from her mouth to force her to the ground. She cried out, but only for a second before he punched her in the face, sending her reeling backwards. Stars danced around the edges of her vision as she stared up at her attacker, terrified and confused.

Why was this happening?

What had she done to deserve this?

His face swam in front of her, unidentifiable in a balaclava. That's when she knew she was going to die.

Lucy began to cry.

Poor Justin.

Not again. Not her as well.

A surge of anger shot through her and she rallied, kicking out, but he had the upper hand now. Sitting on top of her, he forced her hands above her head. Adrenalin pumping, she writhed beneath him, desperately trying to buck him off — but he was too heavy.

She heard him give an annoyed huff, then he hit her again. She almost blacked out, clinging to consciousness long enough to feel him sliding her skirt up her legs.

"No!" she screamed, but it was all in her head. Above her, the rain bounced off the guardrails of the bridge, metallic pings that resonated through the night air. She was too feeble to cry out. Too weak to resist. He kneed her legs apart and, hovering on the edge of consciousness, there was nothing she could do as he undid his fly and mounted her.

Lucy's head spun from the two blows. Her breath came in shallow gulps — she couldn't get enough air. Disoriented, she lay immobile as he penetrated her, grunting with pleasure, or excitement, or both. She didn't care anymore. She just wanted the nightmare to end.

***

The killer saw she was waning and slapped her hard across the face. Her cheeks were wet from the rain, or maybe it was tears. They were sheltered beneath the bridge.

"Hey! Not yet," he hissed. He wanted her awake for this part, wanted to see the terror in her eyes. It was no fun strangling an unconscious woman.

Her eyelids fluttered, and he grinned. "That's it, darling. Stay with me."

Hovering over her, he stared, fixated, at the fear on her face — it spurred him on, faster and faster until he spiralled over the edge. Once he was done, he zipped himself up and leaned forward, as if to embrace her. Instead, he wrapped his hands around her throat.

"Good girl," he murmured into her ear, as he began to squeeze. "You did good."

His pulse thundered in his ears as he watched the life ebb out of her, just like the outgoing tide. Her eyes closed and her face turned an unattractive purple. Finally, her body surrendered, and her arms went limp.

The killer stood up, looming over her. The excitement he'd felt before had left him trembling but euphoric — just like he'd known it would. The rain was a gentle pitter-patter on either side of the bridge. It would stop soon, and then the tide would wash back in to conceal his crime.

One task remaining . . . He lifted her limp hand and slipped the engagement ring off her finger. It was dull — covered in dirt. But it still had a purpose.

When that was done, the killer took one last look at his handiwork, making sure there was nothing he'd forgotten. Then he walked back up onto the wharf and disappeared into the shadows.

CHAPTER 2

PC Trent got the Dispatch call as he drove down Fulham Palace Road on his way to work. A young woman's body had been found under Putney Bridge by a passerby early this morning.

Putney Bridge! Such a public place.

Uniformed police officers were at the scene, but the nature of the crime meant it had been escalated to the Metropolitan Police's Homicide and Serious Crime Command — i.e., them.

The daily commute from Marlow took him a little under an hour at this time of the morning, but since he was approaching the end of his three-month probation period with the Major Investigation Team, he should probably think about moving to London permanently. Still, it wasn't too bad. If he left early enough, he missed the worst of the traffic.

A thrill shot through him as he engaged the siren and flew up the inside lane across the bridge towards the bustling Putney High Street. Once there, he veered left across the intersection and turned into the paved pedestrian area next to an old stone church.

The team had been notified, which meant they were on their way, but Trent was closer and had been instructed to head directly to the scene and make sure the proper protocols were followed.

Not for the first time, he thanked his lucky stars that the Debbie Morris investigation had brought DCI Miller to Marlow, and he — PC Trent — had been fortunate enough to work the case with him. What an experience that had been. He still couldn't believe the DCI had poached him from Thames Valley and offered him a job investigating serious crime with the MIT. The look on grumpy old Sergeant Willoughby's face when he'd told him he was leaving had been priceless.

Trent climbed out of the car and, battling the current of early morning commuters, made his way to the wharf. The fog hung heavy in the air, the damp chill seeping through his coat as he reached the paved riverfront. Leaning over the railing, he peered down at the rocky foreshore.

There, sprawled across the shingle, and partially obscured by the swirling mist and the looming shadow of the bridge, lay the body.

DCI Miller would want him to preserve the scene. With a start, he realised that the tide was coming in.

This was not good.

Hurrying over to the police officer standing guard at the top of the slipway, he said, "How long has she been there?"

The officer gestured to a large man sitting on the low stone wall of a nearby pub, his head in his hands. "I got here just after eight o'clock. Mr Banstead called 999 about half an hour before that, and Dispatch notified my unit. Luckily, I'd just started my shift."

Trent nodded. He knew the uniformed police had shift changes between seven and eight in the morning. Trying to get hold of anyone in a hurry after that was nigh on impossible. They'd already been assigned their locations and were scattered around the Greater London area.

"Mr Banstead found the body?"

"Yes, sir."

He strode over to the man. Time was of the essence, but he would be remiss if he didn't speak to the witness, or at least take down his details. "Sir, do you mind if I ask you a few questions?"

The man glanced out from behind his hands, like he was a child playing hide and seek. *Is it safe to come out now?*

"What time did you find the body?"

"It was around half past seven. I was on my way to work when I spotted an umbrella on the ground." He nodded to it, closed at his feet. "I was just picking it up when I saw her — lying there, under the bridge." Trent glanced at the umbrella, while the man took a shuddering breath. "Not something you expect to see on your way to work, is it?"

Trent shook his head. It certainly wasn't. "Where do you work, sir?"

"Putney Wharf Towers." The man gestured to the large, multistorey, ship-like building jutting out over the Thames.

"What do you do?"

"I'm the concierge. My shift starts at eight." He glanced pointedly at his watch.

Trent nodded. No reason to keep the man here when he was already late. "If you'll just give me your name and a contact number, you can be on your way. We will need you to come into the station and give an official statement later, though."

After the concierge agreed to go to Putney Police Station after his shift, Trent bagged the umbrella, just in case it belonged to the victim, then peered over the railing, glancing suspiciously at the encroaching water. "How long have we got until it reaches her?" he called down to the officer on the foreshore.

"I'd guess about two hours," the officer replied. "It comes in pretty fast along the Tideway."

"The Tideway?"

"The tidal Thames, yeah. We're forever getting calls about missing bikes and even cars that end up being washed away because people don't realise how fast it comes in."

Trent nodded. They didn't have tides in Marlow. The Thames was always the same level.

He thought back to what he'd learned in the last few months. Their priority was to protect the body, and then the crime scene, in that order. But with a river incident, he had to notify the Marine Policing Unit, commonly known as the

River Police. They were adept at dealing with these kinds of situations and would know when high tide was, and the best way to recover her body.

Calling, he identified himself, explained the situation, and asked for their advice. The officer he spoke to was very clear. "Low tide was at 7.03 this morning, so it's pushing. In two hours, it'll have reached the wharf wall, and then your crime scene will be gone."

Two hours. Trent wasn't sure that was enough time.

"Make sure you get detailed photographs of the scene," the MPU officer went on. "Shoot the body from every angle, so you've got context. That's the best you can do." Spoken with the confidence of a man who knew about these things.

Trent had a camera in his vehicle — part of the crime pack he carried around with him for just such occasions. It wasn't a state-of-the-art forensic camera or anything fancy like that, but it came in handy when it wasn't possible to get a crime scene photographer in time. Another tip he'd picked up from his mentor.

"Once you've done that, bag her and get her onto dry land."

Trent's head was spinning. "What about any evidence?"

"Call SOCO, they'll advise. They usually tell us to gather as much shingle and plant life from around the body as possible. That way, if you find anything on the body, you can do an accurate comparison later. I'll put a rig in the water and be with you in fifteen minutes. We can supply you with some buckets and help with the collection."

That was something, at least. "Appreciate that."

Trent hung up and looked around. People were stopping on the bridge and along the embankment to gawk at the body. According to DCI Miller, that was a no-no. He needed to cordon off the entire area.

He turned back to the uniformed officer. "Let's clear the wharf. Get everyone away from the railing and off the bridge."

The officer's eyes widened. "What? Putney Bridge?" He was young, younger than Trent, and obviously hadn't been on the job long.

"Yes, Putney Bridge."

The officer glanced at his watch and then back at the traffic crawling along the bridge. "But . . . But it's peak travel time."

"I know, but it can't be helped." Trent could already see a crowd of onlookers peering over the bridge, trying to catch a morbid glimpse of the pale figure lying below. Another police officer was standing beside the body, guarding it, but as far as Trent could tell, there'd been no attempt to restrict access. "Get on it."

He wasn't used to giving orders, but he felt confident in his instruction.

"It's going to be chaos," the young officer muttered but took out his radio.

He wasn't wrong there. Putney Bridge was jam-packed with traffic at this time of the morning. Traffic that would have to be rerouted, that would back up in Fulham and cause disruption among the commuters — but that wasn't his problem. DCI Miller would insist nobody be allowed on the bridge. Trent had worked with the man long enough to know that.

A quick call to SOCO confirmed what the marine police officer had said, so Trent fetched his camera from the vehicle, deposited the umbrella safely in the boot, and made his way back down the slipway. An apt name for it, he thought as he inched his way over the muddy cobblestones, trying not to slide on the silt-coated stones and fall on his backside.

He approached cautiously, aware that he was solely responsible for making sure the integrity of the body remained intact. The lapping river water, getting higher with every passing minute, served as a constant reminder that the clock was ticking.

The first thing he noticed was her attire, or lack thereof. Her skirt was bunched up around her waist, exposing long, pale legs, now mottled on the lower parts due to post-mortem lividity. Trent gulped, an icy sensation sliding between his shoulders. He knew what that meant — she'd been sexually assaulted. Her blouse was ripped, displaying her belly, but thankfully one side of the camel-coloured trench coat covered her left breast and pubic region, affording her some degree of protection against the onlookers.

As he got closer, he noticed bruising around her throat and marks on her face. A single lock of her hair, matted with blood, clung to her cheek, a poignant indication of the brutality she had endured in her final moments. It looked like she'd been punched or hit with something.

Trent clenched his fists but didn't go any closer. She was so young, likely no more than mid-twenties, with her whole life ahead of her. Now she lay lifeless on the cold, damp riverbank, her dreams and aspirations shattered by this senseless act of cruelty.

This was the second dead woman he'd attended by a river. First Debbie Morris last year in Marlow, and now her . . .

Blinking — the early morning chill made his eyes water — he raised the camera and began taking photographs. First, at a distance, he made sure he got the shingle, the water level, and the general surroundings, including the wharf area and the bridge above.

Next, he zoomed in until her battered face filled the lens. He took multiple shots of the bruising and abrasions on her cheeks, nose and neck. Working his way down her body, he forced himself to capture every bit of damage that had been done to the poor girl. He kept going until he heard the low drone of an approaching motorboat.

A high-speed rigid inflatable boat pulled up, and two officers in black tactical gear — waterproof anoraks, helmets fitted with comms headsets — leapt out, their wellies splashing in the knee-deep water. The Marine Policing Unit had arrived.

One officer secured the vessel, pulling it up onto the foreshore, while the other removed his helmet and approached him. "I'm Sergeant Reynolds. You PC Trent? We spoke on the phone."

He sniffed back the emotion that had gripped him as he'd taken the photos and nodded. "Yes, that's me. Thanks for your assistance."

"No problem." Reynolds' gaze was drawn to the frail, ghostly figure of the victim. Rugged, weathered, with crinkly eyes from squinting against the sun, this was a man used to the outdoors. "Not good, is it?"

Trent shook his head. "No, it isn't."

The marine police officer's practised eye scanned the waterline. "Correction. You've got an hour at most. She's lower down than I thought. Best get her out of here so we can scrape the bank before it's too late."

Trent nodded as his gaze drifted to the large plastic buckets in the RIB.

Where was DCI Miller? He'd want to study this before the tide came in and there was nothing left to see. Above him, Trent heard the sirens, and knew the uniformed officers were cordoning off the traffic on the bridge. Already, the onlookers had been removed from the wharf and no longer stood gawking over the railing.

"I would stop the river traffic," the marine police officer told him, "but I don't think there's much point, and we'd have a hell of a fight on our hands with the ferry companies."

Trent nodded. That was the marine police officer's area of expertise. With the tide surging in, it wouldn't matter if there was wash from the odd ferry.

"I will instruct them to keep to the north side of the river, though." He nodded to his colleague, who pulled out his radio to call it in. "That'll give her some more privacy." Trent noticed Reynolds spoke of the victim with respect, like she was still alive, and appreciated that.

Since SOCO wasn't coming, and DCI Miller wasn't here yet, Trent called Dispatch and asked after the coroner's transport.

"On site now," the operator told him. "Shall I radio them to collect the body?"

"Yes, she's ready." He cleared his throat. "I mean, we're ready."

A couple of minutes later, two men descended the slipway carrying a gurney. They laid the body bag beside her and gently lifted her into it. Both were in their thirties, with knowing eyes and steady gloved hands. Trent bet they'd been doing this a while. One gave him a professional nod before they loaded her onto the gurney and took her back to the transport vehicle.

CHAPTER 3

Rob got to the crime scene just as the private ambulance was leaving, no doubt containing the body of the victim.

Bloody hell.

He was too late. Even though he'd blued-and-twoed it here as fast as possible, he'd still got caught up in the morning mayhem on Upper Richmond Road. His own fault — he'd left later than usual. Jack had a slight fever and, consequently, he and Jo hadn't had a great night's sleep.

"Was that her? Is she gone?" he asked a hovering officer, pointing to the ambulance.

He got a nervous nod in reply. That's when he spotted PC Trent and two marine police officers on the foreshore, collecting shingle in large buckets. Snorting his approval, he descended the slipway and went to join them.

"Constable, how's it going?" He nodded at the two marine police officers, who glanced up but didn't stop what they were doing. The tide was lapping at his feet, and there was less than two metres of foreshore left.

"I had to move her, sir." Trent set his bucket down. "I'm sorry, but the tide—"

"You did good." Rob eyed the area under the bridge where the victim had lain, now clearly marked by a yellow cone, the water covering the base. "You're collecting river samples?"

"Yes, sir. I called the Marine Policing Unit, who advised me. I hope it was the right thing to do."

"Very astute of you, Constable. I'm impressed." Trent had taken control of the situation and done everything to preserve the body and as much of the crime scene as he could. "Did you manage to take photographs?"

"Loads, sir. From every angle, including close-ups."

"Excellent."

Trent glowed.

"What about SOCO?"

"Oh, I called them too, but with the tide coming in, they didn't want to come out — said they wouldn't get here in time — but they told me to gather as much material under and around the body as possible, which is what we're doing."

Another nod. It seemed Trent had it all in hand.

The two officers stopped scraping. "That's it," the taller one with a ruddy, weathered face said. He dusted his hand off on his trousers and extended it. "Sergeant Reynolds, Marine Policing Unit."

Rob shook it. "DCI Miller, Major Investigation Team."

Reynolds' colleague was busy lugging the buckets to the slipway. "We've done what we can here. The rest is up to you."

"Thanks for your help."

Reynolds nodded. "Your man here did the right thing by calling us. Another hour and it would have been too late."

Trent flushed. "Just doing my job, sir." He went to help carry the heavy buckets up to the wharf.

"Did you see the body?" Rob asked Reynolds. He wondered if the marine sergeant ever got used to hauling bodies out of the river.

"Yeah. Didn't look good."

Did it ever?

"Do you think she washed up here?" He may as well try to glean something from the guy's expertise.

"Can't be sure." Reynolds frowned, the lines in his tanned forehead deepening. "Judging by the state of her, I'd say she'd been in the water for some time. My guess is she went in late last night. Maybe here, maybe somewhere nearby."

Rob glanced down as the water splashed onto his boots. They were running out of foreshore. "If she went in late last night, it would have been . . . high tide?"

"Depends. Low was shortly after seven o'clock yesterday evening, so by midnight, it would have been almost high tide. She could have gone in any time between then."

"Then there is a possibility she was killed here and wasn't moved by the tide?" He gestured to the area under the bridge.

"Definitely. The foreshore would have been accessible from about five o'clock yesterday afternoon to about nine, nine thirty, but the pathologist should be able to confirm. Your man took enough samples to compare to any material found on her body."

Rob jutted out his jaw. "If the water hasn't washed it away."

Reynolds shook his head. "Nah, there's always something. Pockets, underwear, skin crevices. Lots of places for trace amounts of sediment and organic material to get stuck." This obviously wasn't Reynolds' first rodeo.

"Thanks, mate." Rob shook his hand again. "You've been very helpful."

Reynolds nodded and backed away to where the RIB was bobbing in the shallows. "Good luck. Hope you catch the bastard who did her in."

"I plan to."

***

The team was positioned around the boardroom table in Incident Room Two, waiting for Rob to start the briefing. Even though they had multiple active cases on the go, in various stages of completion, this one had taken priority.

Detective Sergeant Will Freemont wheeled the whiteboard to the foot of the table and spun it around. The remnants of a previous case, now in the court preparation phase, were on the back. Rob gestured for Trent to come up to the front. The young officer did so, but reluctantly, and Rob could tell he didn't feel he was worthy of being up there.

Rob was about to start, when his boss, Detective Superintendent Felicity Mayhew, sneaked in and stood at the door.

"Carry on," she said curtly, as heads turned in her direction.

Rob began the meeting. "At seven thirty this morning, the body of a young woman was found at Putney Wharf, lying on the foreshore under the bridge. Sergeant Reynolds from the Marine Policing Unit, who are no strangers to pulling people from the water, said he estimated she'd been there since the previous evening, although that has yet to be confirmed."

Felicity's gaze was locked on him from across the boardroom. She cut a formidable figure with her flaming red hair, slender but rigid stature, and folded arms across a smart navy-blue blazer. Rob tried unsuccessfully to pretend she wasn't there.

He gestured to Trent. "PC Trent was on his way to work when the call came in, so he diverted to the scene, and a damn good thing he did too. The tide was coming in, and we all know how fast that happens."

Nods all around. Working this close to the Thames, they were all familiar with the vast tidal changes in water level and the associated havoc that caused.

"So, Trent managed to take some photographs, which Will is putting up on the board now. They're quite graphic," he added as an afterthought, although his seasoned team had seen worse. "Trent also preserved the body and collected samples of the surrounding environment for analysis by our forensic team."

There was a wave of approving nods, causing young Trent to blush. "It was nothing."

"Nonsense," Rob cut in. "It was smart thinking, and you did what needed to be done."

Will stuck the blow-ups on the whiteboard and immediately the chatter halted. Stark images of the victim lying on the dark shale, her bruised body half naked, her skirt bundled around her waist. Celeste grimaced while Jenny glared angrily at the board. Mayhew's expression was unreadable.

Next came the close-up shots of the victim's face. Bruised, battered and grazed. Blood and grains of silt, shale or debris filled her nostrils and mouth and lined her eyelids. *Crevices*, Reynolds had said. Hopefully, that was how the pathologist would find evidence of where she'd gone into the river.

"Trent, talk us through it, since you were the only one who saw the body in context."

"She was in a bad way," Trent began, his voice a bit hoarse. He cleared his throat and carried on. "Her clothes were ripped and it . . . it looked like she'd been sexually assaulted."

"What about the bruises on her face?" Jenny asked.

"There were several," Trent confirmed with a nod, "along with lots of little nicks and marks that could be from the water or from her attacker."

"The post-mortem will confirm," Rob pointed out. "Liz Kramer called and said she'll do it at four this afternoon."

Jenny nodded. Liz was one of the best pathologists Rob had ever worked with, and they'd handled more than a few high-profile cases together. She got to pick and choose her cases now, so he was grateful to get her.

"There were also strangulation marks around her throat," Trent continued. Everybody looked up as Will stuck on a photograph illustrating the deep purple finger impressions on the victim's neck — ugly against her once smooth, pale skin.

"He beat, raped *and* strangled her." Jenny shook her head in disbelief. "I cannot wait to catch this guy."

The rest of the team nodded in agreement.

"What about where she was found?" Rob prompted.

Trent took a deep breath and thought about what the marine officer had told him. "At low tide, a small amount of shingle is visible along the riverbank near Putney Wharf. There's a narrow window when this is accessible — namely, between two hours before and two hours after low tide, which gives us a duration of four hours in every twelve."

Rob prodded the board. "That means if she was attacked where she was discovered, at Putney Wharf, it would have to have happened after 5 p.m. yesterday afternoon and before 9 p.m."

"Oh, the man who discovered the body also found a discarded umbrella on the wharf," Trent added. In all the chaos, he'd forgotten it was still in his boot.

"Where is this man?" Rob asked, frowning. "Did he give a statement?"

"He works at the apartment block at the wharf, but he's agreed to come in this afternoon after work."

Rob nodded. "If that is her umbrella, there's a possibility she was taken there."

"Could she have floated up- or downriver with the tide?" DS Harry Malhotra asked. Harry was usually the most animated member of the team, but right now he sat very still, the haunting images affecting everybody in the boardroom.

It was a good question, and one Rob had asked himself. "Anything's possible until we rule it out. In which case, we may not have found the primary crime scene yet."

"Do we know who she is?" Mayhew's voice carried from the back.

"No, ma'am. We're still waiting on an ID. There wasn't time to inspect the body at the scene, due to the threat of the incoming tide."

Mayhew gave a stiff nod. "Let me know as soon as you do."

Rob relaxed a little. Something about that woman always put him on edge. "Okay, so our priority is to find out who she is. Trent, check all the missing persons reports over the last forty-eight hours. If someone was waiting for her, they would have filed a report when she didn't come home."

"I can do that," Celeste said quickly, before Trent could reply.

Rob nodded. "Will, get whatever CCTV footage you can from the area. We might even be able to see the abduction if she was taken from the wharf."

"Shouldn't we wait until Dr Kramer confirms she was attacked there?" Will asked. Trawling through CCTV footage was probably the worst part of an investigation, and one they usually outsourced. The recent budget cuts meant the surveillance teams were stretched too thin and consequently their turnaround times were largely useless, which was why they were doing it themselves.

Rob shrugged. "We may as well make a start. Give it to Trent. We'll have to look at it anyway."

Will nodded and Trent dutifully made a note on his iPad.

Even if she hadn't been murdered under Putney Bridge, they'd still have to check the waterfront footage to see if they could spot her body washing up, and from which direction it had come. Plus, he wanted to confirm what the concierge had told Trent about finding the body. Every detail had to be checked, to avoid screw-ups down the road.

After the last few cases, they couldn't afford another scandal.

"The crime scene looks vaguely familiar," Jenny mused, her eyes glued to the images on the whiteboard.

Rob frowned. "In what way?"

"I mean, the location is wrong, but picture that woman on the Thames Path near Kew Gardens, with her dress bunched up around her waist, her hands tied above her head, her face covered in bruises. Even the bloodied nose and the marks around her throat are the same."

Rob felt someone walk over his grave. Jenny was right, it was eerily similar.

"Coincidence," he muttered, shaking his head.

"Yeah, obviously." She turned to Will. "Can you access the crime scene photos from the Surrey Stalker case?"

Rob opened his mouth to speak, but Jenny held up a hand. "Humour me, okay, guv?"

He gave a reluctant shrug.

Will's fingers flew over the keyboard as he logged into HOLMES, the system used to manage major investigations.

With his prior permissions, he quickly navigated to the files from their original case.

"Got it." He swung his laptop around so they could all see the screen. An overhead shot of Julie Andrews, the first victim in the infamous Surrey Stalker case of nearly five years ago.

Trent gasped, while the rest of the team gazed in muted shock.

She had the same deathly pallor as the victim on the foreshore, the same matted dark hair and bruised features. Around her throat were dark purple bruises, finger marks from her strangler as he'd pressed the life out of her. Like the Putney victim, Julie had also been raped, and her dress was dirty and ripped, and bunched around her waist.

Rob closed his eyes, trying to block out the visuals. It was impossible. He'd never forget that scene. It had been his first case as a DI for the Major Investigation Team and had spilled over into his personal life too. "There are similarities, I'll grant you that much." He raked a hand through his hair. "But it's not the same."

It couldn't be.

"Who was the perp?" Will nodded to his screen. He hadn't yet joined the squad when Rob had investigated the Surrey Stalker case along with his then partner, Sergeant Mallory. Jenny had been here, as had Celeste, although she'd been more of an admin assistant at the time, trawling through hours and hours of CCTV footage in hopes of catching a glimpse of the killer.

Jenny shot a sidelong glance at Rob. "A man called Simon Burridge."

"You catch him?" Will asked.

Rob gave a stiff nod.

You could say that.

He was now lying in an unmarked grave in Wandsworth Cemetery.

"So it's not the same guy, then." Harry looked around the room.

"Obviously not," Rob snapped, unable to help himself.

Harry shifted his gaze to Jenny, who cleared her throat. "No, of course not. It just reminded me of this one, that's all."

"Shall we move on?" Rob asked.

They all nodded, and Will closed his laptop with a snap. Rob continued with the briefing, but he couldn't shake the uneasy feeling that had crept over him. The goddamn Surrey Stalker case. Back to haunt him.

CHAPTER 4

Back at his desk, Rob made sure nobody was watching, then pulled up the same file Will had accessed in the incident room. He needed to check for himself that the similarity in the two cases was merely a coincidence. Just another sicko rapist targeting women in West London.

Bracing himself, he opened the crime scene photographs and clicked through them. Julie Andrews lying in the foliage beside the Thames towpath, near the allotments at Kew Bridge. Julie with her hands bound above her head, her face marred by the killer's fist. Duct tape stretched across her mouth.

The Putney victim didn't have duct tape over her mouth, nor were her hands tied. That was different.

He zoomed in on the image of the marks around her throat. Widespread fingers, a man's hand. A large man's hand.

Next, he opened the photos Trent had taken and saved on the database. Finding the close-up of her neck, he studied the two, comparing them. Also a large hand. Powerful enough to squeeze the life out of a defenceless woman. He suppressed a shiver.

So what?

Just because the two women were both strangled by men with large hands, didn't mean the cases were related. Lots of victims were strangled, unfortunately, and lots were strangled by men with large hands.

Rob flicked through the remaining photographs, more due to a strange compulsion than because he actually wanted to look at them. This case had changed his life, set him on the course he was on now.

He paused on one of an engagement ring lying in a sterile kidney-shaped metal dish. A platinum band with a solitaire diamond. The promise of love, a future, a new life together. Ripped apart by the killer, a man with a twisted need to stop others from having what he couldn't.

On a whim, he printed out the post-mortem report, stapled it, and set it aside on his desk. It would be interesting to compare it to the Putney victim, once Liz was done.

* * *

"The victim is a young female, in her mid-twenties, currently unidentified," came Liz Kramer's clipped voice over the intercom. Rob sat upstairs in the viewing gallery at the lab, watching as she began the post-mortem.

Liz, wearing a white lab coat and assisted by one of her junior techs, systematically inspected the body. "She has multiple abrasions on her face, possibly due to an assault. There is blood and river debris in her mouth, nose and ears, which would indicate she was either held underwater at some point during her ordeal or submerged soon after. I'm taking samples to analyse."

Using swabs, she carefully removed the material from the victim's orifices and inserted it into test tubes. Her assistant dutifully labelled these and set them aside on a plastic tray.

Turning back to the victim, Liz peered at her neck. "Bruises around her throat and petechial haemorrhages around her eyes indicate she was strangled." She glanced up at Rob. "I'd say this is most likely your cause of death."

"She didn't drown?"

"I can't be sure until I look at her lungs, but it doesn't look like it." Liz worked her way down the body, inspecting the arms and torso, including the belly. "She has numerous scrapes and cuts that were made post-mortem, probably from debris floating in the river."

In the fast-flowing tidal Thames, there were lots of natural and unnatural items that could do damage.

"Any idea of time of death?" Rob asked. It would be good to confirm what the marine police officer had said about the four-hour window.

"Looking at the lividity and degree of rigor, she died sometime yesterday evening. I'm afraid it's a rather wide margin. Anywhere from eighteen to twenty-four hours ago."

Rob exhaled. During the low-tide mark. It fit.

"Liz, can you tell from looking at her whether she was killed where she was discovered, or whether she floated in with the tide?"

"Hmm . . . I wouldn't like to say. I can tell you there are roundish bruises and nicks on her back that indicate she could have been lying on the pebbles of the foreshore when she was attacked, but it's not conclusive." Liz didn't deal in assumptions. If it wasn't backed up by science, it didn't happen. She peered up over her mask. "If the material in her nose and mouth match that which you collected on the riverbank, then I'd say it's likely she was killed there, but you'll have to wait for the forensic report for that."

Yep, he knew that.

Liz pulled the magnified light stand closer and inspected the victim's pubic area. Rob glanced away out of respect. "Definite signs of penetration." Liz's voice was tight. "Tissue damage to the vulva and the vagina. I'll take a swab in case he's left any DNA behind."

Rob clenched his jaw, trying not to think about what the poor woman must have gone through in her final moments. He remembered having a similar thought at Julie Andrews' post-mortem.

"Liz," he said, before he could help himself.

Don't go there.

"Yes?" She didn't look up.

It's a ridiculous notion.

"Is there . . . Is there anything inserted inside her?"

Liz paused, then glanced up at him. "Inside?"

He bit his lip. "Yeah."

"I'll check for you." She bent over and inserted a speculum, then angled the magnified lamp so she could see inside it. "Good heavens."

Rob felt the ground tilt and gripped the railing. "What?"

"There is something wedged inside her." Using a long, thin pair of tweezers, she extracted the item and studied it under the light.

Rob held his breath.

Tell me it's not an engagement ring.

She held it up so he could see. "It looks like an engagement ring."

* * *

"Surely not?" A stunned Jenny gawked at him from across the incident room table. It was half past six in the evening and nobody on his team was giving any indication of leaving.

Rob gave a grim nod. All the way back to the office, he'd been trying to rationalise what he'd discovered, but he couldn't.

"B—But the Surrey Stalker is dead," Celeste stammered, her usually rosy cheeks drained of colour. "You killed him."

Trent, Harry and Will's eyes nearly popped out of their heads. Trent opened his mouth to speak, but Jenny shook her head. He shut it again.

Rob took a shaky breath. "This isn't Simon Burridge. This is someone emulating his MO. It's got to be."

Or as close as dammit.

"A copycat?" breathed Harry, his eyes gleaming with excitement. "We haven't had one of those before."

The department had been getting a reputation as the Met's unofficial serial offender unit, before they'd invited a killer into their midst and unknowingly given him full access to their investigation.

Now they were a laughing stock, and they might never live it down. Not even solving the high-profile Debby Morris case last year had restored their reputation. Mayhew's career had stalled, they were in the Mayor of London's bad books, and nobody wanted to work with them, as if they might be tarnished by association.

Rob still didn't know how the Superintendent had prevented them all from being moved on elsewhere, but he'd bet it had taken all her persuasive power and an indecent amount of schmoozing. Still, if anyone could do it, Mayhew could. He'd never met a more manipulative woman — and he'd met a few.

The team couldn't afford to put a foot wrong.

"This is not good." Rob pictured the potential media fallout and winced. "If the press gets wind of this we're going to be in the firing line again, and I don't think we've got many lives left."

"Particularly if they link it to the old case," Jenny added.

"Nobody mentions the ring." Rob focused his steely glare on each one of them. "No one. Got it?"

They all nodded sombrely.

"We kept the ring detail back from the press last time too," Jenny pointed out.

"Then how did the killer know about it?" Trent whispered, speaking for the first time.

"That's the million-dollar question." Rob shook his head. "He couldn't have."

"Not unless he was connected to the original case," Jenny said.

There was a long pause.

"Maybe a journalist mentioned it?" Will broke the silence. "After someone divulged it by accident." He'd been hoodwinked into giving away important information by a conniving reporter before, so he knew how easily it could happen.

"It's a possibility," Celeste conceded. "We didn't release it, but that doesn't mean someone else didn't."

Rob frowned. "I don't recall reading about it."

"Me neither," Jenny added. "That's something the press would have blown out of proportion had they known."

"A lot of people worked on that investigation." Rob's mind shifted to a different incident room five years ago. Chief Superintendent Sam Lawrence had been the guvnor then — his mentor and the man who'd had the biggest influence on him.

Damn, he wished he could talk to Sam about this. The guv had always known how to point Rob in the right direction, making him think for himself. He could almost hear his deep, booming voice now.

Start at the beginning, he'd say. *Work your way through it. You'll find the source.*

If there was one to be found.

"We're going to have to dig out all the old case files." Rob fought the descending weariness. He'd hoped to never have to revisit *that* investigation again. "I'll talk to Vicky Bainbridge and ask to see all our press releases, just in case we missed something."

Jenny arched an eyebrow. "Look on the bright side, at least it's a lead."

She had a point. If the Putney Bridge killer was mimicking the Surrey Stalker's MO, he had to have prior knowledge. It gave them a place to start.

"I'll make a list of everyone who was involved in the original investigation," Celeste said. "That should help us narrow it down."

"Okay." It was a good plan. "The rest of you, keep going on the victim. Let's see if we can put a name to her, then we can look at her friends and family, and cross-reference them against the list Celeste is making."

The mood changed. The initial shock had worn off and they had a solid starting point. Now he just had to tackle Mayhew.

CHAPTER 5

"Please tell me you're joking?" Superintendent Mayhew's glacial blue eyes burned right through him.

Rob stood in front of her desk, hands on his hips. "I'm afraid not. It looks like we've got a copycat."

"Oh, for fuck's sake." Her Irish accent was always more pronounced when she was angry.

He knew exactly how she felt.

She rubbed her temple. "How do you know? How can you be sure that this is the same MO?"

Rob sat down and told her about the rings. "No one knew that detail."

She stared at him for a long time, her mouth open. He waited, letting it sink in.

Eventually, she pulled herself together. "Okay, then. I guess that confirms it." Her voice was hoarse.

He nodded.

"How do you plan to proceed?"

"We don't have an ID on our victim yet." He chose his words carefully. He didn't want to set her off on a rant about the precarious state of the department. He already knew that. He knew she'd stuck her neck out for them and was grateful, but she didn't have to keep rubbing their noses in it. "But as soon as we do, we'll follow up all available leads. Whoever killed her knew she was going to be at the wharf last night. He may even have followed her there."

"CCTV?"

A quick nod. "On it. We're also pulling all the old Stalker case files, and we're going to make a list of everybody involved in the original investigation."

Mayhew tensed. "You definitely think the perpetrator is connected with that case?"

Rob shrugged. "How else could he have known?"

"God forbid the media get wind of this." She gnawed on her lower lip, white teeth on a slash of red.

"I know. I've already warned the team. Mum's the word."

"Okay, Rob." She took a steadying breath. "Proceed carefully on this one, and I mean really fucking carefully. Keep it close to you. I don't even want Galbraith or Linden's teams to know that level of detail."

"Understood, ma'am." The fewer people who knew, the less likely it was to be leaked. "Unfortunately, I can't speak for the techs at the lab."

"I'll call Liz Kramer myself," she said.

"Liz wouldn't say anything, but she did have an assistant at the PM, and there's the forensic team doing the testing."

"I'll make it clear she needs to have words with them."

Rob nodded. It would be better coming from Mayhew. Liz didn't take kindly to people telling her what to do, even lowly detective chief inspectors like him.

* * *

Vicky Bainbridge was one of the most efficient women Rob knew. Everything about her screamed speed and productivity — her minimalist office with a bright desk lamp on a swivel; her thin, silver laptop over which her fingers paused as he walked into her office; her stylish, no-frills office attire. The only concession to frivolity was the wine-coloured lipstick that brightened up her face.

She smiled warmly and pushed her chair out to greet him. "Rob, it's been ages. How are you?"

He never knew whether to shake her hand or not. It seemed too formal after everything they'd been through together, but they weren't quite at the hugging stage yet. Vicky had at one point been very obviously interested in him, and he didn't want to overstep or give her the wrong idea. Not that she would still be interested — a lot had happened since then.

He wasn't a rookie anymore, that's for sure. After an eye-watering list of serial offenders, knife-wielding maniacs, corrupt cops, human traffickers, sexual predators and dirty politicians, among others, he'd earned his stripes. The stress had taken its toll, he knew that too. Grey hairs peppered his temples, and fine lines cracked around his eyes when he laughed, which wasn't often enough these days.

"I'm great," he lied. She didn't need to know how he really was. "How have you been?"

"Oh, you know. Never a quiet day in this job."

"I can imagine." Even when his team weren't making headlines for all the wrong reasons, the two other major investigation teams stationed at Putney were still churning through their caseloads. Statements, appeals and press releases were always in demand — not to mention the carefully managed leaks to trusted reporters, keeping the media on side without compromising the investigation. Vicky was a pro.

She arched an eyebrow. "What can I do for you?"

He hesitated. "I need a favour. Remember the Surrey Stalker case?"

She narrowed her eyes. "How could I forget?"

"Well, I need all the press releases and any media communication we issued during and after the investigation. Official statements and anything we briefed off the record."

"Oh, er . . . yeah, sure. There's quite a bit in the system."

"I need all of it, Vicky."

She studied him, openly curious. "Can I ask what this is for?"

He gave what he hoped was a nonchalant shrug. "Another case. There are some crossovers, and we're comparing potential links between the offenders."

Her expression sharpened. "Crossovers?"

"I'm afraid I can't go into detail at this stage."

She gave a quick nod, knowing it would be useless to press him. "I'll pull everything together for you by the end of the day. Do you want it printed or will digital do?"

"Digital's fine. Thanks, Vicky. I owe you one."

"Yes, you do." She flashed him a burgundy grin as he turned and left her office. If there was any mention of the rings in any of those press releases, he'd find it. He also wanted the team to look at any staff reporters and freelancers covering the story. They'd have sources, and those sources may be connected to the case.

"Do we have an ID yet?" Rob strode back to his desk through the squad room.

"Good day to you too," DCI Galbraith said, side-stepping to let him pass. He'd only just got in, having also been delayed at a crime scene earlier that morning.

Rob nodded at the Scottish detective, but didn't stop to chat. The clock was ticking. Every minute took them further away from finding the perpetrator. Memories dried up, evidence got compromised, and offenders had time to manufacture excuses. It was imperative they find out who this woman was today.

"I'm on the phone to the lab." Jenny placed her hand over the receiver. "They're running her prints now."

"We can do that. Get them to send them through," he hissed. Jenny tilted her head back as if to say, *Hang on*. Seconds later, she broke into a smile. "That's great. Give me her name."

She grabbed a pen and turned to a fresh page on her notepad. Rob loomed over her, while the rest of the team fell silent, fingers paused over keyboards.

"Excuse me?" Jenny blurted, going a whiter shade of pale. The pen remained poised over the pad. "Can you say that again?"

Rob scowled. "What is it?"

Nobody moved.

Slowly, Jenny began to write.

Lucy Andrews.

For the second time that day, Rob felt the ground shift beneath him.

What the—? It couldn't be.

Jenny hung up the phone and stared at him. "The victim was Julie Andrews' sister."

CHAPTER 6

Felicity Mayhew was living a nightmare, and it was only going to get worse.

Nobody had warned her this job was going to be so hard — or so damaging to her career. If they had, she'd have run like a sinner from a priest. She'd had offers from the National Crime Agency as well as Interpol, before settling on the Major Investigation Team.

She paced up and down her living room, massaging her temples. Still, they closed cases, despite the mayhem they left in their wake, and that was a good thing, right?

Wrong.

The fallout wasn't worth the reward.

Felicity had just got off the phone with her boss, Assistant Commissioner Matthew Gray, who wanted an update on the young woman found under Putney Bridge. Apparently the evening papers were awash with images of her partially naked body, grainy in the early morning dawn, and were warning youngsters, particularly females, not to walk home alone.

"She washed up in front of thousands of commuters," he'd barked at her, as if it was her fault. "Have you seen the pictures circulating on social media?"

"No, sir." But she could imagine. Nothing was sacred these days. PC Trent had moved fast, but by the time they'd closed off the bridge, more than a few rubberneckers had managed to snap photos of the victim below. Anyway, it only took one to go viral.

"Do we even know who she is?"

"Yes, sir. Her name is Lucy Andrews." She'd shut her eyes, praying he didn't make the connection. He didn't.

"I take it your team is questioning her family?"

"Of course." She'd gripped the phone in annoyance. What did he think? That they were a bunch of amateurs? The entire team was working overtime, as they did with every major crime. She felt bad leaving them to it, but she knew her presence made them nervous. They didn't want her peering over their shoulders while they worked. "DCI Miller's team are a competent unit," she'd said, "and they're doing everything in their power to get to the bottom of this." Probably more than most.

"I want updates, Superintendent. Updates, you hear me?"

"Yes, sir."

Felicity blew a hair out of her face. What a dick. After the high-profile Debbie Morris murder last year in Marlow, their professional relationship had broken down. It was a miracle Gray was still allowed to do his job, but the Met's internal investigation had ruled that he had not been involved in the crime or impeded the investigation in any way — an outcome she felt was debatable — and they'd swept the whole thing under the proverbial rug.

She poured herself a very large glass of Sauvignon Blanc and took it over to the sofa, along with her briefcase packed full of files. There must be a lot of very dirty rugs at Scotland Yard.

They were hanging on by a thread, she was well aware of that. Her superiors braced when they saw her coming. They didn't want to deal with her department, despite all the good they were doing. They'd rather just ignore her and hope it went away.

She collapsed onto the soft cushions. Nobody ever mentioned the other side of it. All they cared about was the Met's failing reputation, and how they had to be "paradigms of professionalism". Dickhead's words.

Since she'd come on board, she'd done nothing but put out fires, and she was sick to death of it. She took a large gulp, curling her feet beneath her. If these two cases were linked, she needed to familiarise herself with the Surrey Stalker investigation.

Of course she'd heard about it — there were few in law enforcement circles who hadn't — but it had been before her time, and the finer details of the investigation would be important. She couldn't be caught on the backfoot. Not again. When the questions came, as they inevitably would, she wanted to be ready.

Halfway through the police report on Julie Andrews' murder on the Thames River path, her mobile phone buzzed. She glanced at the screen, but didn't move to get it.

The message displayed automatically for a few seconds, before disappearing.

Can I come round?
Tom.

Her lips twitched. She could use a little stress relief tonight. It was Friday after all, and it had been a hell of a week.

They'd met at this little wine bar where she went some nights after work when she needed to unwind. It was a good way to evaluate the day and plan for the next while enjoying a glass of wine and trying to pretend she had a normal social life, before going home to her empty house.

He'd knocked into her at the bar, spilling her drink. After apologising profusely, he'd offered to buy her another one, and that had been that. Darkly handsome, with a boyish charm that she found endearing after all the hard-hitting detectives she dealt with in her work life, he was just the tonic she needed — and she had to admit, she was getting very used to their late-night booty calls, if you could call them that at her age.

As far as she knew, he wasn't married. No ring. No tan mark either. He'd been at the bar with some golfing friends, whom he'd had no problem ditching to go home with her. Smiling at the memory, she picked up her phone and texted him back.

Have to get some work done. See you at ten?

It buzzed again.

Great!

Putting her phone aside, she returned to the report. Another few minutes of reading and she'd forgotten all about what was going to happen later.

Julie Andrews.

Attacked while walking home along the Thames Path. Beaten, sexually assaulted and strangled. What type of monster did that to a young woman?

Felicity shook her head but kept going. The shocking thing was it could happen to anyone. To her. Her sister. Her nieces. She closed her eyes briefly, not wanting to think about that.

There were some crime scene photographs attached to the report. She looked through them, one after the other, swallowing over the lump that formed in her throat.

Breath hitching, she stared at the engagement ring that had been retrieved from the victim.

Jesus.

The wine helped fortify her, and after a long moment, she closed the report and moved on to the next one.

Sara Bakshi. Attacked while jogging in Richmond Park. Same cause of death as Julie. Found later that evening by a dog walker.

Her phone buzzed again. This time it was her sister.

Felicity hesitated, debating whether to answer or not. Faith was going through a tough time. The divorce was messy — custody battles, arguments over finances, fighting over every goddamn thing there was to fight over. Funny how the person you once loved could be the one to tear your life apart. If she ever needed a reason not to settle down, Faith was it.

Felicity had tried to be there for her, had got drunk with her, talked about what a two-timing wanker Mike was, how betrayed Faith felt, how broken. Tonight, however, she couldn't dredge up the energy to pick up the pieces. With what she was reading, she just didn't have the capacity for more drama. She let it go to voicemail and turned to the last report — Miller's account of what had happened at Wimbledon Common.

It was brief and to the point, as if written by a robot, but she read between the lines. There she sensed anger.

No. Anger was too mild a word.

Fury.

As she read about the capture and death of Simon Burridge, the Surrey Stalker, Felicity realised how little she truly knew Rob Miller. A man of few words and many secrets, he kept his emotions locked down, never revealing anything personal — yet somehow, his team still idolised him.

They were the tightest unit she'd ever worked with, and though she'd never admit it, being a loner didn't make teamwork easy for her. Part of her craved their camaraderie. Another, darker part questioned if she was even capable of it.

Sighing, she set down the document and stretched. Her thoughts drifted back to their elusive leader. She'd never broken through Rob's armour, and she doubted she ever would. Maybe he had a problem with authority. Or maybe he just didn't trust her.

She scoffed. She couldn't blame him there. He knew her dirty little secret — the real reason she'd been promoted to superintendent — but he wasn't talking. Then again, she knew his secrets too. Several of them.

They were both holding on to them, stockpiling them like ammunition, in case there was ever a gunfight. She hoped to hell that day would never come.

The doorbell rang.

Crap, she'd forgotten about Tom.

Taking a deep breath, she tried to push work out of her mind. Getting up, she checked her appearance in the hall mirror, then went to answer the door.

CHAPTER 7

The first twenty-four hours after a murder were crucial — and chaotic. Every moment counted, and every decision could make or break the case. Now that they had identified the victim, it was all systems go.

"I know it's late, but we need to talk to her family," Rob said grimly. Statistically, the perpetrator was likely someone connected to her. Most victims knew their killer.

"It's strange, though, isn't it?" Jenny stood in front of the incident room whiteboard, studying the crime scene photos. The fluorescent lighting made everything seem brighter, starker. "We've dealt with this family before. We know her parents. We even know the victim, sort of. I remember talking to Lucy five years ago."

Rob grunted. He couldn't deny that it was surreal, like history repeating itself.

"There's something else," Celeste said, her face flushed.

Rob turned to her. "Yeah?"

"You're never going to believe this."

"What is it?" asked Jenny, frowning.

"Lucy was engaged — to Justin King."

It took a moment to register, then Rob sucked in a breath. "Not the *same* Justin King?"

Jenny stared at her. "Her sister's fiancé?"

Celeste nodded.

"Oh, my God," Jenny murmured.

"What are the chances of two women in his life being murdered?" Harry wondered out loud. With his prominent cheekbones and ridiculously long eyelashes, he looked more like a film star than a police detective.

"Remote," Jenny replied.

"Not possible," Rob muttered, making for the door. He'd spent the last few hours going through the media pack that Vicky had compiled. There had been no mention of the rings — nothing to suggest any member of the press had even known about them. The closest the Met had come was hinting they'd held back a few key details, just enough to filter out false confessions or catch suspects off guard during interrogations.

The leak hadn't come from them.

"Justin knew about the rings," he murmured.

Jenny gave a tight nod.

While he and Jenny went to visit Lucy's fiancé, Harry and Celeste were going to question her parents. The middle-aged couple had already been notified about their daughter's death, so Rob had warned them to tread gently.

Will, the team's self-appointed computer whiz, was checking the victim's phone data, credit cards and online profiles. So far, he'd come up with nothing of note.

Trent was working with the lab to analyse the material found in her nose and mouth, and reports on the various swabs were coming in all the time. As the newest member of the team, he was also trawling through CCTV footage around the Putney Wharf area at the time of the murder.

"Anything?" Rob paused at Trent's desk on his way out.

Trent looked up. "Nothing on the CCTV yet," he replied. "But it looks like Lucy was killed where she was found. The soil samples on her body match those we collected under the bridge."

"Good work," Rob acknowledged. "That narrows it down. At least we're not looking for another primary crime scene."

Trent flushed.

"Keep going on that footage. If she was attacked at the wharf, we must have him on tape."

"Will do, sir. Oh, and Mr Banstead, the man who found her body, came in and gave his statement. There was nothing new in it."

Rob grabbed his keys. "Thanks, I'll look at it later." With Jenny beside him, he left the building.

* * *

"He's moved," Rob muttered, tapping Justin King's address into the satnav.

"Not surprising." Jenny pulled out of the police car park and joined the evening traffic. "There were probably too many memories at his old place."

"Justin's the common denominator in both Julie and Lucy's murders," Rob murmured, settling back in his seat.

Jenny turned to him. "You don't think he had anything to do with it, do you? I mean, he was devastated after Julie died, and we both know who was responsible for *her* murder."

The long-dead Simon Burridge.

Rob grimaced. "I know, but what if all this is about Justin? I mean, think about it. Simon murders Justin's fiancée five years ago, and now he's engaged again—"

"To her sister," Jenny cut in.

"Yeah, which is weird enough in itself, but it does happen. Now *she's* been murdered. Maybe someone's trying to send him a message."

"Plus, she was murdered in almost exactly the same way as her sister," Jenny pointed out. "Which means whoever killed her must know how Julie died. That has to narrow down our suspect pool."

"Agreed." Rob scowled as they crawled along Putney High Street. "Why is the traffic always so diabolical around here? It's after nine, for Pete's sake."

"It's Thursday night," she muttered, coming to a stop at a set of traffic lights. "I read that it's replaced Friday as the most popular night to go out in London."

"It's a work night," he said, then realised how old he sounded. It wasn't that long ago he also used to go to the pub with the crew on a Thursday night.

The corners of Jenny's lips lifted. "I think you need to get out more, guv."

He smirked. Maybe he did. Life hadn't been much fun the last few years. Maybe he'd talk to Jo. They should both take some time off and go away in the summer. The thought cheered him.

"I've asked Becca to meet us there," he said, as the lights turned green. Becca Townsend was an experienced family liaison officer with a background in trauma counselling. Calm but compassionate, she empathised with victims' families, but what Rob liked about her was that she was sharp. Sharp enough to earn their trust, delve into their lives without making it obvious, and gather information useful in investigations.

The traffic was crawling. Rob was tempted to tell Jenny to put the lights and siren on, but this wasn't a police emergency, not really, even though time was of the essence. It didn't warrant the full bells and whistles.

Jenny wrinkled her forehead. "Wasn't she the FLO on the original Stalker case?"

"Yeah, she knows Justin. She'll be able to talk to him, get him to open up about Lucy's friends, exes or anyone who might have a grudge against her — or him."

A short while later, they pulled up in front of a narrow Victorian terrace. A lamp outside the door cast a soft glow over the carefully kept front garden. As they walked up the path, Rob noticed a series of pot plants arranged on one side, and a fledgling apple tree on the other. The couple had been making this house into a home for a life they now wouldn't have. The thought saddened him, and he felt a renewed anger at the killer who'd so ruthlessly destroyed their world.

Before he could knock, Becca opened the door. She gave a kind smile. "Rob. Jenny. Come in. We're in the living room."

They followed her into the house, where Justin King sat hunched on the sofa, gazing into an untouched mug of tea. He looked positively haggard.

The years had not been kind. His naturally unruly hair was greasy and stuck up in all directions like he'd been clawing his fingers repeatedly through it. His features were sagging and dull, and there were deep purple shadows beneath his heavy-lidded eyes. The poor guy looked like he'd aged years in the last twenty-four hours.

"I'm so sorry." Rob echoed the same words he'd uttered when Julie had died, and just like back then, they made little difference.

Justin turned his vacant, glassy eyes on him and nodded vaguely.

Rob couldn't get Jenny's words out of his mind. *What are the chances?*

What were the odds that the same guy would lose two fiancées in the same way, half a decade apart? So infinite as to be almost impossible. There was a connection here — they just had to find it.

"Do you feel up to answering some questions?" Rob asked, keeping his tone light.

Justin nodded weakly, his gaze flicking to Becca, who gave him a small, reassuring smile. "Okay," he whispered.

Rob sat on the edge of the armchair across from Justin, careful to keep his tone soft. "When was the last time you saw Lucy?"

Justin's breath hitched. "Yesterday morning. She left for work like usual, around seven thirty."

"Where did she work?"

"The Design Centre at Chelsea Harbour."

He knew of it but had never been there. "What was her role?"

Justin took a shaky breath. "She was an admin assistant for a design company there. They specialise in textiles, I think."

Rob glanced across at Becca. "We'll need her company details." He'd get one of the team down there to question her boss and colleagues. They'd need to know what time she left.

"I've already got them for you," Becca said.

Rob leaned forward. "And after work, you were supposed to meet her?"

"Yeah, we were going to meet at Coppa, the pub down by the wharf." Justin's voice wavered. "It was our date night."

Date night. How long since he'd had one of those with Jo?

He gave a sympathetic nod but pressed on. "Can you tell us what time you left to meet her?"

Justin blinked, his brow furrowing in confusion. "I . . . I left around twenty to eight."

"You walked from here?" Rob made a note of the details.

"Yeah," Justin nodded. "It's only twenty minutes. I got to the pub a little before eight. I waited, but she . . . she never showed up."

Rob glanced at Jenny before gently asking, "Did anyone see you on your way to the pub? A neighbour, perhaps? Maybe someone you passed on the street?"

Justin rubbed his face with both hands. "No . . . I don't think so. I just walked straight there." He paused, then shook his head as if frustrated with himself. "There was a guy running with his dog, but I didn't know him. I . . . I was just thinking about getting there, you know? I wasn't really paying attention."

Rob kept his expression neutral. "When she didn't arrive, did you try calling her?"

Justin inhaled shakily. "Of course. I called her phone, but it went straight to voicemail. I thought she had got caught up at work. I texted her too, but . . ." He broke off, staring at his hands.

"What did you do when she didn't respond?"

"I stayed there for about an hour, waiting, thinking she'd show up." He took a deep breath. "When it started getting late, I began to get worried, so I called her parents."

"Had they heard from her?" Rob asked.

Justin shook his head. "No. That's when I called the police." His voice cracked, and he buried his face in his hands. "I can't believe this has happened again."

Rob exchanged a glance with Jenny. "We didn't hear about a missing person report."

"That's because they told me it was too soon to report her as missing." There was a bitterness in his tone now. "I knew that would happen. I don't know why I bothered."

It was something they could check out anyway. The call would be logged on the system. Jenny got up and left the room.

"I'm sorry," he murmured, but he meant it. Protocol dictated that they wait the obligatory twenty-four hours before reporting a missing person, particularly an adult and with no extenuating circumstances. Most missing persons turned up within that time frame — except not Lucy. It wouldn't have mattered if he'd reported her missing, because by that time, she was almost certainly already dead.

"If only I'd waited outside for her." He dropped his head into his hands. "This would never have happened."

"You couldn't have known," Becca said quietly. "This isn't your fault."

Justin let out a trembling breath, but Rob could feel his regret. He sighed. On that, he could relate. Maybe if Justin had gone to look for her, if he'd just glanced down at the foreshore... but there was no point in dwelling on the maybes. Rob learned that a long time ago. The man's fiancée was dead — and he was going to have to live with that.

Jenny returned and gave Rob a quick nod. That was the confirmation he needed. Justin had indeed placed the call when he'd said he had. So far, he was telling the truth. Still, he could have placed the call after he'd murdered her, pretending to be concerned. Without anyone to confirm his whereabouts, his alibi still hung in the air, unverified.

Rob studied the man in front of him. He looked shattered. There wasn't a hint of calculation in his demeanour — just raw pain.

He gave him a moment before he moved on to the next question, careful to keep his tone as gentle as possible. "I know this is difficult, but had Lucy mentioned anyone bothering her recently? Any issues at work or with anyone from her past?"

Justin lifted his head, eyes clouded with confusion. "No, nothing like that. Lucy was well liked. She never had a problem with anyone."

"Was she nervous about anything in the days leading up to . . ." Rob trailed off, letting Justin fill in the blanks.

"No," Justin said, his voice weak but certain. "She was excited about the wedding. That's all we talked about. We were making plans for the reception."

"And you didn't notice anything unusual? No strange phone calls, no one paying too much attention to her?" Rob pressed.

Justin blinked, his brow furrowing as he tried to think back. "You mean like . . . ?"

Rob nodded.

"No, nothing like that. She was always a bit stressed with work, but that was normal."

Okay, so no stalker that they knew of. That, at least, was different. "We're going to need a list of everyone who knew you and Lucy were planning to meet at the pub last night. Friends, family, anyone you might've mentioned it to."

Justin's gaze had become a blank stare. "It was just us. I didn't tell anyone. It was supposed to be our quiet night together."

"Okay. And Lucy didn't mention meeting anyone before you?"

"No," Justin said. "It was just supposed to be me and her."

Rob scratched his chin, now prickly with stubble.

Well, someone knew she was going to be there.

Jenny took up where he'd left off. "How did you and Lucy get together?"

Justin gave a tired nod, as if he'd been expecting the question. "I know it sounds a bit incestuous, but we were united by our grief after Julie's death. I think we both needed someone to talk to — about her, and then about other things. We became friends, and then we fell in love."

Rob supposed it was five years down the line. Not so weird, now he'd heard Justin's explanation.

Jenny smiled sympathetically. "I'm so sorry for your loss, Justin."

He sniffed as his eyes filled with tears.

Becca looked at them and shook her head. *Enough*, she was saying.

For now.

"Thank you, Justin." Rob got to his feet. "I just want you to know we're doing everything we can to find out who did this."

Justin didn't reply, but silent tears streamed down his desolate face.

Becca followed them to the door. When she spoke, her voice was a whisper. "His grief seems genuine to me. I don't think he's hiding anything."

Rob tended to agree. The guy was too distraught to be involved, although they'd have to verify his movements, just to be sure. If they could pinpoint where he was when he made the 999 call, that would verify his location; however, it would also place him at the scene of the crime.

It was a tough one. Justin would have a hard time proving he *didn't* murder his fiancée.

"Whoever killed Lucy knew she was going to be meeting Justin at the wharf yesterday evening. We need the names and contact details of everyone they spoke to. As it stands, all the evidence currently points to Justin. Add to that, his previous fiancée was murdered in exactly the same way." He shrugged.

All that was missing was a motive.

Becca gave a grim nod. "Leave it with me."

As they left, Jenny said, "Anyone can see the pain he's going through."

Rob grunted as he got into the squad car. "That doesn't necessarily matter. A jury may not care."

"Well, they should." She climbed in and scowled into the darkness.

"Let's focus on who knew they were meeting up. This was well planned. The tide was out, it was dark enough so nobody could see the attacker, and Lucy was exactly where he expected her to be."

She nodded, but didn't speak.

"You okay?" He glanced over at her.

She sighed. "I just feel bad for him, that's all."

"It's hard not to," Rob agreed.

Jenny took a deep breath, her hands on the steering wheel. She had yet to pull away from the kerb. "So, we're assuming the killer knew Lucy?"

"Or Justin," he added.

She pursed her lips, thoughtfully. "He also knew about the Surrey Stalker investigation."

"Correct."

"There can't be many people at the centre of that Venn diagram."

Rob stared out of the windscreen into the darkness. "Exactly."

CHAPTER 8

Back at the office, they went through the list of people with intimate knowledge of the Surrey Stalker case. It turned out to be a lot longer than they'd anticipated. Once you included all the detectives in the different jurisdictions, support staff, lab techs, and the victims' families, it was close to fifty suspects.

"Those are just the ones who could have known about the rings." Jenny swept a stray hair off her face. "If you include everyone involved in the original investigation, it runs into the hundreds."

They had assembled in the incident room for an impromptu update. Even though the office was nearly deserted at this hour, the blinds were drawn and the door was kept locked to ensure the utmost secrecy. He wasn't going to risk anyone wandering in and seeing their notes on the whiteboard or the old case files littered across the boardroom table.

"DC Evan Burns and DC Mike Manner have left the force," Rob said, pointing to their names on the list, "so we can rule them out." Evan had moved back to America with his family some years ago, while Mike had left to work on an upliftment programme for Mayor Raza Ashraf. While Rob had zero time for Ashraf, he did respect what his former DC was doing on the rough South London housing estates.

"Do we have Justin King's contact list yet?" Will asked.

"No, Becca's still working on it."

"Justin was in no state to remember anything when we were there," Jenny pointed out. "The guy is broken."

Will cringed. "His mobile phone puts him close to the crime scene last night. It's not looking good."

"There's no way he did it," Jenny insisted. "If you'd seen him, you'd know that. Nobody's that good a liar."

"He had no reason to kill her," Rob stated. "We need to widen the net." He turned to Harry and Celeste. "How'd it go at the parents' place?"

They glanced quickly at each other before Harry said, "Not well. They're barely keeping it together."

Celeste added, "Mr Andrews didn't say much, and his wife sobbed the whole time we were there."

"Did they confirm Justin called them last night?" Jenny asked.

"Yeah, they showed me their phone. I took a photo of the screen, but it's as he claimed. He called them at eight forty-five."

"Forty-five minutes after Lucy was due to show up. That's a reasonable time frame." He might do the same if — God forbid — Jo didn't turn up somewhere.

Jenny nodded in agreement. "Did they know who Lucy may have told about meeting Justin?"

Harry shook his head. "They hadn't seen their daughter in over a week. Mrs Andrews had spoken to her on the phone, but she pretty much lived her own life. According to her father, Lucy was very independent."

He sighed. They wouldn't be able to help, then. "Did they say anything of interest?"

"Only that she was excited about the wedding. It was scheduled for next month at Pembroke Lodge in Richmond Park."

"Can we get a guest list?" Rob asked. Pembroke Lodge was a popular local wedding venue.

"I'll call Becca." Jenny picked up her phone and headed for the door.

"Tell her we need that list of names ASAP," Rob called after her.

Will briefed them on Lucy's phone data and bank records. "Nothing out of the ordinary. I've made a list of all the phone numbers she called in the last two weeks, and I'll identify who they are, particularly the ones that aren't in her contact list."

"Thanks, Will. Follow up and find out what they spoke to Lucy about."

"I can help with that," Trent said hopefully.

"You've got enough on your plate with the CCTV and the river samples," Rob said, his tone brooking no argument.

Trent glanced down, but gave a little nod. His new constable was eager to help, Rob got that, but he didn't want to stretch the team too thin. That's how details fell through the cracks. "I need your full attention on that footage," he added. "I'm relying on you to find whoever did this. The killer has got to be on some camera somewhere within the time frame."

Trent perked up. "Yes, sir."

Jenny came back, her eyes shining. "Guv, I've got the list from Becca. She took a photograph of it and sent it to my phone. Thirteen possibles."

"Thirteen? Justin talked to thirteen people in the week before Lucy's death?" Other than work, he was lucky if he made one or two personal phone calls per week.

"He *was* planning a wedding," she reminded him.

Fair point. "Let's see it, then."

Jenny walked over to the whiteboard, and they all watched as she wrote out the names. Most of them were people he'd never heard of before. Next to the names, Jenny added a description: wedding planner, caterer, best man, friend, and so on.

The thirteenth name on the list was Natasha Wakefield, the maid of honour.

"Natasha Wakefield." Rob rubbed his forehead. "Why is that name familiar?"

"I questioned her five years ago in relation to Julie's death." Jenny glanced over at him. "She was the best friend, remember?"

"Oh yeah. The one Julie had lunch with the week before she was killed."

"That's right. She confirmed Julie had a stalker. We picked him up on CCTV following her home from the restaurant where they met."

He gave a thoughtful nod. It had been a defining moment in the case. A darkly clad figure, lurking in the shadows. He dragged himself away from the memory. "I suppose it would make sense they'd know her, but maid of honour?"

"Maybe we should go and talk to her?" Jenny said.

Will, who'd been tapping away on his iPad, nodded. "She's one of a handful of suspects who knew both victims."

"Who are the others?" Rob asked.

"Justin, of course. Julie and Lucy's parents, who we've already spoken to. You, Jenny and Celeste. Becca Townsend." Will glanced up. "That's it."

"And if we rule out the fiancé, the parents and our team, you get Natasha." Rob grabbed his jacket off the back of his chair. "Jenny, let's go."

* * *

Natasha Wakefield lived in a sleek, modern apartment block within easy walking distance of Putney High Street, yet far enough to escape the relentless hum of the busy neighbourhood. The building was quiet, sheltered from the commuter frenzy that usually came with city living.

They drove through the whisper-quiet electric gates, which closed with a soft, mechanical thud behind them. They parked near the entrance, where a sharp-eyed concierge stepped out to greet them. "Is there a problem, Officers?"

"We need to speak to someone on the fifth floor," Rob replied, curt but polite. The man nodded before retreating to his station behind a polished reception desk.

The lift took them straight up, and after pressing the doorbell several times, a sleepy Natasha answered. She stood in the doorway in her pyjamas, her hair tousled, eyes squinting into the bright light of the corridor. "What's going on?"

"Ms Wakefield, we need to talk to you. Can we come in?"

She frowned, confused. He didn't blame her. It was past 11 p.m. "Now?"

"Yes, now."

She blinked, then reluctantly stood back to let them enter. "Is this about Lucy?"

"You've heard, then?"

"Of course I've heard. I'm her maid of honour." She gulped and sank down into a pale leather armchair. "*Was* her maid of honour."

Jenny, wanting to put the woman at ease, sat down on the matching sofa, but Rob remained standing. They weren't going to be here that long, and he preferred to keep people on their toes.

"I apologise for the late hour," he said, "but we're trying to understand Lucy's last movements on the day she died. Did you know she was going to be at Putney Wharf?"

Natasha stared at them, her eyes a little glazed. "Putney Wharf?"

"Yes, where she was attacked."

Her eyes widened in understanding. "Oh, right. Er . . . no, she didn't tell me about that. We were planning the wedding — that was my job. I was helping her organise the recep—" She choked on the words, her voice crumbling into a sob.

Jenny shot him a look, and he gave an imperceptible nod, letting her take the lead. "I'm sorry for your loss," she said gently. "Were you and Lucy close?"

"She was my best friend," Natasha whispered.

"Like Julie?"

Natasha nodded. "I met Julie first, but after she died, Lucy and I became close. I think it's because we both missed her so much."

Jenny smiled in understanding. "We believe you spoke to her fiancé, Justin, on Monday, two days before she died. Can you remember what that phone call was about?"

Natasha blinked as if searching her own memory, or perhaps weighing up how much to share. Rob couldn't tell if she was fabricating something or genuinely trying to recall the details.

After a moment, she spoke. "Oh, yes. He was planning a surprise for her and wanted my opin—"

"What kind of surprise?" Rob cut in.

"A live band for the reception." Her eyes glistened. "They were trying to keep costs down, using a playlist for the disco. But he thought hiring this band would make it special."

"What did you think?" Rob asked.

"I thought it was a great idea." She wiped a tear from her cheek, her gaze dropping to the floor.

A live band — one more detail that would never come to pass, like the dress, the cake and everything else that comes with a wedding. Rob had never made it down the aisle, but thanks to Yvette, the woman he'd briefly been engaged to, he had a good idea of what went into planning a wedding. It was no mean feat.

"Natasha, was there anyone in Lucy's life who didn't want them to get married?"

"Like who?" She stared up at him blankly.

"I don't know. Maybe a jealous ex-boyfriend?" Women, in particular best friends, had a way of picking up on the subtle tensions, the undercurrents of hostility that most men would overlook.

"No, there was nobody like that. Lucy hadn't dated since Julie died. It's only been Justin."

He sighed internally. So much for that theory. "What about Justin? Anyone on his side who resented their relationship?"

She shook her head. "He started dating Lucy a couple of years after Julie died. They were friends before that. There was nobody in between."

"I seem to remember Julie having an ex-boyfriend." Jenny scratched her head.

Natasha raised her eyebrows. "Oh, that prick Jamie."

"Jamie?" Rob scowled. The name didn't ring a bell.

"Yeah, he was a piece of work. She was well shot of him."

Rob glanced at Jenny. Natasha's tone suggested a lingering anger towards this previous boyfriend, which was strange, given the amount of time that had passed.

"Tell us about him," Jenny coaxed.

"Oh, there's nothing to tell, really." She bit down on her lower lip as if regretting her previous flash of anger.

"It didn't sound like nothing," Jenny probed gently. "Did you know him?"

Natasha stared at her hands clenched in her lap. Rob noticed her fingernails were bitten to the quick. "Natasha?"

A sigh. "Okay, Julie broke up with Jamie because he was possessive and controlling. It wasn't evident at first, but after a few months he started keeping tabs on her, asking where she'd been, that sort of thing."

"Did she report him?"

"No, it was nothing that serious. She broke up with him, that's all."

Rob gave a thoughtful nod. "How long before she met Justin did this relationship end?"

A shrug. "Six months or so."

Jenny's gaze locked on his, and he knew they were both thinking the same thing. Why was this only coming up now?

He turned back to Lucy's friend. "Natasha, we interviewed you after Julie's murder, do you remember?"

She nodded.

"You didn't mention her ex-boyfriend then. Was there a reason why?"

She swallowed, and a bad feeling crawled into Rob's gut. "Natasha?"

She exhaled, slow and low. "Because he didn't have anything to do with her murder."

Rob frowned. "You couldn't have known that."

Her eyes darted to the thick darkness outside the window as if she longed to disappear into it. "I could. I mean, I did know that, because he was with me when Julie was killed. We were on holiday together in Marbella."

There was a stunned silence.

Rob processed the new information, turning it over in his head. "You and Jamie . . . You were an item?"

"We were in a relationship, yes."

"Did Julie know?" Jenny asked.

Natasha wouldn't meet her gaze. "No, she didn't."

CHAPTER 9

"What the actual—!" Jenny hissed as soon as they'd left the apartment and were out of earshot. It was now nearly midnight, and they were both wired from too much coffee and adrenalin. "I questioned her five years ago, and she said nothing about a bloody Jamie."

"She was sleeping with her best friend's ex-boyfriend," Rob said grimly. After Natasha's surprise revelation, they'd got the rest of the story out of her. Jamie was good-looking in a brutal, rough kind of way — a typical bad boy. Six months after Julie had dumped him, Natasha had bumped into him at a local club. They'd got talking, and several tequila shots later, she'd ended up at his place.

"I know he was probably only shagging me to get back at Julie," Natasha had told them miserably, "but I really liked him."

The relationship lasted maybe two or three months, the highlight being a week-long jaunt in Marbella, after which he'd told her it was over and he was moving on.

"I was devastated," she'd confessed, though Rob couldn't quite grasp why. Then he thought about his own past with Yvette, how unsuitable she had been for him, and he started to understand. There was something undeniably alluring about those borderline reckless relationships that brought with them an exotic blend of excitement and chaos.

"Still," Jenny continued, prodding the key fob to unlock the squad car. He could tell she was thoroughly annoyed that she'd missed a crucial line of enquiry in the original case. "He would have been a person of interest."

"It wasn't him," Rob concluded, opening the passenger door. "It doesn't matter now. If we'd followed that lead, it would have just taken us down another blind alley." They'd had enough of those during that case as it was.

"That's not the point," she argued, getting in behind the wheel.

"I know, but we'll talk to him now. He might still be pissed off enough at Justin for stealing his girlfriend to wish him harm."

Jenny glanced over at him. "Pissed off enough to murder his new fiancée?"

Rob inhaled. "I don't know. That's what we need to find out."

A swift call to Will at the office gave them Jamie McNamara's home address. He lived above a fish and chip shop in Hammersmith, West London, although the takeaway was shut — just like everything else in the small parade of shops — when they ramped the pavement outside.

A homeless man eyed them from a doorway, his bed sheets oil-stained chip paper, probably scavenged from a nearby rubbish bin. At least it kept some of the cold from seeping through from the concrete.

"Whadayawant?" he slurred, his head lolling back to get a better look.

Rob ignored him and pressed the buzzer on the door beside the chip shop.

Jenny stood on the pavement and looked up. "The lights are off," she whispered.

"Not surprising at this hour," he murmured. They could've waited until daybreak, but by then Jamie might be at work — or worse, on his way out of the country if he was guilty. Or, with enough time, he might have crafted a perfect alibi. No, it was always better to catch people off guard, even if it meant showing up in the dead of night.

Like Natasha, it took several rings to rouse him, but then the door buzzed open. They walked up a dingy flight of stairs, a naked bulb wobbling from the stained ceiling above. The carpet had a dark, unidentifiable print on it and felt slightly sticky underfoot. "Nice place," Jenny murmured.

The door to the flat above was open, and silhouetted against the light stood a male figure. "Jamie?" Rob asked. "Jamie McNamara?"

A frown. "Who wants to know?"

"We're police detectives." Rob showed his ID card. "DCI Miller and DS Bird. Can we come in?"

"Jamie's not here," replied the barefooted man, who was wearing a hastily pulled-on T-shirt and a pair of jogging bottoms.

Rob frowned and glanced behind him into the flat. "Who are you?"

"His flatmate."

"You got a name?"

He scowled, clearly unhappy to share it. "Gregory Randall."

Rob stared at the man in the dim light. He had dusty blond hair and was taller than the rough description Natasha had given them. "Where is Jamie?"

"Quite honestly, I have no idea. He travels for work."

"What does he do?" Jenny asked.

"He's a reporter. Works for the *Guardian*."

Rob pursed his lips. "How long has he been doing that?"

"As long as I've known him, and that's been several years. Sorry, but what's this about?"

"A friend of his was killed yesterday." Rob decided to share only what was needed to get Jamie's whereabouts. "We wanted to inform him of her death."

The flatmate shuffled back, clearly surprised by the news. "Shit, man. I mean, that's awful. Who was it?"

"You know Lucy Andrews?"

He thought for a moment. "Nah."

"Well, Gregory, do you know how we can get hold of him?"

"Um, yeah. I can give you his number. That's all I got. I don't know where he went. Probably some war zone somewhere."

"How long has he been away?"

A shrug. "At least two weeks."

Rob's stomach sank. This was a dead end. Jamie couldn't have killed Lucy, and he sure as hell didn't kill Julie, which meant he was in the clear. They'd run his mobile anyway, just to fact-check the story, but he didn't think they'd find anything untoward. "Right, thanks."

Jenny took down Jamie's mobile number, and they left. They drove back to the office in a weary silence, Jenny at the wheel, lost in her own thoughts.

Rob stared out of the window at the dark, murky Thames and wondered what secrets it held. If only it could reveal who the murderer was, cough them up when the tide came in, just like it had with Lucy Andrews' body.

But that would be too easy.

Back at the squad room, it was eerily quiet apart from the whir of the computers and the faint ticking of a clock on the wall. Will was staring unblinkingly at his screen, while Celeste was free-pouring sugar into yet another cup of coffee, and Trent was mindlessly watching CCTV footage on quadruple speed, his eyes red-rimmed and glassy. They all glanced up as Rob and Jenny entered.

"Anything?" Will asked, tiredly.

Rob shook his head. "Wasn't him. He's been abroad for two weeks on a job. Will you run his number for me to confirm?"

"On it." Will took the piece of notepaper Jenny handed him.

It was nearing 4 a.m. when Trent gave a sharp gasp. "Sir, I think I've found something."

"CCTV?" Rob peeled himself out of his chair. Every muscle complained. The rest of the team gathered around Trent's computer, peering hopefully over his shoulder.

"It's the camera outside one of the rowing clubs on Lower Richmond," Trent said excitedly.

Having driven that road often, Rob knew that section of the river was lined with school and university boathouses, all using the tidal Thames as their training ground.

Trent replayed the footage. The timestamp said 8.47 p.m. The waterfront was well lit, and still quite busy. They spotted dog walkers and joggers, a trailer of eight boats parked to one side, teenage girls dressed in skimpy outfits, and strapping young lads with broad shoulders wooing them with easy, public schoolboy charm.

"I don't see anything out of the ordinary," Rob muttered.

"Wait." Trent hunched over, his body poised.

The video continued. More laughing students, a van driving past and then . . .

"There!"

A dark shadow passed behind the trailer, visible only between the racks. It was quick, like he was walking fast, head bowed, shoulders hunched as if he didn't want to be noticed. Trent paused the video, catching the man at the edge of the screen.

"Looks furtive," Jenny said, nodding at Trent.

Rob studied the figure. His constable must have had eagle eyes to spot that. Side on, it was hard to tell what type of build he had, or how tall he was, or even if it was a male. By the slouched shoulders and hoodie, he guessed it was a man, but he knew better than to assume anything. "The damn boats are in the way," he growled.

"Play it again," Jenny said, leaning in even closer. "Slowly."

It ran at half speed, the black-and-white images clear but jerky.

"I'd say he's at least six feet," Will said, "judging by the height of those boats on the top of the trailer."

Rob nodded. "Agreed. Physique?"

"Average. Nothing remarkable. Not skinny, but not wide either. Certainly not as broad as those guys." Will nodded to some rowers.

"If it is our killer, why is he coming this way?" Rob asked, thinking out loud.

"He could live close to there," Celeste suggested.

"There are no buses or trains in that area," Will confirmed. "Only the river path that leads to Lower Putney, and then Barnes and Mortlake."

"He could have parked up one of those side roads," Trent suggested. "Away from the crime scene, but easy to get to afterwards, especially if he walked along the foreshore."

"Trent has a point," Jenny looked up. "The tide was out, so if he wanted to avoid notice, he could have crept along below the embankment wall. He'd have been totally hidden down there, and in shadow."

"Plus, it was already dark," Rob added.

"Yeah, it would have been impossible to see him," Jenny finished.

Rob took a deep breath. "So he comes up the slipway on the west side of the bridge and melts into the crowd on the embankment."

"*If* it's him," Harry pointed out, running a hand through his thick hair. "I don't mean to play devil's advocate, but that could be anyone walking home along the embankment in dark clothing."

He was right. Another assumption.

Rob sighed. "It's the closest thing we've got to a lead. Let's try to pick him up down the line." Trent nodded. "But not now. I want you all to go home and get some shut-eye. Let's pick this up first thing tomorrow morning."

If they were lucky, they'd manage three or four hours' sleep, which would stave off the exhaustion and the accompanying mistakes that came with it.

The office emptied out, until it was only Rob and Trent left. *Shit*, Rob realised, the constable lived in Marlow. By the time he'd driven home, it would be time to turn around and come back again.

"You're welcome to crash at mine," he offered awkwardly, as Trent leaned back in his chair and closed his eyes.

The young PC jerked up with a squeak. "Oh, er . . . thank you, sir, but I'm okay here."

Rob frowned. "You sure?"

"Yeah, I can sleep anywhere."

"Okay, then." Rob said goodnight and left the office. His was the only other car besides Trent's in the car park. Luckily, his house was only two miles away, and at this time of night, it would take less than ten minutes.

As he drove along Upper Richmond, enjoying the rare freedom of the uncluttered road, he thought about Natasha Wakefield and Jamie McNamara. Two people he hadn't even considered in the Julie Andrews case, purely because he hadn't known about their relationship. How differently things might have turned out if he had.

And not for the better.

They'd never have cottoned on to Simon Burridge, never have reached Yvette in time, never have . . .

He shook his head and concentrated on the road ahead. Sometimes, fuck-ups were a blessing. The problem was, there was no way of knowing it at the time.

CHAPTER 10

Jo was fast asleep when Rob got home, so he didn't wake her. He simply slipped into bed and, within seconds, was out cold. When he woke up three hours later, his head was surprisingly clear, the fog of exhaustion lifting, though he knew it wouldn't last. Three hours of sleep wasn't enough — not for what was coming. He lay still, staring at the ceiling, feeling the weight of the investigation pressing down on him.

"You okay?" Jo's voice was soft, sleepy. She rolled towards him, her arm draping over his chest. "I didn't hear you come in."

"New case," he murmured, breathing in her vanilla-scented hair, so warm and familiar. He wrapped an arm around her and drew her close.

"Is it bad?"

He hesitated. "Yeah."

"Want to talk about it?" Her voice still had that gravelly undertone — remnants of the attack that had almost taken her life. It had been nearly ten months now, and while the emotional trauma would take longer to fade, the silver scar at her throat was thinner and less raised.

Jo's resilience amazed him. She never mentioned it, never complained, not unless he specifically asked how she was doing, and even then he could tell she didn't relish talking about it. It wasn't that she was holding it in or blocking it out. She'd been to therapy, faced it head on, and was now determined to move on with her life.

But him? He couldn't shake the memory, couldn't forget the sound of her choking, her blood spilling onto the kitchen tiles. In his darker moments, the horror still gnawed at him. Horror and guilt. Because he'd let it happen — trusted the wrong man. He should've seen it coming. Should've known the guy was a ticking time bomb. But he didn't. He'd missed the signs, and Jo had paid the price.

"Maybe later." His arm tightened around her, fingers gripping her nightgown as if she might slip away again if he let go. "Right now, I don't want to think about it."

She snuggled into him. They stayed that way, shutting out the world for a few blissful minutes, before they heard a snuffle and movement in the next-door bedroom.

"I'll go," he said, throwing back the covers.

Jo had started working again, though mostly from home, which enabled her to be more hands-on with Jack. From what he could gather, she was coordinating logistics, liaising with MI5 field agents and gradually easing back into her old routine. She had a separate work phone, some high-security thing encrypted with all the latest tech, and a government-issued laptop.

Before she could even start, Rob had been vetted, answering what felt like an endless stream of probing questions. Surprisingly, or maybe unsurprisingly, they'd even asked about his father, a man he hardly ever saw and had nothing to do with.

Even their nanny, Tanya, had gone through the process, much to her alarm. But they'd cleared everyone without issue. Or at least, he thought they had. Tanya would have passed with flying colours. He wasn't sure about himself.

After scooping Jack up and making his way downstairs, Rob nearly stumbled over Trigger, their overzealous golden Labrador who never failed to greet him like he'd been gone for days. Jack giggled, making him grin in response. "Come on, then. Let's go eat."

He got them both fed — Jack with his porridge, Trigger with his kibble — the familiar motions comfortable and grounding. A brief moment of normality before the chaos of the day began.

He made himself a coffee, finally having mastered the Nespresso machine, and made a second cup for Jo. Handing it to her as she walked in, he lingered for a moment, savouring the sight of his little family, the messy comfort of it all. "Sorry, I can't stay. Still early days." He hadn't even left yet and he could feel the job clawing at him.

Jo met his gaze, nodding. She knew the drill.

"Good luck." Her fingers brushed his, a small, fleeting gesture of reassurance. With one last glance at Jo, Jack and a forlorn-looking Trigger, Rob slipped out the door, his mind already shifting gears back to the hunt.

* * *

"I've enlarged the stills of the suspect," Trent told him as he walked into the office. "They're on the incident room whiteboard." The constable's normally crisp white shirt was wrinkled, his black tie crooked, but his eyes were alert. Looked like he'd managed to get a decent few hours of sleep.

Rob shrugged off his jacket and threw his keys onto the desk. "Any luck tracking him further down the embankment?"

"Not yet, but I've only just started going through the actual footage. One of the cameras was down for maintenance, and another had the wrong timestamp. Took me an hour before I realised I was looking at the wrong day."

Celeste, who was already at her desk, said, "You'll find that happens a lot."

The joys of council CCTV.

Rob dispatched Harry and Celeste to the Design Centre in Chelsea to interview Lucy's colleagues. "Get the exact time she left work and see if she mentioned anything before she went missing."

"We're on it," Harry said, eager to visit London's stylish design hub.

Rob turned to Will, who was still scrolling through the victim's call list, filling in a spreadsheet with notes. "Any luck with those contacts?"

"Nothing yet," Will muttered, eyes glued to his iPad. "Everyone I've spoken to so far is wedding-related. Some of the vendors didn't even know Lucy was dead. Can you believe that?"

Rob raised an eyebrow. "That's not surprising. Justin must be too shaken to think about notifying anyone."

Jenny walked in with a takeaway coffee and heard the tail end of the conversation. "Cancelling the wedding is probably the last thing on the poor guy's mind."

Rob nodded, remembering Justin's hollow, broken look when they questioned him. "I'll get Becca to step in. She can help with that."

Jenny went over to help Trent, who was still painstakingly reviewing CCTV footage. Rob, meanwhile, made his way to Mayhew's office, his gut tightening as he knocked and stepped inside.

"Have you seen this morning's papers?" Mayhew slid a tabloid across her desk.

Rob glanced at the headline. *PUTNEY GIRL MURDERED ON RIVERBANK* screamed across the cover in bold black letters.

With a grunt, he scanned the article. No mention of the Surrey Stalker case or the rings, thank God.

"We're in the clear — for now," Mayhew said, as if reading his thoughts.

"Let's hope it stays that way. We don't want them drawing any parallels."

"They won't, *if* we keep the original details away from the press. Five years is a long time. That's a lot of news cycles."

Still, Rob knew it only took one eagle-eyed reporter to connect the dots. He was surprised at her optimism — that wasn't like Mayhew at all. Usually, she was all caution and dire warnings about what would happen if they crossed the line again.

Now that he thought about it, she did look different today. Prettier, somehow. The sharp edges of her face had softened, a hint of colour warming her normally pale cheeks. And there was something new in her eyes. A sparkle that he hadn't seen before.

There was only one thing that could explain it. She was in love, or if not love, then lust. He was willing to bet that Mayhew had got laid last night. The woman was practically glowing.

Thank God for that. He didn't know who the guy was, but he wanted to thank him personally. Mayhew in a good mood would make all their lives easier.

"We will do our best, ma'am."

"I reviewed the old case files last night," she said.

Rob frowned. So much for his romance theory. "The similarities between Lucy's and Julie's murders are . . . uncanny. Sisters, both engaged to the same man. Are we *sure* this is the work of a copycat?"

"It has to be." Rob's voice was steady but cold. "Burridge is dead."

She hesitated for a moment, then said, "What about the fiancé, Justin King?"

"What about him?"

"He's the common denominator here. Does he have an alibi for the night of the murder?"

"We're still verifying it." Rob wasn't in the mood to tell her Justin's alibi was shaky. "But Justin didn't kill Julie, and I very much doubt he killed Lucy. The guy's a wreck."

"Have you at least considered the possibility that he copied the Surrey Stalker's MO to get rid of his girlfriend?"

"Of course, but he has no motive. He loved Lucy. They were planning their wedding, a new life together. Why would he kill her?"

"I don't know. Maybe he felt obligated, maybe he was trapped. Who knows? People do all sorts of crazy things."

She was right, they did. But not this time.

"Justin did not do this."

Mayhew fixed her arctic-blue eyes on him. "Then how do you explain the connection?"

"I can't. Not yet. But we're working on it."

CHAPTER 11

Celeste looked up as they walked into the Design Centre. The glass-and-chrome structure gleamed under the midday sun, bright and airy, like the centre-page spread in a glossy style magazine. Huge windows flooded the surrounding showrooms with light.

Both she and Harry paused, taking a moment to absorb everything, watching as designers and clients strolled around, sipping coffee, chatting about fabrics or discussing the next big trend in luxury living. Everything looked so polished, so perfect — it was hard to imagine anything bad ever happening here.

It was possible, however, that someone had hovered in plain sight, watching Lucy Andrews before following her home. Celeste shivered. "Which company did she work for again?"

"Del Castillo Fabrics." He glanced around at the ground-floor showrooms. "Can't see them on this level."

They walked up a storey and found it almost immediately. The showroom was a sprawling, elegant space that looked more like an art gallery than a fabric store.

"This is it." Celeste walked inside, the draping fabrics — velvets, silks and linens in every imaginable shade — catching her eye. Subtle lighting showcased the textures, and she resisted the urge to reach out and touch them.

A large, wooden table stood in the centre, neatly stacked with artfully arranged swatches, while a petite woman in an expensive-looking outfit — Chanel, maybe? — strutted around, keeping a sharp eye on everything.

"It's hard to imagine Lucy in a place like this," Harry whispered. "She wasn't the type."

It was true. The crime scene photos showed a woman with a more casual style. Even though her skirt had been pulled up around her waist, they could still tell it was a high-street brand — nothing designer. Her blouse, torn and ripped, was viscose, the kind you'd find in any chain store.

Celeste decided to take the lead. As the constable who'd been with the Met longer, it was time she pushed herself out of her comfort zone. She was no longer the rookie, and if she didn't step up, Trent would surpass her in no time. He'd caught DCI Miller's eye, and she'd have to work hard to impress her senior now. The time she thought she had to learn the ropes had run out.

Harry opened his mouth, but she got in first. "Hello, I'm DC Parker, and this is DC Malhotra from the Met's Major Investigation Team. We'd like to ask you a few questions."

Harry glanced at her in surprise.

"Is this about Lucy?" the woman asked.

"Yes. We understand she worked here."

A nod.

"Such a terrible thing to happen. Lucy was . . . well, she was an asset to the team."

Fairly generic response, Celeste thought.

"What was her position here?" She studied the woman's carefully composed expression.

"She was our admin assistant," the woman said. "She took orders and arranged shipping and so on. She'll be missed."

So she was a back-office worker. That made more sense. Celeste got the impression she'd be missed more for her efficiency than anything else.

"Did she ever help on the showroom floor?" Harry asked.

Celeste bit her lip. That was an angle she hadn't considered — that someone had seen her on the shop floor and targeted her that way. It was a highly visible position. Hundreds of people came through here every day.

The woman shook her head.

"What is your name?" Celeste asked.

"Tabitha Hilton-Ross."

"And what is your position here?"

Tabitha tossed her mane of blonde hair over her shoulder. "I'm the showroom manager."

"Tabitha, was Lucy acting strangely at all in the days or weeks before she was . . . before she died?" If she'd learned anything from the guv, it was not to give out more information than was necessary, even if it had been splashed all over the papers. In her peripheral vision, she saw Harry nod. She appreciated that he was letting her run with it.

"Not that I recall. I mean, we didn't talk much. She was in the office most of the time."

Celeste glanced towards the rear of the showroom, where an insignificant door blended seamlessly into the background. "I understand. So she didn't appear to be scared or agitated at all?"

"I don't think so."

"Could you tell me what time she left here on Wednesday?"

"We close at five. She always leaves promptly, especially when she's meeting Justin."

"Oh, you know her fiancé?"

"Of course. He's been in a few times to meet her for lunch." Tabitha offered no opinion on Justin, and Celeste got the impression she didn't consider him worthy of being friends with.

Tabitha was something of a snob.

"Did you know Lucy was meeting Justin on Wednesday night?" she asked.

"Oh yeah. She'd been looking forward to it since Monday. Date night, she called it." Tabitha barely resisted rolling her eyes.

Celeste wasn't warming to her.

"Anyone else know?" Harry looked around the showroom. A woman was browsing in one corner, holding up fabrics to the light.

"Um, Neville was here when she told us. He's our distributor."

"Neville?"

"Neville Foster. He works for the shipping company."

"We'll need his details," Celeste said.

Tabitha was looking over at the customer, itching to rush over and assist.

"Now, please." Celeste shot her a pointed look, and didn't miss Harry's surreptitious grin.

"Okay, give me a moment." She rushed off to the office.

"Nice work," Harry whispered.

She gave a grateful nod.

Tabitha returned within two minutes. "Here you are. The details of the company and Neville's personal mobile number."

"Thank you."

"If you'll excuse me?"

Celeste nodded, and Tabitha darted across the room as fast as her Louboutins would carry her.

"Everyone knew Lucy had a date with Justin," Celeste summed up as they walked back to the squad car.

"Yep. I can't see Tabitha being involved. Murder would be beneath her."

Celeste grinned. "Indeed. That leaves Neville Foster, the delivery man."

"We'll get on him as soon as we get back to the office. Let's go report to the Chief."

Celeste couldn't help feeling a sense of accomplishment as they drove back to Putney. Her first solo on-the-spot interrogation, and she'd uncovered a lead. DCI Miller would be impressed.

CHAPTER 12

"Good work," Rob said once Celeste had told him what they'd discovered. Harry had stood beside her while she briefed him, which meant she'd taken the lead on this one. He was glad she was stepping up. He addressed them both. "Get an address for Neville Foster and go pay him a visit. We need his alibi for Wednesday evening."

They nodded in unison. Harry began the DVLA search while Celeste stood beside his desk, not even bothering to remove her jacket.

Will beckoned Rob over. "The best man, Nathan Sheldon, knew that Justin was meeting Lucy that night. Nathan suggested getting together over a pint to discuss the ceremony, but Justin told him he couldn't do Wednesday as he was meeting Lucy. They rescheduled for Monday."

"Sounds believable." Rob suppressed a yawn. Damn, he needed a decent coffee and not this awful office crap. "We'd better check him out anyway. Does he have an alibi for Wednesday night?"

"Says he and his wife were at home."

"She vouch for him?"

"Not yet," Will replied. "She works at a recruitment firm in Clapham."

"Well, let's go talk to her. You up for an excursion?"

"Sure." Will didn't get out of the office much. "It'll be good to step away from the computer."

"Great." Rob needed to clear his head. The discussion with Mayhew had blackened his mood, and he didn't want to take it out on his team.

* * *

"How do you think Trent is doing?" Rob asked Will as he drove to Clapham.

Will, in the passenger seat, set down his iPad. "Great. He puts in a lot of effort, he's trying to learn the ropes, and he's astute. I think he'll make a great detective."

Rob gave a pleased nod. He was glad he'd listened to his gut on that one. The kid was wasted in Marlow.

"I'm not sure Celeste is as happy," Will added.

"Celeste? Why's that?" Had he missed something?

"Well, she used to be the new kid on the block, but now Trent has that honour, and he's arguably getting more attention than she did."

He frowned. That much was true. "Has she said something to you?" The last thing he wanted was for a member of his team to be unhappy. Celeste may not have the same policing style as Trent, or wear her heart on her sleeve as much, but she was a grafter. She put in the hard work, always dotting the i's and crossing the t's. They needed someone steady like that on the team.

"No, but I've noticed the way she's taken some subtle swipes at Trent. Nothing major, just thought you should be aware of it."

"Thanks," he said distractedly. She had questioned Lucy's colleague at the Design Centre, taking the initiative, but he didn't want animosity in the team. He made a mental note to have a word with her as soon as he could.

Will's iPad vibrated, and he glanced down. "I've just got the results of the location lookup I ordered on Jamie

McNamara's mobile phone. Interconnect services put him in Lebanon at the time of the murder."

"Expected as much." Julie's former boyfriend and Natasha Wakefield's fling wasn't a suspect. They had several other leads to follow up on anyway, starting with Sheldon's wife.

* * *

Rosy Sheldon was a curvaceous blonde woman in her early twenties with a cherubic face and enormous, smiling blue eyes that instantly clouded over when he mentioned Lucy's name.

"We were devastated to hear the news," she said sombrely. They were sitting in a vacant interview room at the recruitment company, around a small, square table. The glass walls were shuttered, and there was no window, which made it rather claustrophobic for job applicants, Rob thought. "Lucy was such a lovely person, and she and Justin were so happy."

"I believe your husband was the best man?" Rob asked.

She sighed sadly. "Yes, he had a speech prepared and everything."

"We understand your husband asked Justin to meet him to discuss the arrangements on Wednesday night?"

She frowned. "He didn't go out on Wednesday night. Justin said he couldn't make it. He was meeting Lucy. Something about a date night."

The stories aligned. Looked like Nathan was in the clear too.

"Nathan tell you that?"

She nodded. "I think they changed it to Monday, not that it matters now." She hung her head.

"You were at home with your husband on Wednesday evening?" Rob asked, just to be clear.

"Yes, we watched the start of that new series on TV. You know, the one where the husband suspects his wife is having an affair? It's got a French-sounding name."

"*Double Entendre*," Will supplied.

She snapped her fingers. "That's it."

"What did you think?" Rob asked.

She blinked, a little thrown by the question. "Of the episode?"

"Yeah. Was it any good?"

She shrugged. "I thought the wife was great, but the husband . . . not so much. Too much of a wimp. I get why she strayed. A woman wants a man to be . . . well, a man, right?"

Rob nodded, unsure how to respond, so he changed the subject.

"Do you know if there was anything bothering Lucy or Justin? Anyone hassling them or giving them a hard time about getting married?"

"Oh heavens, no. They were the perfect couple. Everyone was so happy for them, especially after what happened to Julie." She gasped, her hand flying to her mouth. "Oh my God. You think someone was trying to stop them from getting married?"

"It's just a line of enquiry we're following," Rob said hastily.

Her eyes grew even larger. "I don't think so," she whispered. "Like I said, everyone was very happy for them."

"Any money troubles?" Will asked.

"Who doesn't have those?" she scoffed. "But no, they both worked. As far as I know, they were sound."

Will nodded. Rob knew he'd looked at their bank statements and hadn't found any red flags.

"Okay then," he said, standing up. They had what they'd come for. Nathan's alibi checked out. From what he could gather, neither he nor his wife had a motive for wanting to murder Lucy or hurt Justin.

***

Rob and Will got back to the office to find Jenny pacing up and down behind Trent's desk like a caged tiger. "It's like he magically disappeared," she said, turning to face them. "There is absolutely no trace of the suspect after that quick glimpse behind the trailer."

Rob walked over. "There must be something."

She put her hands on her hips. "Well, if there is we can't find it."

Rob turned to Trent. "You checked every camera along that stretch?"

"Yes, sir. All the boat clubs have them for security and we've been through them all for the designated time frame. He's nowhere to be seen."

Jenny raked an agitated hand through her hair, which was loose now — no longer pulled back in the efficient ponytail she'd had earlier. "We think he slipped between the clubhouses and headed up to Lower Richmond."

"But we'd have picked him up there." Rob shared her frustration.

"Unless he got into a car parked on one of the side streets near the river," Trent suggested. "It's the only way he could've vanished without a trace. If he was on foot, we'd have him by now."

Rob rubbed his forehead. "I suppose checking the nearest ANPR camera is out of the question."

"Too many variables," Jenny replied. "Too many routes out of the area. He could have gone towards Barnes, up to East Sheen, over the bridge into Fulham. We'd be shooting in the dark."

She was right.

"Okay, thanks for trying. Let's leave it there. Take a break. You guys have been at this for hours."

"I was going to take Trent through the original case files," Jenny said. "If that's okay with you? It might be useful to look at everything with fresh eyes."

He gave a stiff nod. "It can't hurt."

It was like a cruel joke. His worst moment on the job, the low point that had almost got him kicked off the force before he'd even begun to develop his career, was the latest point of scrutiny. Everyone in his team would know his shame.

Sure, he'd been exonerated, the killing justified, but he still had to live with the stigma. Five years ago, it had been a tough thing to get over, but he'd managed. Now it was being dredged up again.

He sighed. There was fuck all he could do about it. They needed to revisit that investigation, needed to rake through it with a fine-tooth comb. Someone connected to the case was copying the Surrey Stalker's MO. Whether they'd been actively involved in the original investigation, or they had access to the files, he didn't know. Either way, Jenny was right. It needed to be done — and there was nobody he'd rather do it than her.

Rob's inbox was overflowing, as usual, so he sat down and scrolled through it. One email immediately caught his eye. It was from Liz Kramer.

Clicking it open, he scanned the contents.

Just three sentences. Direct. Efficient.

Typical Liz.

We found a strand of hair in the victim's mouth. Attached the profile for you to run. Lab report to follow. Liz

"Holy shit," he breathed.

DNA. And it wasn't the victim's.

Pulse racing, he opened the attachment.

Liz had sent him the DNA profile early, before the official forensic report had been processed. Normally, everything went through formal channels, and running DNA through the national database required proper authorisation. But with a backlog and delays at the lab, Liz knew how much they needed a break in the case. Sending it now wasn't bending the rules too far — everything would be officially recorded in the forthcoming report, keeping the chain of custody intact. This just gave him a head start.

Rob followed the official procedure and logged into the national DNA database. If he got no hits, he'd run it against HOLMES and, if necessary, expand the search internationally through Interpol's DNA Gateway.

"Got something?" Jenny asked, carrying a cup of machine coffee.

"Maybe." He filled her in on the DNA discovery.

"Seriously? This could be our breakthrough, Rob." Her eyes glistened as she looked at him. "It could be the killer's DNA."

He didn't want to get his hopes up.

"I'm surprised they found anything on her body, considering she'd been in the water all night." Rob copied and pasted the DNA profile into the database.

"It could have got lodged in her mouth when she fought off her attacker," Jenny reasoned. "Particularly if her mouth was open."

Like when she was screaming.

"Okay, here goes." Rob hit the search button and sat back. To his surprise, it settled on a match almost immediately.

"The owner is in the system!" Jenny peered over his shoulder.

Rob clicked on the result, and his heart skipped a beat.

No way. It couldn't be.

It simply wasn't possible.

"Oh Lord," Jenny whispered, placing a hand on his shoulder to steady herself.

The name that the system returned was Simon Burridge.

CHAPTER 13

"It can't be right," Rob croaked, staring at the Surrey Stalker's name on the computer screen.

"Run it again." Jenny's hand tightened on his shoulder.

He ran the DNA profile a second time, but it returned the same result.

Simon Burridge.

Rob exhaled like he'd been punched in the gut. "There must be some mistake."

Jenny stood up and bit her lip. A long moment passed where neither of them spoke.

Eventually, Jenny said, "Okay, let's think about this. Assuming this is not an error, the only way for Simon Burridge's DNA to appear at that crime scene is if it was planted there. Correct?"

Rob nodded, but in his mind he was spiralling back to that night.

The chase through the woods. The struggle. He could still feel the rough edge of the rock in his hand as he brought it down on Burridge's skull, over and over, until the man crumpled. In that moment, he'd lost all control. Something primal had taken over, blind fury driving him until Jo had yanked him back to reality, pulling him off Burridge's limp body.

It was self-defence. That's what the inquiry had ruled and that's what he'd told himself over and over, but seeing Burridge's name now, like a ghost from his past, brought all the guilt and doubt flooding back.

Jenny continued her train of thought. "As well as the original details of the case, the killer also managed to get some DNA."

"A strand of hair," Rob muttered. His fingers twitched as he recalled throwing down the bloody rock. Burridge's hair would have been on that.

"Exactly. Now, how would someone go about getting that?"

Rob scratched his stubbly chin. This case was getting more bizarre by the minute. "Assuming he wasn't at any of the original crime scenes, he would need access to the evidence collected."

"Which means visiting the Met's Forensic Services Command Unit."

Rob nodded. "He'd need clearance. There are strict protocols in place." His voice sounded distant, even to himself.

What kind of sick game was this?

Burridge was dead.

I killed him.

Yet his DNA was here, haunting him — taunting him — from beyond the grave.

Jenny faced him, her eyes searching his. "Are we saying whoever did this is law enforcement?"

There was a pause as they both considered this possibility.

"If someone accessed the unit," Rob said, "there would be a digital trail. He'd have to request it and that would be on their system."

"Let's start there, then." Jenny straightened up. "We'll drive to the storage facility now and check the logs. That will tell us if anyone has accessed the evidence since the case was closed."

"We can't take this to Mayhew yet," Rob muttered. "Not until we find out what the hell is going on."

Jenny nodded. "Agreed. If someone has tampered with evidence, she's going to want to know who."

* * *

"Someone's screwing with us," Rob growled as they drove to the forensic storage unit, based in Central London.

Jenny glanced across at him. "It certainly seems that way, but who'd want us to think Simon Burridge is responsible for murdering Lucy Andrews?"

"The real killer," Rob stated flatly. "This is his way of diverting attention from himself."

"But to go to these lengths?" Jenny shook her head, keeping her eyes on the road. "Surely there are easier ways to frame somebody. I mean, did they really think we were going to believe a dead man killed Lucy Andrews?"

"He wants us to revisit the original case," Rob said. "That takes time. While we're distracted, scrambling to justify the outcome of the original investigation and trying to figure out who it could be, he's in the clear."

"This might not be a serial offender at all," Jenny said. "Just some guy who wanted Lucy dead and replicated her sister's murder to do it."

"That's my guess, but what's his motive? Lucy was well liked by her colleagues and friends, she was planning a wedding, she was happy. There's no reason to want her dead."

"Unless Justin was the indirect target all along," Jenny said. "Maybe the killer wanted to cause him pain."

"But why?" Rob slumped in his seat. "There isn't any obvious motive. Unless Becca can find one."

The Met's Forensic Services Command Unit was a squat, grey structure with tinted windows that hinted at the secrets hidden within. After parking, they passed through a revolving door into a secure entrance hall manned by several uniformed officers.

Rob and Jenny both showed their ID cards and were escorted down a long corridor to the warehouse-style evidence lock-up. "You need to sign in," their escort said, before turning and walking back the way they'd come.

"Names and badge numbers," the duty officer said. He was positioned behind thick Perspex with pockmarked holes through which to talk. His voice sounded muffled and disjointed. The name on his shirt badge said *Mullins*.

They dutifully handed them over, and Mullins began entering them into his computer.

"Do you do this with everybody who comes here?" Rob asked.

Mullins glanced up. "Have to. It's procedure. Nobody's getting in here without the proper authorisation."

"Good to know. If we wanted to check the logs for an old investigation, you could give us that information?"

He frowned, then glanced at Rob's ID card. His rank afforded him the necessary clearance. "Sure, Detective Chief Inspector Miller. I can get that information for you. Do you have the case number?"

Rob gave it to him, and Mullins set about pulling up the evidence log.

They waited while the officer peered at the screen. "Haven't had anyone request those files in . . . let's see . . . four years. Last check-in was right after the case was closed."

His stomach sank. "Nothing recent?"

"Nope."

"Who viewed them four years ago?" Jenny asked.

"That would be Chief Superintendent Sam Lawrence," the officer said.

Rob glanced at Jenny and shook his head. Sam would have reviewed the evidence for the inquiry into the death of Simon Burridge. Nothing suspicious there.

"You're absolutely sure nobody else has accessed that evidence since then?"

"One hundred per cent, sir."

"And there's no way of getting past you?"

"No, sir. Me or my colleague are always on duty. We never leave the post unmanned, and nobody can get in without being buzzed through by one of us."

"What happens after hours?" Rob asked.

"The entire building is locked up and we have surveillance cameras in the lobby and above your head over there." He gestured to the ceiling above them. They both looked up. A bulbous camera lens gazed down at them.

"So you'd know if anyone breached the room?"

"The alarm would go off," Mullins said. "It's pretty secure."

"Thanks." Heart sinking, Rob turned to Jenny. "This is a dead end. Whoever planted that evidence didn't get it here."

She gave a reluctant nod. "I'm with you on that."

* * *

Before he went back to the office, Rob told Jenny he was going to grab a decent coffee, but he desperately needed some space to think.

Putney High Street was bustling, the afternoon sun drawing shoppers to the centre, the shops and the river. Rob moved through the crowd on autopilot, his thoughts circling the same impossible question.

How had the killer got hold of Simon Burridge's DNA?

He walked mechanically, the crowd a blur around him. The closest coffee shop was Caffè Nero, but he couldn't face the possibility of running into any of his colleagues right now. Not with his mind reeling like this.

Instead, he headed down towards the bridge, to a little café adjoining St Mary's Church. It was community run, only open during certain hours, but whoever was in charge knew their coffee — it wasn't half bad. Rob wasn't even sure if he cared about the coffee today, he just needed to be away from people, away from *that name* flashing in his head.

They could rule out the Forensic Unit. It was almost a relief, knowing the perpetrator hadn't been a dirty cop. At least they wouldn't have to endure the damning media fallout. The facility hadn't been breached, so unless Officer

Mullins was lying to them — and he didn't think he was — that lead had been shut down.

Yet, somehow, Burridge's DNA had turned up in Lucy Andrews' mouth, as if the dead man had returned to invade their lives.

On the opposite side of the river, lorries and trailers lined the embankment, loaded with camera rigs, scaffolding and branded equipment. Crews were already hard at work, setting up for the Oxford–Cambridge Boat Race next weekend. Temporary stands were going up, dark and light blue flags fluttering in the breeze.

Normally, he'd have at least a passing interest in the chaos. It was always a raucous weekend, with students flooding the towpath, pubs overflowing, local police stretched thin trying to contain it all. But right now, he couldn't dredge up much enthusiasm. If not the Forensic Unit, then how had Burridge's DNA got there?

As he joined the queue at the café, he went through the various options. The strand of hair could have come from something personal. A hairbrush, a comb, clothing — something that Burridge had used before he died. If the killer had somehow got hold of one of his belongings, that would explain how they had planted the DNA. But who would have kept Burridge's things after all this time?

He made a mental note to dig into Burridge's family and known associates as soon as he got back to the office. Someone in Burridge's past, someone with access to his personal effects, could be the one playing games with them. With *him*.

If that was true, it meant the killer had been meticulously planning this for years, holding on to an object that would connect Burridge to a new crime. The thought made his skin crawl.

He reached the counter, eyes scanning the room out of habit. And that's when he saw her — Felicity Mayhew. She was sitting at a corner table, talking to some man whose back was towards him. Rob froze. His instincts screamed to turn around and leave before she spotted him.

Shit.

Of all days . . . He couldn't deal with her right now. But if she saw him sneaking out, it'd only be worse.

And of course, she looked up.

Double shit.

There was no way out now. He nodded at her — quick, professional — then turned back to face the counter. He didn't care about her response. She was probably schmoozing some councillor or businessman, always working an angle, plotting her next move. That's how she operated. But today, he didn't have the energy to talk to her, not when Burridge's ghost was looming over everything.

When the coffee was ready, Rob snapped the lid on and headed for the door, ignoring Felicity completely. Even the best coffee couldn't clear the bitter taste in his mouth. He needed to get back to the office and start digging into Burridge's connections.

The killer had gone to extraordinary lengths to plant that DNA, possibly even holding on to a piece of the dead man's life for all these years. Rob took a scalding sip and swore under his breath. He resented feeling lost in the past, chasing shadows, while the killer moved freely in the present.

CHAPTER 14

"I've updated the team," Jenny said as Rob walked into the incident room. Mayhew still wasn't back, thank God, but the team were primed and ready to discuss this new development.

"There could be a mix-up in the database," Will said, leaping straight into the brainstorming that they were so good at. "I mean, Julie was Lucy's sister. It's not unfeasible that the DNA was entered against the wrong name."

He frowned. "As far as I recall, there was never any DNA found in Julie's mouth. Liz specifically said they found this hair in Lucy's mouth."

Will shrugged. "It's worth checking."

"Do it." He gazed around at the team. "Any other suggestions?"

"It was obviously planted," Celeste said, her voice hesitant. "But if they didn't get it from the evidence lock-up, they must have got it from another source."

"Exactly." Rob took a deep breath. He'd wanted someone else to say it. Proof that he wasn't grasping at straws. "What other sources are there?"

"Well, his mother is still alive," Jenny said.

Rob's eyebrows shot up. "She is? I didn't think that scumbag had any living relatives."

"Oh yes, but she changed her name after he was arrested, and moved to Mortlake. Can you believe it?"

"Here? She moved *here*?" Rob stared at her. Jenny had been busy while he'd been out, her thoughts moving along the same lines as his, but while he'd been spinning out in the coffee shop, she'd been doing some actual police work.

Jenny gave a tight nod. "You know that rambling property on Mortlake High Street? The overgrown one with the paint peeling off the front?"

"Yeah, it's a real eyesore," he muttered.

"That's hers."

Rob let out a slow hiss.

"It's quite a coincidence that she moved to the area, isn't it?" Harry glanced around at the team. "I mean, why?"

"Her son is buried at Wandsworth Cemetery." Rob forced his brain into gear. "Maybe she wanted to be nearer to him."

"Bit macabre." Celeste recoiled.

"But she could possibly still have some of his belongings," Jenny pointed out.

Rob allowed himself the briefest of grins. "That's where our killer would have got his DNA. It has to be. I was thinking he'd have to have held on to an item all these years, like some sick, twisted fan, but maybe it's simpler than that."

"I'll still check the true crime groups and forums and see if there's any mention of a Burridge fan club," Will said. "It's not a completely crazy idea. Those freaks do exist."

"Good." Rob felt a flicker of control returning as the fog in his mind started to lift. "What about known associates or friends? Anyone who might still have something of his — clothing, a hairbrush, anything that could hold DNA."

Trent frowned. "Wouldn't a hair sample from five years ago degrade? I thought it had to be from a living person."

Celeste scoffed, even though it was a fair question, especially from a constable with only three months as an investigator.

"DNA can last for years, even decades," Rob explained, frowning at Celeste. She immediately flushed and looked down at her hands. "As long as the hair still has the root or follicle attached, we can extract a viable sample."

"Anthropologists have recovered DNA from centuries-old remains, under the right conditions," Jenny added.

Trent, oblivious to any undercurrents, frowned. "Can they tell how old the sample is?"

Now that was a better question.

"Unfortunately not," Jenny said. "DNA is DNA, no matter the source, and forensic labs don't have a way to date it." She glanced at Rob. "If they did, we could prove it didn't come from a living person."

"Nothing we can do about that," he said. "Jenny, let's go and pay Mrs Burridge a visit."

Harry stood up. "Neville Foster, the delivery man from the Design Centre, was a dead end, by the way. He has a concrete alibi for Wednesday evening. He was at a local theatre with his wife, watching their teenage daughter in *A Midsummer Night's Dream*."

"Okay, cross him off the board, then." Rob had almost forgotten they'd gone to speak to him. He paused, eyeing a still-pink Celeste, who hadn't said a word since he'd given her that sharp look. "Celeste, Jenny was going to run through the original case files with Trent. You take over. Get him up to speed on the Surrey Stalker case."

For a moment, Celeste looked like she might refuse, but one glance at his face and she thought better of it. "Of course, guv."

* * *

Jenny did up her seat belt. "That was either very clever or very foolish."

"What do you mean?" He glanced across at her.

"Celeste and Trent. You know they didn't get off to the best start."

"It was brought to my attention," he said dryly as he turned out of the car park. "I thought they might like each other more if they got to know each other."

"Could go either way," she warned.

He smirked. "We'll soon find out."

He navigated through the high-street traffic, turning onto Lower Richmond Road before reaching the bridge. He headed towards Barnes Common and after weaving down Barnes High Street, they finally arrived at the road that ran along the river towards Mortlake.

On their right, the Thames sparkled in the late-afternoon sunlight. It was low tide, the foreshore pebbly and exposed. A man with a metal detector swept back and forth under Barnes Bridge, hoping to find something of value. Usually, all they discovered was old scrap metal or a rusted trinket that had meant something to someone once but was now long forgotten.

"How old is his mother now?" Rob asked as they passed a row of quaint terraced houses.

"Late sixties, I'd guess," Jenny said. "I didn't have time to pull up her particulars."

"This is the one, isn't it?" He slowed outside a three-storey property in a blocky Georgian style, masked by ivy-covered oak trees and barely visible through the chaotic curtain of leaves. A low brick wall, faded with age and in desperate need of sprucing up, was all that separated the property from the road, but since the house was set back more than its neighbours and was blocked by the trees, it didn't command attention. In fact, it was so nondescript as to be almost invisible.

"Hiding away, just like its owner," Jenny murmured.

They pulled into the drive next to the house, though it was more of a vacant gravel plot than a driveway.

"It's a sizeable property." Rob climbed out of the car and looked around. "How'd she afford a place like this?"

"We'll ask her," Jenny said, her feet crunching on the gravel.

A car door slamming made them turn around, just in time to see a rusty old Ford pull away from the kerb. A man stared back at them — dark hair surrounding a white face, sunglasses covering his eyes.

"Who was that?" Jenny murmured.

"I didn't get a plate, did you?" Rob scowled at the car, which had zipped into the traffic on Lower Richmond.

"No. Maybe Mrs Burridge will be able to enlighten us."

As it turned out, the front door wasn't in use. The dark wood had warped and the exterior was covered in thick, unbroken cobwebs. Even the windows were firmly closed, with white metal burglar bars across them, and more webs holding them together.

"Spooky." Jenny glanced up at the second level. "All the curtains are drawn. Maybe it's been abandoned."

Rob frowned. "Let's check around the other side."

They trudged back through the gravel car park and down towards the river. Sure enough, once they'd fought their way through a path criss-crossed with brambles, they reached a wooden porch with a rocking chair on it overlooking what could generously be called a garden — though it looked more like a wilderness, overtaken by vines and unruly shrubs.

The porch steps groaned as they walked up them, as if protesting the intrusion. Rob banged on the sliding doors. From the street, they could still hear the low hum of traffic, but the heaviness enveloping the place seemed to smother it.

Beside him, Jenny stared at the overgrown sprawl, a swamp of tall grass and half-submerged trees. "I can't believe anyone lives here."

Rob was surprised when a blurry figure of a young woman appeared on the other side of the mottled glass. She turned a key and slid open the doors.

"Hello? Can I help you?" The expression on her face told them she was as surprised at having visitors as they were at finding the house inhabited.

"Yes, we're looking for Mrs Burridge."

This woman must be a care worker or housekeeper. She sounded foreign — Eastern European, Rob guessed — and she wore an apron over skinny jeans and a plain blue T-shirt. On her hands were a pair of bright yellow kitchen gloves.

"Come in." She moved aside, allowing them to enter.

Rob stepped into a dated living room that resembled a scene in *Great Expectations*. A sagging green-velvet sofa faced the garden, the upholstery faded and worn thin in places. A threadbare rug, possibly Persian, sprawled across the floor, the once-rich reds and purples muted by age. Against one wall stood a dark wooden cabinet with glass panes, displaying a china dinner set, what looked like crystal wine glasses, and a silver-plated cutlery set, all untouched. Relics from another era. Rob doubted they'd seen the light of day in decades.

"Monica is in the library. I show you."

The library. He glanced at Jenny, who arched an eyebrow.

"What's your name?" Rob asked, before she could swivel around.

"Oksana," she replied.

"Oksana who?"

"Oksana Petrenko."

"Do you work for Mrs Burridge, Oksana?"

She nodded. "I am carer, but I do cleaning too." Clearly she could understand English but struggled a little with the spoken word.

"Was there a man here?" Jenny asked. "With glasses?" She signalled to her eyes.

"Ah, yes. That is Paul."

"Paul? Who's he?" Rob asked, rather bluntly.

Oksana's face hardened. He could see she didn't like his tone, so he softened it. "Was he here to see Mrs Burridge?"

She gave a stoic nod. "He help her to move."

"Move?" Rob glanced at Jenny. "Like a physio?"

She shrugged.

"Okay, will you take us to see Monica?"

Oksana nodded and set off down a dark corridor. The wooden floorboards creaked as they walked, the narrow threadbare runner doing little to soften the sound. The interior of the house was cold too, and dark, with no light spilling in from the other rooms.

At the end of the corridor was the unused front door. It was locked and bolted from the inside, no doubt out of use for years. Rob wondered why she didn't use it. Why she'd let the place go. The property had loads of potential, and probably had developers scrambling to get their hands on it.

Oksana led them into a spacious parlour, which — had the curtains been open — would have offered a view of the street. The room had a cosy, olde-worlde charm, with floor-to-ceiling bookcases packed with paperbacks, hardbacks and a few leather-bound volumes.

In the corner, sitting in a comfy armchair with a reading lamp poised beside it, was Monica Burridge. She glanced up as they entered. Rob reached for his warrant badge and was about to show it to the elderly woman when Oksana said, "Police, Mrs Burridge."

So much for that. He held it up anyway.

Oksana nodded to her boss before quietly exiting the room and closing the door behind her. Once Oksana's footsteps had faded away, Monica Burridge spoke. "You're the police?" She peered at them from behind her spectacles. The book she'd been reading was poised precariously on her lap, which was covered by a blanket. He couldn't see the title.

"Yes, Detective Chief Inspector Miller and Detective Sergeant Bird from the Putney Major Investigation Team. Do you mind if we ask you a few questions?"

Her eyebrows rose. "Has someone died?" she sniggered, and then started coughing. She had the deep rattle of a lifelong smoker.

Rob frowned. "Why would you think that?"

A shrug. "Why else would you be here?"

"As a matter of fact, yes. Someone has died."

She took a shuddering breath. "I have no living relatives, so I don't know why you're here to see me. And if it's my ex-husband, I don't give a damn."

"Your ex-husband?" Rob glanced around the room. There wasn't a single photograph in sight. The library felt strangely impersonal. Aside from the towering bookshelves, the only other furniture was a small coffee table in the centre and two low, shell-shaped armchairs on the opposite side. On each chair was a neatly placed blue cushion, unruffled, as if no one had sat there in a long time.

She scoffed. "Left me. Couldn't handle the fallout."

Rob didn't pretend not to know what she was talking about. "You mean after your son was outed as . . ."

A sick, psychopathic, murdering rapist.

". . . the Surrey Stalker?"

A nod, and another shuddering breath. She looked around as if for a cigarette, but then leaned back with a resigned sigh. "Had to give up. My doctor won't let me smoke anymore. Damn shame. It was the only bloody enjoyment I had."

"Where is your ex-husband now?" Rob asked.

"Then he's not dead?" She shrugged and stared vacantly into the past. "Pity."

"No, we're not here about your husband, madam."

"Oh?" A flicker of interest. "Who, then?"

Rob cleared his throat. "We want to know if anyone has visited you in the past few weeks asking about your son, Simon."

"Simon?"

"Yes." Rob glanced at Jenny, wondering if the woman was all right in the head.

"My son is dead."

A flat, simple statement that spoke volumes. Like her absent husband, she'd obviously never recovered from his death, or from the shock of what he'd done.

"I know, but we need to know if anyone has been to see you, asking about him. A journalist, perhaps?"

"You lot killed him."

Rob sighed internally. He couldn't keep her focused on the question.

"They thought he was this . . . this . . . monster from the newspapers. But he was my gentle, kind boy. Simon never hurt anyone."

He met Jenny's gaze.

The woman was delusional.

"He was killed while attempting to murder a victim he'd abducted," Rob blurted out, then bit his lip. *Shit.* He shouldn't provoke her — they needed her help.

"It was a mistake. All a mistake," she muttered.

Damn. They weren't getting anywhere. The woman couldn't see her son for the bastard he was. He looked at Jenny for help.

"Monica," Jenny cut in, coming closer. "May I call you that?"

The woman nodded.

"Monica, do you live alone here?"

"Yes, dear."

"Do you have any visitors?"

"Only my carer. She comes in three times a week to make sure I'm still alive." Monica gave a hoarse laugh. "I pay her to do some extra cleaning. This is a big house."

Jenny nodded sympathetically. "So nobody has come to see you lately? No visitors other than Oksana?"

Monica shook her head, and her wrinkled hand fluttered around the room. "Who would want to come here?"

Good point, Rob thought darkly.

"What about the man outside? We thought we saw somebody leaving as we arrived. He's got dark hair, wears glasses."

"Oh, that's just Paul, my physio-terrorist." She coughed again.

Jenny arched an eyebrow. "Do you know his last name?"

"No, dear. He was sent by the council to make sure I'm still breathing."

Jenny glanced at Rob. He shrugged. He'd get Will to track him down later.

"Do you have any of your son's belongings here?" Rob tried a different tack.

She seemed puzzled. "Simon never lived in this house."

"I know, but did you keep any of his things after he died?"

A sad smile played on her lips. "Oh yes. A few little keepsakes."

He was about to ask if they could see them, when she was hit by another crippling coughing fit. When she recovered, Jenny leaned forward. "Are you okay, Monica? Do you want me to call Oksana?"

She reached over for her inhaler, took a hard suck, then closed her eyes.

"Monica?" Jenny asked, concerned.

"I'm fine, dear. Just need a moment to catch my breath."

Jenny straightened up. "Okay, well, I think we'll leave you to rest."

Rob shot her a panicked look. He didn't want to go.

Not yet.

"Do you mind if I use your bathroom?" he asked.

She frowned, but nodded weakly. "It's down the hall on the left."

Rob nodded, shot Jenny a pointed look and exited the room.

CHAPTER 15

The old wooden staircase creaked under his weight as he crept upstairs. *Shit*. He didn't want Oksana to hear and come and investigate. He could hear water running in the kitchen, and hoped she was washing the dishes or cleaning up and hadn't clocked that he'd gone up to snoop around.

He got to the top and looked around. Several closed doors stared back at him. How many rooms were in this house? Starting with the first one, he opened the door and poked his head inside. A bathroom. Nothing there.

The next one was a spare bedroom, vacant, the bed not even made up. The curtains were drawn and it smelled musty from lack of use. There were no personal items or trinkets in the room or on the ancient dresser but, just to be sure, he darted inside and checked the wardrobe. It too was empty save for an old pair of Wellington boots with decades-old mud caked around the heels.

Moving on. He listened for any sound downstairs, but it seemed quiet. From up here, he couldn't hear Jenny's voice or the kitchen taps. It was as if the house was holding its breath — or was that just him?

He came to the master bedroom, which was at the end of the property overlooking the shambles of a garden. Beyond the verdant chaos twinkled the Thames, lazy, thick and full. With the late-afternoon sun reflecting like a mirror and the idle meander of the bend, it looked like it was flowing at a leisurely pace, but he wasn't fooled.

Underneath the surface, those currents were brutal. Many a hapless watercrafter had been fooled by the river's subterfuge, lulled into a false sense of security and forced to make an emergency docking when they ran out of steam. He turned away from the window and checked under the bed for boxes, then in the wardrobe, and finally in the wide drawers of the cabinet.

Nothing.

Damn. Where were those keepsakes she'd talked about?

Gritting his teeth in frustration, he moved on.

What's behind door number four?

Another spare room, or rather, a dumping ground. He'd hit paydirt. This room was filled with boxes and belongings yet to be unpacked, or maybe repacked and stashed here, unwanted. Parts of Monica Burridge's life that she was trying to forget. If she'd kept anything of her son's, it would be here.

Where to start? There was too much stuff. He glanced around, but none of the boxes was labelled. Some were sealed with duct tape, some still open. One burst at the seams with Christmas decorations, a sad trickle of tinsel hanging out onto the floor. He doubted Monica put up a Christmas tree — but then would he, if he were living alone like this, his spouse having walked out, his child dead? He gulped, not wanting to think about it.

A noise downstairs caught his attention, and he quickly left the room, creeping back along the landing to the bathroom. "Where is policeman?"

Oksana's voice, a mixture of concern and suspicion.

"He's using the bathroom," Jenny replied, loud enough so he'd hear. A warning. He ducked into the bathroom and quietly closed the door after him.

"Upstairs?"

Floorboards creaking told him someone was coming up to investigate. He flushed the loo and opened the door just as the carer reached the top of the staircase.

"Sorry," he muttered, stepping past her and jogging down the stairs.

"Thank you," Jenny called up. "We'll show ourselves out."

They left the same way they'd come in.

***

"Find anything?" Jenny asked once they were back in the car.

"Well, there's a storage room with a ton of stuff in it, all boxed up. I didn't get a chance to go through it, but if she kept any of her son's belongings, that's where they'll be."

"Do we need to go back?" Jenny asked, frowning.

"I'd like to, but we'll need a warrant."

"You won't get one for a sick old lady," Jenny said through her teeth.

"Sick?"

"Yeah, she has lung cancer. According to Oksana, she has monthly treatments at Kingston Hospital."

"Easy enough to check," Rob murmured, still thinking about the boxes in the room.

"Oksana doesn't remember anyone visiting either," Jenny told him. "But she only works three days a week. Anyone could have come to the house on the other days and we'd never know."

"Do you think Monica Burridge has all her mental faculties?" Rob glanced over at her. "I wasn't sure. She seemed fuzzy at times."

"The chemo could have affected her memory," Jenny said slowly. "She's not that old, but she's frail, and clearly sick. I got the sense there was something not right."

"Yeah, me too."

"I'll follow up with her doctor, and Will can check her medical records."

"What about Oksana? Do you think she could have stolen the DNA and given it to someone?"

"I don't know. It's worth considering. She wasn't exactly forthcoming."

"Language could be a barrier," Rob said.

"I think her English is better than she's letting on," Jenny murmured.

Rob arched an eyebrow. "Let's look into her as soon as we get back. Oksana Petrenko. That's Ukrainian, isn't it?"

"I believe so. She got the position through a care agency. Daffodil Care. They'll have some background on her. They have to vet all their staff and do DBS checks and the like."

"What about things like groceries and medication?" Rob was enjoying the sunshine on his face as he drove back to the office along Lonsdale Road. Damn, that house was creepy.

"Oksana places an order with Ocado once a week, using Monica's credit card. It's part of the tailor-made package she pays for. She also does some light cleaning and makes supper for her on the days she's there."

"You found out quite a bit," Rob said, impressed.

She grinned. "You were gone for so long, I had to find ways to keep them distracted."

He acknowledged that with a tilt of his head. Somehow, the killer had got into that house and stolen some of Simon Burridge's DNA, he was sure of it. Now, all they had to do was find out how, and who. That was not going to be easy, but at least it was a lead. Something that made sense.

After the shock of the morning's forensic result, Rob desperately needed a way to make sense of it all, so he didn't feel like he was going mad. So that a dead man wasn't ridiculing him from beyond the grave.

CHAPTER 16

The sun was setting when Trent got out of Celeste's squad car at Wimbledon Common. They'd parked near the Windmill Café, a cosy-looking coffee shop that, much to his disappointment, closed at five. He could have done with a pick-me-up.

"So this is where it happened?" He surveyed the park area, surrounded by tall oaks, their branches rustling in the breeze. It was very picturesque. Not quite as beautiful as Marlow, mind you, but then he was probably a little biased.

"Nope, not here. Down *there*." Celeste pointed to the edge of the car park, where a dirt track disappeared down a hill and into a dark wood.

Trent's eyes widened. "He tracked the Stalker into the woods?"

"Yep. I honestly don't know how he did it. He had like a sixth sense or something. Maybe it was because the Stalker had Yvette, his fiancée at the time, and he knew he had to find them or she'd be killed."

Trent gave a sombre nod. He could fully believe DCI Miller capable of a kind of crime-fighting sixth sense honed over the years.

"It's hard to imagine him with anyone other than Jo." Trent really liked Jo. She'd been with him in Marlow when they'd discovered Sir Leland Ainsworth's body, and again when they'd apprehended his killer. He'd thought she was friendly, competent and very intuitive. He considered the last two of those three qualities to be essential in a successful investigator. Being friendly was just a bonus.

"Yvette was stunning, French and a complete handful, if rumour is to be believed. Apparently, she was a lingerie model." Celeste tossed her wild, curly brown hair over her shoulder. She was short, only about five foot two, and at least two inches of that was hair. He didn't know her very well yet but was grateful she'd agreed to show him this place. While it hadn't been strictly necessary to see the place where the guvnor had been attacked by and subsequently killed the infamous Surrey Stalker, he'd been intrigued.

"Seriously?" Wow. The guvnor sure knew how to pick them.

"Yeah, but nobody really liked her. She didn't come to many office functions, and didn't like the fact that he was a detective. It was never going to work out."

"Hmm . . ." Trent knew how that felt. How many times had he been told by his father that being a police officer didn't make for a happy home life? He was determined to disprove that theory when he eventually found the right girl to settle down with. Someone pretty and clever, who understood the responsibilities of the job — when he had any. Someone like Jo.

"You planning on sticking around, then?" Celeste asked, as they set off down the path. It dipped at an almost forty-five-degree angle into the tangle of trees. Due to the setting sun and the thickness of the overhead coverage, it was dark down here, and much colder than he'd expected.

"Definitely, if the guvnor will have me." He pulled his jacket closer around his body. A scurrying immediately to his left made him swing his head round and peer into the darkness. Two squirrels were chasing each other around a thick trunk, their nails clawing and scratching at the bark. At least they were having fun.

"He rates you," Celeste said stiffly. "I'm sure if you wanted to stay, he'd be more than happy to keep you on the team."

"You think so?" Trent beamed.

"Yeah, he doesn't treat me the same way as you and I've been working for him for almost five years now, although I've only been on the team for the last two or so."

"I'm sure he does," Trent said loyally, although, truth be told, he hadn't really noticed how the guvnor treated Celeste. She seemed to be a quiet but effective member of the team and did a lot of the desk work.

"Didn't you have a girlfriend in Marlow?" Celeste asked.

He was glad the dim light meant she wouldn't see him flush. "Not really a girlfriend, but there is someone I've been seeing — when I have the time." Weekends, mostly, and only when they weren't working on an active investigation. "We're taking it slow."

She nodded.

"How about you?" he asked, peering across at her.

"Me?" She tripped over an exposed root and stumbled, but he was quick on his feet and reached out an arm, steadying her.

"You okay?"

She glanced up at him, nodded, then took a step back. "Yes, thanks."

They carried on walking. "Yeah, you married or dating anyone?" He was just trying to make small talk, being friendly, but she seemed uncomfortable. He bit his lip, wishing he could take it back.

"No, I'm not seeing anyone." She pointed to a shimmer of water up ahead. "That's the duck pond. Follow me."

Trent had to walk faster to keep up. The dark, oval-shaped body of water looked cold and uninviting, like an oil slick in the middle of the woods. Hulking oaks and other trees bowed over it as if in worship, and one or two lone ducks paddled around, quacking resolutely. The sound echoed around the trees.

He suppressed a shiver. "Bit creepy, isn't it?"

She shot him a rare grin. "Yeah."

He bet she was one of those people who loved horror films and always dressed up at Halloween.

They skirted the pond and then ascended another narrow path leading into even denser foliage. It was so tight they had to walk single file, and brambles and thistles clawed at his legs. "How the hell did he find them here?"

"It's a mystery, but this is where it happened."

Celeste came to a halt in a tiny clearing marred by several thick stumps, remnants of ancient oaks that had been chopped down for safety reasons, and a few scrubs and bushes. The ground was dry underfoot, but they could still smell the dampness that surrounded the pond. "The killer, Simon Burridge, had Yvette on the ground and was about to rape her when Rob found them."

"Jesus," Trent whispered, picturing the scene. He couldn't imagine the DCI losing it — he was always so controlled, so together — but apparently that's exactly what happened.

"Yeah, the killer got the jump on him and when he regained consciousness, he was tied to a tree with duct tape. Somehow, he managed to break free, bulldozed into Burridge and hit him on the head with a rock. Killed him outright."

Trent stared around the clearing, picturing the final grisly tableau. "At least he got him."

"Yeah. Jo was working the case with him. She followed him out here and called the paramedics. Apparently Yvette had been drugged and was in a bad way."

"Where is she now?" Trent asked.

Celeste shrugged. "No idea. He never mentions her. I know they got married in France, but divorced shortly afterwards. Think the relationship was doomed from the start."

Trent arched his eyebrows. "Sounds like it."

They gazed at the spot a while longer, and then Celeste took him back to the car park, walking back the same way they'd come. "Best not mention where we've been," she told him as they drove back to the office.

He stifled a yawn. It was cosy and warm in the vehicle after the cold woods, and he was surviving on three hours' sleep. They all were. He forced his eyes open. "I won't, I promise. Thanks for showing me."

She gave a tight little smile. "You're welcome."

Neither the guvnor nor DS Bird were back when they reached the office, and Detective Superintendent Mayhew had already left for the day. Trent was glad — he didn't like her much. She scared him, but then she was an intimidating woman. Sometimes he caught her watching him, silently judging, probably wondering what the hell he was doing there, which always made him uncomfortable.

One thing Trent knew, however, was that he'd never been happier than he had these last three months, and that was thanks to DCI Miller. He wanted to be a permanent member of this team, and he'd do everything he could to make that happen.

CHAPTER 17

Rob had barely opened the front door when he was nearly bowled over by a thoroughly overexcited Trigger. "Hey, boy. It's good to see you too." He fondled the dog's ears.

Jo came out and kissed him. "You look shattered."

"I'm okay."

He'd got back to the office with Jenny after the doom and gloom of Monica Burridge's house and realised he couldn't do it anymore. He longed for the soft comfort of home, and his family — and he desperately needed some sleep.

They all did. The team were running on fumes. So he sent everybody home and said they'd reconvene first thing. They were all aware of the importance of finding out who'd planted the evidence at the crime scene. Tomorrow morning he'd have to have it out with Mayhew, who was still in the dark. He wanted to tell her before she read the official forensic report that had no doubt come in during the day. Mayhew liked to keep abreast of all their major investigations, and he knew she did the same with Galbraith's and Linden's cases too. Something of a control freak, was their charming superintendent.

"Come and sit down. I made a chicken casserole for supper, but we've already eaten." By we, she meant her, Jack and possibly Trigger, who often got a little human food mixed into his kibble if he was a good boy. He was particularly fond of chicken gravy.

This is what it's all about, he thought as he collapsed at the kitchen table. *Family.*

Not murdering scumbags, copycat killers, ghosts from the past.

"I'm so glad I've got this to come home to." He wound an arm around Jo's waist as she stood at the table dishing up for him. "I just wanted you to know that."

"I know." Her smile was tinged with concern. It wasn't like him to get so gushy. "Have something to eat and, if you like, we can talk about it."

She poured them each a glass of wine and sat down opposite him. "What's got you so rattled?"

"You can tell?"

"You haven't been yourself since that girl's body washed up under the bridge in Putney." Jo hesitated. "The crime scene looked eerily similar to another murder on the towpath not so long ago."

She was astute, that's for sure.

"It was almost identical," he muttered.

She nodded. "Must have brought back some unwanted memories?"

He couldn't deny that. "I've been too busy to think about it," he lied, knowing she'd see right through him.

A gentle smile. "I know, I've hardly seen you these last few days."

Jo knew better than most how the major investigation teams ran — she'd run her own for the National Crime Agency at one point, which is how they'd met. The first few days after a major incident were busy, stressful and urgent as they rushed to gather as much evidence as possible, speak to witnesses and act on the information they had. It usually calmed down a few days in, when the team fell into a natural rhythm, following leads and formulating hypotheses. They were at that point now — with just one small difference.

The fucking Surrey Stalker angle.

He sighed but picked up his knife and fork and began to eat. Trigger lay down across his feet under the table, while Jo sipped her wine and watched him contemplatively.

"Want to talk about it?"

"In a sec." He began to feel better as he ate, or maybe it was just being away from the case and having this welcome normality to ground him.

"Oh, I've got something to show you." She smiled, changing the subject, and reached for her phone on the countertop. He watched while she flicked to the photographs and showed him a gorgeous one taken in Old Deer Park of Jo crouching down beside a grinning Jack. The wind was ruffling their hair and they both had rosy cheeks from exertion.

"It's great. Was that today?"

"Yeah, in the park. A man walked past and offered, so . . ." She shrugged. "Nice, isn't it? I think I'll put it in a frame."

He squeezed her arm. "You should put it on the mantelpiece."

They chatted about Jack, baby group and developmental milestones. It felt good to take his mind off the investigation, even temporarily. Jo filled him in on the gossip in the group and things she'd observed. Once a detective, always a detective.

"Mel's jealous because her wife, Pippa, is still in touch with their baby's biological father. He was supposed to cough up the sperm then disappear, but now he wants more of a say."

Rob couldn't blame him.

"Kendra and her husband are having money problems. He's just lost his job in IT and is working at Sainsbury's, so she's going to have to go back to work, which she's not happy about. She doesn't want to leave baby Elmo with her mother-in-law, who's — and I quote — 'a controlling bitch'."

Rob grimaced. Thankfully, they didn't have to make those kinds of decisions. He'd never be wealthy on his salary, but it was decent, and they could survive on it until Jo decided to go full-time again.

"How's work going?" he asked.

"Oh, fine. I'm glad it's only a couple of days a week. I like having this time with Jack while he's young. There'll be plenty of time for everything else when he's at nursery school."

She had her priorities straight, but then that was Jo. Sensible, logical, clear-headed. He couldn't ask for a better partner.

Fiancée.

He glanced down at the ring on her finger. Last Christmas, he'd proposed and, to his relief, she'd accepted. He thought about Lucy Andrews, the ring Liz had found in her body. Just like her sister, Julie. They'd never had the chance to see their own weddings.

"We should set a date."

She followed his gaze and smiled. "I know. I was thinking the same thing. How does October sound? The wedding photographs will be stunning with the trees turning."

He grinned. "Sounds perfect."

They didn't want anything fancy, and Jo had no family left to speak of, while he only had his father, who he rarely saw, although their relationship was better now than it had been. A small ceremony at the registry office followed by an intimate reception at their place, only close friends and colleagues.

"I thought maybe I'd invite Mallory and Sylvia round for dinner."

"Sounds great. You want me to call them and set something up?"

"Would you mind?" It would be good to pick his former sergeant's brain about the original investigation. Mallory, now a DI, had an almost photographic memory and could retain information that Rob didn't even realise he'd forgotten. He might remember something useful.

"Of course." Jo didn't push about the case, but after he'd finished eating, Rob picked up his glass of wine and leaned back. "There was a surprising development today."

"Oh yeah?" She studied him, her clear blue eyes seeing a lot more than he wanted.

"We found some DNA on the victim. A strand of hair lodged in her mouth."

Jo's eyebrow quirked. "Really? That was lucky."

Too lucky.

"Yeah, I ran the profile today."

She watched him, her gaze unwavering.

"It belonged to Simon Burridge."

There was a long pause while she processed this. Her gaze darkened, and she slowly set her wine glass down on the table. The only sound was the ticking of the kitchen clock behind their heads, and a shuffle as Trigger shifted position.

"It can't be," she whispered eventually.

"I know."

She gnawed on her lower lip, thinking. "Is someone messing with you?"

He loved that she got it. Jo had been there at the end — she'd seen what he'd done to that murdering rapist and she knew there was no way in hell he'd survived. That meant someone had managed to get hold of his DNA and plant it at the scene. She'd skipped all that and got straight to the point.

He gave a little shrug. "Must be. I can't explain it otherwise."

"Did you check the evidence logs?"

"Yep, no breach. Nobody has accessed those items for four years, and even then it was only Sam." Jo had known and worked with his late chief superintendent, so she knew he was above board.

She frowned. "And there's no mistake?"

"Ran it twice. Besides, Liz doesn't make mistakes."

The clock ticked on, hollow and ominous.

Half a minute lapsed before she murmured, "So how did the killer get his DNA?"

"That's what I've been trying to figure out." He shook his head, weariness making his lids heavy. "Simon's mother is still alive. We went to see her today. Can you believe she lives in Mortlake?"

Jo frowned. "That's a bit of a coincidence, isn't it? What's she doing here?"

"Hiding, I think. She bought that rambling old place on Mortlake High Street. You know, the run-down property set back from the road."

"With the tangled garden that you can see from the river path?" Jo asked.

"That's the place. She's lived alone since her husband walked out. Couldn't deal with what happened, apparently."

Jo nodded. "It must be hard coming to terms with the fact your son's a monster."

Rob couldn't even begin to fathom. "Still, she rattles around in there, she's got lung cancer and sits in her library reading all day. It's not much of a life."

"You ask her about the DNA?"

"Not directly. She's bitter about her son's death. Thinks he was innocent, and a gross miscarriage of justice took place."

Jo scowled, outraged. "Denial, obviously. A mother refusing to believe her son is guilty isn't uncommon."

"Yeah, but she's adamant."

"Does she know it was you who killed him?"

"I didn't think it wise to mention that part."

"Probably not, no." She tilted her head contemplatively. "How are you going to find out if that's where the killer got the DNA to plant at the scene?"

"I can't. Not legally. Nobody will issue a search warrant for a harmless old lady. I could ask outright, but she'd probably refuse once she knows who I am."

"You want me to try?" Jo slowly twirled the stem of her glass. "I could befriend her, get into her house and take a look around."

Rob hesitated, tempted, but he didn't want Jo involved unless it was strictly necessary. Not that he didn't think she was capable — she was more than qualified — but after what she'd been through, fieldwork might be one step too far right now. She was still recovering from the attack that had nearly taken her life.

"Not yet. Let me see how this pans out, and I'll let you know."

"Okay. You know I'm here if you need anything."

He took her hand across the table. "Thanks, Jo. I mean it. For this. For everything."

She grinned, blue eyes sparkling. "October. Don't forget."

He smiled back. "It can't come soon enough."

CHAPTER 18

Next morning, Rob found the rest of the team assembled in the interview room, waiting for him. It seemed the case was plaguing more than just him.

"I've updated everyone on the latest developments," Jenny said.

Rob nodded and locked the door behind him. He didn't want Mayhew slipping in as she was prone to do, not until he'd briefed her.

"Where's the boss?" he asked.

"Not in yet." Jenny shot him a look. She knew he'd be facing down a dragon when he told her about the DNA.

He turned and a dark, grainy photograph pinned to the whiteboard caught his eye. "What's that?"

"A private security camera up Festing Road. Our uniformed team knocked on doors and asked if anyone had surveillance cameras pointing onto the street the night of the murder. This came in last night, and Trent found it this morning. We think it's the same guy."

Rob strode over to the board and took a good, hard look. This was a clearer photograph, and he could make out the man's height and build. Head down, hoodie pulled up, shoulders hunched over like he was in a hurry. His hands were thrust into his pockets, so they couldn't tell if he was wearing gloves or not.

"He could have parked somewhere along Lower Richmond," Trent supplied.

Rob didn't respond. There was something bothering him about this photograph, like he'd seen it somewhere before. A chill crept up his spine. "Jenny, have you compared this to the CCTV images we have of Simon Burridge?"

"No, of course not. We know it's not Simon."

"I hate to say it, but he *does* look similar," Celeste murmured.

Jenny nodded to Will, who opened his laptop and flicked through several folders, eventually coming to the CCTV images they'd kept from the original Surrey Stalker investigation.

He spun his device around so Rob and Jenny, both of whom were standing at the foot of the table, could see. Jenny gave a sharp intake of breath. The figures were so similar to be almost identical.

"It's not him," she whispered. "It can't be him."

"No, but someone is going to an awful lot of trouble to mimic him," Rob muttered.

"You think this is deliberate?" Will glanced away from the image on his screen.

"It's uncanny otherwise. Both men are tall, lanky and walk with hunched shoulders. If we didn't know better, we'd think they were the same man — and I think the killer is banking on that."

"You think he wants everyone to think this is the Surrey Stalker?" Trent asked.

Rob gave a tight nod. "He either doesn't know the real Stalker is dead, or he wants everyone to think we got the wrong guy."

"But why?" whispered Celeste, her eyes wide.

"Maybe he has a grudge against the cops," Rob suggested with a shrug. "I don't know, but what I do know is everything he's done so far is to cast doubt on our original verdict."

"Which is indisputable," Jenny insisted.

"Is it?" Rob asked.

Jenny frowned. "What do you mean?"

"I mean, think about it. We caught him because he kidnapped Yvette. I traced him to Wimbledon Common."

"Yes, but we linked him to all the other victims," she insisted. "Starting with Bridget Kane, the first girl who rejected him."

"I know, but the evidence was largely circumstantial. Burridge worked at Harrods, which meant he used their gift registry to target young, engaged women in West London." Rob spoke slowly and deliberately. "But so did a lot of other people. We never had to argue that in court, because the suspect was dead before it even got to trial."

"There was an official inquiry," Jenny said, putting her hand on her hips. "They cleared you. It was a justified kill."

"I'm just playing devil's advocate. If this gets out, we're going to be slaughtered in the press. Our heads will be on the chopping block this time if we can't prove we got the right guy."

"What are you doing, guv? Why are you second guessing yourself? We were right the first time around. You know that. This guy is messing with us, that's all. He fancies himself a copycat."

Celeste nodded. "We got the right guy then, and we'll get the right guy now."

He forced a smile. "I know. I'm just covering all the bases."

"Well, let's not revisit that theory again," Jenny said tartly. "We don't need to be questioning our own judgement on this."

True. He shook off the bad feeling and turned to the rest of the team. "Where are we on the care worker, Oksana, and Monica Burridge?"

"I've spoken to the care agency," Celeste said. "Oksana Petrenko is a Ukrainian refugee who travelled to the UK with her four-year-old child and elderly mother when the war broke out. She's staying in temporary accommodation in Witton and joined the agency to find work. She was a nurse back in Kyiv."

He'd suspected her backstory would be something like that. "What about DBS checks?"

"She passed all the relevant police checks, although there is obviously no history of her in this country. The agency assures me she had no red flags in Kyiv either."

"Run her through Interpol's database just to be safe," Rob said, although he doubted she was involved in Lucy Andrews' murder. No motive. No connection to the original case. No reason to lie.

"Someone may have paid her to access the house," Jenny reasoned. "If she was desperate enough, she might take a bribe."

Rob rubbed his jaw. "Not sure how we're going to confirm that unless we bring her in and come down hard on her. I'm not ready to do that yet."

Jenny nodded. "Fair enough."

"What about the physiotherapist, Paul Someone?"

Will glanced down at his tablet. "I contacted the council. They outsource all that stuff to an agency. Still waiting for them to get back to me with the name."

"Okay, let's follow that up when it comes back," said Rob. "Not sure he's a priority since he'd have no previous knowledge of the case. What about Monica Burridge's health records?"

"She's been registered with a health centre on Sheen Lane for two and a half years, ever since she arrived in the area," replied Will, "but that's all they'd tell me. We'd need a warrant for her records."

"What about Kingston Hospital?" Rob asked, frowning.

"They were more forthcoming, but that's because I know one of the radiologists there." He flushed slightly. "She checked on the system for me. Monica Burridge is midway through an aggressive chemotherapy regimen. Oksana was right. She goes in once a month for treatment."

"NHS or private?" Rob wanted to know.

"NHS."

"So she doesn't have unlimited funds. Have we accessed her bank statements?"

"Yeah, she has ample disposable income in her current account, but then she doesn't really buy anything other than food and medicines."

"Where's it come from?" Rob asked.

"As far as I can tell, she gets several monthly payments from estate agents. I'm guessing she owns multiple properties."

"Find out where," Rob said, "but that's great work for first thing in the morning."

Will nodded.

"And say thank you to your radiologist friend for us."

He grinned. "Will do."

A knock on the incident room door made them all jump. They turned in horror, praying it wasn't Mayhew.

A hulking shadow hovered behind the tilted blind. "Galbraith," Rob muttered.

"What does he want?" Jenny jumped up and turned the whiteboard around, just in case.

Rob opened the door a crack. "Yeah?"

"Hello to you too," came the Scot's booming voice.

"Sorry, we're in the middle of something," Rob replied.

"Won't interrupt, just thought this could be important." Galbraith handed him a standard-sized cardboard box secured with layers of duct tape. Across the top in thick, black marker pen was written: *ATT. DCI ROB MILLER. CONFIDENTIAL.*

"Oh, right. Thanks." He took the box, peering at it suspiciously.

What the hell was this?

Galbraith nodded. "You're welcome." He swivelled on his heel and strode off.

Rob set the box down on the boardroom table.

"What's that?" Jenny asked.

"I don't know."

"It could be a bomb." Harry backed his chair away from the table.

Celeste looked frightened, while Jenny frowned. "I assume it passed through the metal detectors downstairs?"

"I assume so."

"Then it's not a bomb," she assured them.

Trent leaned forward to read the writing on the top. "You don't recognise the handwriting?"

"Nope."

Then his phone buzzed.

Taking it out, he read the message.

Did you get my package? Found this stuff among Lucy's belongings and thought it might be useful. Becca.

He exhaled noisily. "It's okay. Becca sent it. It's Lucy's stuff."

"Oh, thank God," Jenny breathed, leaning forward and peeling off the tape. "I'm not sure I can handle any more unwanted surprises."

"You and me both," Rob muttered.

Becca had packaged all the items individually in clear sandwich bags. Inside each bag was a yellow sticky note with a brief explanation.

"She's good." Jenny held up a bag with a dainty silver necklace inside.

Yep. That's why he liked working with her.

"What does it say?" Trent asked.

"Justin doesn't recognise this," Jenny read. She glanced up at Rob. "Now, that is interesting."

"It could have been given to her by her ex, Jamie," Celeste suggested.

Rob grunted. Could have been. They'd have to confirm that when they spoke to the guy. "Any idea when he's back?"

"Not even his editor at the *Guardian* knew," Will said. The computer whiz had already confirmed with the newspaper that Justin worked there and was indeed on assignment in the Middle East. "It's an ongoing issue."

It sure was. "Okay, let's shelve that for now."

Jenny set the necklace aside and pulled out a handful of cards. "Congratulatory cards," she said, tight-lipped. A brief silence fell on the table as they all contemplated how tragic that was. "They all have notes attached."

"Wow, Becca's been busy." Harry picked one up. "*Best man*," he read. "*Bridesmaid. Maid of honour. Mother. Mother-in-law. School friend.*"

"That's smart." Rob watched as Harry went through them. "Any unidentified?"

"Yes, two." Harry set them aside.

Rob picked them up and looked inside. One was blank and said, *Congratulations!* in slanted handwriting. The other read, *Congratulations On Your Engagement*, in a printed font. On the sticky notes, Becca had written: *Justin isn't sure* and *Unknown*.

"Okay, so we've got two cards unaccounted for. Let's go through those contacts and see who sent them." He glanced at Will, who nodded. "It would be just like this killer to pre-empt the attack by sending her a card."

"You think?" Trent's eyes widened. "That's diabolical."

"That is the type of man we're dealing with," Rob said grimly. "He likes to play games. He's staging this murder to mimic Julie Andrews' murder, and he's planted evidence to mislead us. If he's toying with us, I'm willing to bet he toyed with his victim too."

CHAPTER 19

Felicity glanced up as Rob entered her office. She could tell straight away that something was up. He seemed stiffer, his shoulders tense, as though he was bracing himself to give her bad news.

She put down the report she was reading. "What is it?"

Without waiting to be asked, he pulled out the chair opposite her and sat down. He only ever did that when it was serious. Something they'd have to discuss at length.

"We have a development in the case."

She waited.

He took a breath. "I don't know if you've read the forensic report yet, but Liz Kramer found a strand of hair in the victim's mouth. We managed to trace it back to someone in the system."

Her pulse leapt. "That's good news, right?" Why did he look like someone had rained on his parade?

"Because that person is dead," he growled. "The DNA says the hair belongs to Simon Burridge."

There was a pause as his words sank in.

Simon Burridge?

The Surrey Stalker?

"How can that be?" she whispered.

"It's obviously a plant," Rob said. "We think the perp got the strand from the dead man's mother, who coincidentally lives not too far away."

Felicity shook her head, struggling to connect the dots. "But . . . but why?"

"That's what we don't know yet." Rob bunched his hands into fists. "It could be he's trying to confuse us, to muddy the waters."

The ramifications hit her like a blow to the chest. Bloody hell, this was bad. It would look even worse if it got out.

"What the hell am I going to say to the Deputy Commissioner? I can't tell him a dead man's DNA showed up at a crime scene."

Rob didn't reply. Granted, that wasn't his problem, but she was damned if she was going to come out of this looking like a fool.

"Rob, I say this with the utmost respect, but there's no doubt the man you killed on Wimbledon Common was Simon Burridge, right?"

His cold stare drilled into her, giving her a small taste of what those suspects across the table must feel. "No. There's no doubt."

"You understand how this looks, don't you?"

"I know." He hesitated. "I think that's what he intended — to make us look like fools."

"It's going to raise an awful lot of questions," Felicity admitted quietly. "Questions I hope you're prepared to answer."

She'd have to answer them too.

"I know, ma'am."

She sighed. No matter how hard she tried, she couldn't get him to call her anything other than "ma'am". So formal. It made her feel more of an outsider, less a member of the team. Maybe this was what being the boss meant: you could never really be part of the team.

"Have you spoken to the mother?"

"Yes, but she's convinced we got the wrong guy too, and that her son was innocent all along, so she's not going to help us. I could try to get a warrant to search her premises, but we both know it'll just be declined."

Felicity shook her head. "Agreed. It's more likely he got the DNA from the evidence lock-up."

"We checked. Nobody's accessed that in years."

Damn.

"So we have a copycat who has access to the original killer's DNA. Could it be a friend of his? Someone who wants to avenge his death and thinks this is the way to do it?"

Rob studied her with something almost like respect. "We're looking into Simon Burridge's history, but he was a loner. He kept to himself. Apart from colleagues, he didn't have any friends."

"Keep me posted," she said. Tracing his friends and colleagues wasn't her job.

Rob got up. "Will do, ma'am."

The meeting was over. Once he'd left her office, she dropped her head into her hands and sighed. It felt like the universe was conspiring against them.

She had the sense she was on a speeding train heading for a precipice and the brakes didn't work. One of these days they were going to go flying over the edge, and nobody would be there to catch them.

* * *

The meeting at Scotland Yard hadn't gone well. It might have been the coward's way out, but she had decided to keep the information about the DNA to herself for now. To be fair, if Rob hadn't told her about it, she wouldn't have known, not having read the post-mortem report yet. But there it was, tucked in her briefcase like a time bomb waiting to explode. She couldn't face it, not tonight.

Luckily, she was a pretty good liar, though it was more an omission of truth than an outright lie. That's all she seemed to be doing lately — skirting the truth. She couldn't tell them about the pattern with the first murder, the ring or the DNA. Hell, she could barely admit it to herself. The more she kept back, the more it felt like they weren't doing their jobs properly. And on reflection, failure was what she dreaded most.

"Damned if you do, damned if you don't," she muttered to herself as she left the building. Glancing back at the towering grey walls, she imagined the Deputy Commissioner staring down at her, shaking his head in disappointment.

Screw it. She needed a distraction.

She pulled out her phone and texted Tom: *Free this evening?*

The response was quick. *Sure. Wine bar?*

She sent him a thumbs-up emoji, but the knot in her chest tightened. She knew this was reckless, irresponsible even, but for once, she didn't want to think about how precarious her position was, how complicated this case was turning out to be, or how, once the news of a copycat got out, they were all going to be in the firing line.

There was no point pretending it wouldn't happen, that they could keep it under wraps. That's not how these things worked. Sooner or later, someone was going to make the connection, and the whole thing would blow up in their faces. They might be able to keep the detail about the ring back, but there were too many other similarities, including the fact that the two victims were sisters.

In fact, she was amazed the old case hadn't been dredged up yet. Still, it was only the third day of the investigation. Give it time.

Soon.

By the time she reached the wine bar, her nerves were frayed. Tom wasn't there yet, so she sank into a chair at the back and ordered a bottle of Sauvignon Blanc. He'd stick to beer, but she didn't care. She had no trouble polishing off a bottle these days, especially on nights like this.

Maybe she should leave the department, jump off the sinking ship before it went down and took her with it. If she were happy, she could lay off the booze, get a life, maybe even a boyfriend.

Tom walked in wearing a leather jacket over a hoodie and jeans. He looked good. Sexy. She didn't kid herself into believing he was anything more than a casual fling. They had nothing in common, and he was several years younger than her. Conversation was limited to sport, food and current affairs, and, while he wasn't stupid, he wasn't a genius either.

What he was, was easy on the eye and not bad in bed — the two things she needed right now.

He grabbed a beer and walked over to the table. "Hey, gorgeous," he said, sitting down. "This is a nice surprise."

Usually, they didn't meet twice in one week.

She pasted a smile on her face. "I felt like letting my hair down."

"Bad day at the office?"

He knew she was a police officer, but didn't know in what capacity. She'd never said she was a superintendent or that she worked for the Major Investigation Team and not the local station.

"You could say that."

More people arrived, and the bar filled up. Soon, Felicity was onto her second glass, and the anxiety about the case began to fade. Another glass, and the crime scene photos began to blur until she couldn't see them anymore, replaced by Tom's slightly crooked smile and his knowing eyes, filled with a thousand exciting promises.

"Want to get out of here?" he whispered across the table.

She didn't need to think twice. Reaching down, she grabbed her briefcase from under the table.

"Let's go."

CHAPTER 20

Rob gave his old sergeant a half-hug, half-thump on the shoulder in that awkward way men do, before inviting him and his wife, Sylvia, into the house. Mallory looked much the same, aside from having lost even more hair.

It was good to see him.

"Congratulations," Mallory said, grinning. "I heard via the Met grapevine that you two are getting married."

Rob was momentarily thrown by the well wishes. He'd been so caught up in the grim nature of the investigation, he'd forgotten they'd announced their engagement to a select few a couple of months back.

"Yes, yes we are." Rob managed a smile. "Thought it was time."

"I'm really pleased for you both."

"Thanks. How's Woking?" He changed the subject.

After leaving the murder squad, Mallory had transferred to Woking CID, where they'd been in desperate need of a DI.

"Great," Mallory grinned. "Although not nearly as exciting as the Major Investigation Team."

"A blessing in disguise," Sylvia murmured, but her brown eyes were twinkling.

Rob chuckled. "I can imagine." Apart from one notorious case involving a deranged serial offender known as the Shepherd, who they'd caught a couple of years ago, he doubted Woking saw much in the way of high-profile murders. Burglaries, domestic disputes, maybe a few drug-related crimes — definitely not the sort of cases that kept the MIT up at night. But, as Sylvia had implied, that wasn't necessarily a bad thing.

"How are the girls?" Rob asked.

"They're good." Mallory gave a slightly frazzled grin. After a whirlwind romance, he had proposed, and nine months after the wedding, Sylvia had given birth to twins. Much to Rob's chagrin, he hadn't met them yet — life had been too hectic, especially after Jo's narrow escape.

"Keeping us on our toes," Mallory added.

Sylvia took off her coat, which Rob hung on one of the pegs in the hallway. "They've just started at nursery school, so calm has been restored," she said.

At that moment, Jo appeared from the kitchen to greet her guests. "It's been too long!" She gave them a warm hug.

"How are you?" Sylvia asked, concerned. "We were so sorry to hear about what happened."

"I'm fine. Almost back to normal." Trust Jo not to dwell on the incident that had almost ended her life. "Come on in. Let's get you both a drink."

Mallory held up a bottle of red. "We brought this, if you fancy a glass?"

"Perfect." Smiling, she took the bottle from them.

"Oh, and we found this envelope outside on the doorstep," Sylvia said. Rob took it and set it on the sideboard.

In the kitchen, Rob opened the wine and poured them each a glass, after which he and Mallory adjourned to the living room, which doubled as the dining room when they had guests.

After they'd sat down at the dining table, Mallory looked at him. "Why are we really here, Rob?"

Rob grinned. He couldn't fool his old partner. "What makes you think I don't just want the pleasure of your company?"

"Because you're in the middle of a complicated case, and you never interrupt that unless you either need to or you're after something."

He smirked. "You know me too well."

"Wouldn't have anything to do with a certain case we worked on about five years ago, would it?" Mallory arched his eyebrows.

Rob stared at him. "How'd you know?"

"I've been reading about it in the press. The way they found Lucy Andrews' body, the location, the fact that she's Julie's sister . . ." Mallory didn't need to say any more. Trust his former sergeant to piece it together before anyone else, though Rob knew it was only a matter of time before the media latched on.

"It's a shitshow," Rob admitted. "We've got a copycat, and he's taunting us."

"Seriously?" Mallory set his glass down. "Tell me everything."

Rob outlined the details of the case — the post-mortem findings, the DNA found in Lucy Andrews' mouth, the eerie similarities to her sister's murder. When he finished, he leaned back and said, "Tell me I'm not going mad, Mallory. We did catch the right guy, didn't we?"

"Definitely," Mallory said without hesitation. "Don't let him mess with your head. That's exactly what he wants."

"There was enough evidence to tie Burridge to all the victims, wasn't there?"

Mallory frowned. "You think that investigation is going to come under scrutiny?"

He gave a reluctant nod. "Unfortunately, yeah. Once this gets out, people are going to question everything we did during the initial investigation. Every piece of evidence. Every step we took to track Burridge down."

Mallory exhaled. "Well, there were the trophies found at Burridge's place. I suppose a good solicitor might argue they could have been planted. But the DNA found on Greta Ansley, one of his original victims, is irrefutable, as is the fingerprint on the duct tape he used to gag Sara Bakshi, the woman we found in Richmond Park."

He paused, thinking back to the details of the original investigation. "We also traced Burridge's mobile phone to the Kew riverside area where Julie was killed on the night of her murder. One might call that circumstantial, but he was in several locations where the other victims were killed too."

"Also circumstantial," Rob sighed.

"Sure, but when you put all that together, it's pretty compelling. A jury would have convicted on it."

"Except we didn't get that far," Rob ground out. Maybe if they had, the case wouldn't come under scrutiny now.

"No," Mallory breathed. "We didn't."

Dinner was ready, and the conversation shifted as they all gathered around the dining table. Rob tried to enjoy himself, but he knew Mallory's mind was working through everything he'd heard, analysing it, looking for any holes.

Jo and Sylvia carried most of the conversation, discussing schools, kids' activities and the best family holidays. Sylvia ran her own small indoor plant business from home. As for Jo, neither Mallory nor Sylvia knew she worked for MI5. Most people assumed she was just a stay-at-home mum, and she did nothing to alter that impression.

Once the plates were cleared, and Jo and Sylvia had gone into the kitchen to make coffee, Rob and Mallory faced each other across the dining room table. Rob opened a folder and took out Lucy Andrews' crime scene photos, spreading them across the table.

"I'm looking for differences," he said. "Something the killer missed from the original investigation."

"There's not much," Mallory muttered as he studied the images. Rob knew the original crime scene photos were forever burned into his former sergeant's brain. It was one of the reasons Mallory had left the Major Investigation Team — he couldn't unsee any of it. Most people's memories dulled with time, but not Mallory's. Everything stayed, crisp and vivid, as if replaying in high definition. Rob couldn't imagine what that must be like.

"If I compare this to Julie's murder," Mallory began, his eyes glazing over, "the positioning is similar, but while Julie's hands were tied above her head, fastened to a tree, Lucy's weren't bound. Julie's dress had been ripped up to her waist, exposing her underwear, which he tore off before . . ." He let the sentence hang in the air.

"Lucy was wearing a skirt," Rob pointed out. "But it was pushed up in a similar fashion."

Mallory nodded. "It was raining the night Julie died. Her body was wet, and her handbag was found beside her body."

"It was drizzling the night Lucy died too, but she was drenched from the outgoing tide. She'd been lying on the foreshore all night. There was no handbag."

"The markings around Lucy's throat look similar, if not identical," Mallory continued, now staring at a close-up of the bruises. "The handprint seems the same size, the bruising pattern identical."

"They were both punched in the face prior to strangulation," Rob said, "probably to subdue them."

Mallory looked up. "The question is, how did the killer know all these details?"

Rob shook his head. "He must have seen the original crime scene photographs."

"He didn't get everything right," Mallory pointed out. "He didn't bind Lucy's hands or gag her with duct tape — and her handbag was missing."

"He could have tossed it into the river."

Mallory gave a stiff nod. "Either way, it's not exactly the same MO."

Rob thought for a moment. "What if he only saw some of the original photographs? Maybe he didn't know about the duct tape or the handbag?"

"Maybe." Mallory hesitated, his brow furrowing. "There's another difference."

"Yeah?"

"Julie didn't have a strand of hair in her mouth. We didn't find any DNA on her body."

"He's planted that to mislead us," Rob growled.

Mallory let out a slow breath. "Well, he's doing a pretty good job so far. Even you're doubting yourself."

"I don't doubt we got the right guy. I'm just worried that if this comes out, we might not be able to prove it."

"Especially if there are more murders," Mallory said darkly.

Rob tensed. "You think he'll kill again?"

"If he's sticking to the Surrey Stalker's MO, then yes. It's just the beginning."

Rob felt his stomach lurch. "Let's hope we catch him before that happens."

* * *

"I can draw up a profile of your copycat if you like," Jo offered later that night, once they were in bed. "It might help to give you some perspective."

"You can do that? With so little information?" Rob asked, surprised.

"Yeah, although I'll need access to the crime scene data, the photos, and any evidence you've collected."

"I'll have to clear that with Mayhew," he said. As much as he wanted her help, he knew there'd be pushback. Jo was a DCI, but she wasn't exactly active anymore and wasn't officially attached to any police department. He'd need approval to give her clearance.

"You think she'll go for it?"

"Maybe. I can ask."

"Would it help if I came in?" she suggested.

Rob smiled. "It might. Come and meet our esteemed superintendent and impress her with your credentials. If you're there, it'll make it harder for her to say no."

Jo laughed. "Deal. I'll pop by tomorrow after Tanya gets here."

Their nanny, Tanya, was a godsend. Not for the first time, Rob thought how lucky they were to have found her. She'd become part of their little family, her support unwavering despite everything that had happened.

"What do you think a profile will tell us?" he asked, as Jo laid her head on his shoulder. Her hair brushed softly against his chest. He loved feeling it there.

"The psychology of a copycat is different from that of a typical serial killer," Jo said. "There's some overlap, of course, but the underlying motivation is different. I'd have to study the case notes to be more specific."

"I've got to find this guy, Jo," Rob murmured, his voice thick with frustration. "Before he kills again. If this gets out . . . it'll destroy us. After everything that's happened, we won't be able to weather this storm."

"Are things that bad at work?" She tilted her head to look up at him.

"Yeah." Rob frowned. "I'm afraid they are."

CHAPTER 21

"It's happened." Rob marched into the office, his arms full of newspapers. He'd raided the vendor in the high street, bought as many as he could carry.

"I know. I heard it on the radio," Will replied.

Mayhew's office was still empty, but she'd be livid when she arrived.

Rob dumped the newspapers on his desk. "How much do they know?"

"Enough," Jenny said, walking in with a coffee cup from Nero. "I've been reading the article in the *Mail*. They've connected Lucy with Julie, and you have to admit, it makes for quite a story — two sisters killed the same way, half a decade apart."

Harry strolled in wearing his leather jacket, his hair perfectly coiffed despite the stiff breeze outside. "Conspiracy theories are flying around," he said. "They're saying the two women must've known something and were silenced to stop them from talking."

"Known what?" Celeste scrunched up her forehead.

"Julie worked at the National Archives," Harry pointed out. "There are a lot of classified documents there."

"Yeah, but Lucy was an admin assistant at a textile showroom," Celeste added.

"Could've been a front." Harry held up a paper.

Two sisters, two murders, one question: What did they know?

"What a load of tripe." Rob shook his head. "They've even published a photograph of Julie's bruised and battered face. How the hell did they get that? No member of the press was at the crime scene that night. I know, because I was there. This picture—" he jabbed the paper — "was never published."

"We know the killer has access to the original investigation," Jenny said, though Rob could hear the strain in her voice. "Someone's been digging in our files."

"Or someone's feeding him information." Rob looked around. "We might have a leak in the department."

"Who?" Celeste asked, alarmed. "No one on our team would give away that kind of information, and no one else knows what's going on. We've been so careful not to disclose any details."

"I'm not saying it's one of us," Rob said, "but someone who has access to those files, certainly."

"I'll check HOLMES to see if anyone's accessed the data." Will swung back to his computer. "There should be an audit trail."

Rob felt the beginnings of a headache as he scanned the front page of the *Times*. "At least they haven't found out about the DNA yet. If they had, it'd be front-page news."

"God forbid," Jenny muttered.

Just then, the sliding doors hissed open and Mayhew stormed in, carrying a newspaper. He couldn't tell which one. Her lips were a tight red line, her posture rigid, her hair wild and loose — she was fuming.

"Oh boy." Celeste ducked behind her desk. Harry did the same, while Will hid behind his screen.

"Rob, I take it you've seen this?" Mayhew held up the broadsheet but didn't break stride.

"Yes." He fell into step beside her.

They marched up the aisle between the desks to her office, which she unlocked before throwing her handbag down and turning to face him. "We are so screwed."

That surprised him. He'd expected fury, reprimands, an attempt at damage control — anything but fear.

Mayhew was scared.

Like him, she knew they were down to their last lifeline.

"How'd it get out?" She threw her hands into the air.

"It was bound to come out eventually," Rob tried to reason with her. "The two girls were sisters. They shared the same last name. It wasn't going to take long before some journalist connected the dots."

"Fuck."

He couldn't agree more.

"They're already questioning your initial investigation." She sat in her chair, then immediately got up again. "The top brass are going to be on the phone any minute, demanding answers. What the hell am I supposed to tell them?"

"Tell them the truth," Rob said. "Someone killed Lucy just like they killed her sister. We can't hide that it happened. Why they did it, we don't know yet, but we're working on it."

"Work faster." Mayhew sank down again. She looked exhausted, with shadows under her eyes — and was that a hickey on her neck?

She must have noticed him staring, because she adjusted her scarf to cover it. "And, for God's sake, keep a lid on the DNA. The last thing we need is these bloody reporters getting hold of that."

"Understood, ma'am."

Her desk phone rang. She sighed and nodded for him to leave. He didn't need telling twice and slipped out of her office, leaving her to her difficult phone calls. That, right there, was why he never wanted to be superintendent.

* * *

Around midday, Jo breezed into the office like a breath of fresh air. Everyone was pleased to see her, and after they'd all caught up, Rob took her in to see Mayhew. The Superintendent had been on the phone most of the morning, and her hair looked even wilder now that it had when she'd arrived, if that was possible.

Rob introduced them and was surprised by Mayhew's warm response. He realised the two women had a lot in common. Both had risen to the top in a world that, until recently, had been dominated by men. Both were sharp, perceptive and undeniably driven. They had fought their way up through sheer tenacity, though Jo's path had been rockier of late.

He explained that he wanted clearance for Jo to see the case files, to do a criminal profile of the copycat. "She was involved in the original investigation," he added.

Mayhew nodded. "I've read the original reports. Why don't you tell me what qualifies you to profile our killer?"

Rob sat back while Jo gave a summary of her skill set, her degree and subsequent training. Mayhew was impressed, he could tell — and it took a lot to impress her. It helped that Jo had been involved in the original investigation and had been instrumental in bringing down the Surrey Stalker. It meant she had prior knowledge that would be useful.

After they were done, Mayhew nodded. "I don't see a problem with it. We need all the help we can get."

Rob thanked her.

"Just make sure the same protocols apply," she warned, before they left her office. "Not that I expect you'll leak information to the press, but we have to make sure nobody else knows the details of this case."

"Understood," Jo said with a nod.

Rob's desk phone was ringing when he finally got back to it after walking Jo out. "DCI Miller," he barked, eyeing the pile of paperwork in front of him.

A breathy voice with an unmistakable French accent said, "Oh my God, Rob. Is it true?"

He sighed. "Hello, Yvette."

"I couldn't believe it when I read the papers this morning. Is there really someone out there replicating the murders?" Her voice quavered.

Already highly strung, he didn't want to spook her unnecessarily. "It's early days still. Too soon to tell." One murder didn't make for a copycat. He was still hoping it was a one-off, a killer desperate to cover up after himself, and so he assumed the infamous Surrey Stalker's MO. At this point, anything was possible.

"But this Lucy girl. She was Julie's sister, no?"

"She was, but we think it was someone who knew her. The man who abducted you is dead, Yvette. You know that."

"I know you said you killed him."

"I did kill him." He was pronounced dead at the scene. Simon Burridge had taken his last breath attempting to strangle Yvette, when Rob made sure he'd paid for it. He closed his eyes, trying to erase the image of Burridge lying on the ground, his head a bloody mess.

It didn't help.

"Should I be afraid, Robert?"

She only called him Robert when she was angry with him — or scared. He cringed, the painful reminder making his chest tighten. He didn't want to revisit those days. Yvette had tied him up in knots, figuratively speaking. He'd been in turns blissfully happy and then wracked with despair, unable to give her what she wanted. What she needed. In the end, he realised, that wasn't him.

"There is no need to worry, Yvette," he said, more gently. She'd had an awful time of it, after all, being abducted, drugged, tied up and very nearly raped and murdered. Like the others. "You are not at risk."

Her subsequent post-traumatic stress disorder had made him feel even more guilty. She'd had therapy, and then finally they'd agreed to get divorced. She'd gone back to France to live with her sister, and they'd lost touch. But now, it seemed, she was back in London.

"Are you sure?"

"This is not the same man. You have nothing to worry about."

He heard a sniff and knew she'd been crying. Still fragile, she was the type of woman men fell over themselves to look after. Stunningly beautiful, with the body of a lingerie model, she oozed sex appeal. When they'd started dating, he'd thought he was the luckiest man alive, until her insecurities had started to show.

Everything had been a problem. His work, his lifestyle, the way he treated her. Then came the Surrey Stalker case and things had got way out of hand. He'd become obsessed, and she'd become a victim. He was still dealing with the guilt — all these years later. The whole relationship had been doomed from the start. He only wished he'd seen it sooner.

"Okay."

One word, fragile in its simplicity.

He hesitated, about to say something else, something about the past, about what had happened, the way it had ended, but he stopped himself.

There was no point.

He'd moved on. Yvette was firmly in his past, and he didn't want to dredge up those old, toxic emotions. He had enough on his plate.

"Goodbye, Yvette."

Her response was a whisper. "Goodbye, Robert."

CHAPTER 22

Rob got home to find a mob of photographers and journalists camping outside his house.

"Who killed Lucy Andrews?" called a woman from the *Times*.

"Is the Surrey Stalker back?" asked the *Mail*.

"Did you get the right man?" shouted the reporter from the *Guardian*.

"No comment," he growled, pushing through the mêlée. He managed to get to the front door, which thankfully opened before he had a chance to insert his key into the lock.

"Hurry, come in," Jo said, as he slipped through the gap. She bolted the door behind him and rolled her eyes. "They've been there since I got back."

"Shit, I'm sorry." Bloody journos. Still, he couldn't deny it was a newsworthy story. "We could set Trigger on them?"

Jo managed a smile. "Not sure it would help. He's such a softie, he'd probably roll over as soon as one of them petted him."

Trigger appeared, tail wagging, as if to say, *You called?*

"It was bound to come out eventually." Rob hated how helpless he felt. "There were too many similarities and coincidences for it not to."

Jack lumbered into the hallway, arms outstretched. "Da-da."

Smiling, Rob bent and picked him up. "Hello, little man. How are you?"

Jack gurgled happily. Suddenly none of it mattered anymore. The investigation, the planted DNA, the potential leak, Yvette, the media attention. For a moment, it all faded into the background as he looked at his son's face.

Jo put a hand on his back. "Come into the kitchen. I was just about to give him his supper."

"I'll do it," he offered, not wanting to let go just yet.

She smiled and nodded.

"I finished the profile," she said, ladling stew into a bowl. Trigger sat at her feet gazing up at her longingly. "No, this is not for you, Trigs."

Rob put Jack in his high chair and sat down next to him. "That's great. You want to give me a rundown or shall I read it later?"

"That's okay. I can give you the highlights."

He nodded, spooning food into Jack's mouth. Now that he was on solids, the boy had a healthy appetite.

She slipped into a chair opposite. "I think we're dealing with a highly insecure but deeply motivated individual. This guy isn't just a copycat. He's got a very specific psychological need he's trying to fulfil."

Rob wiped his son's mouth with his bib. "Go on."

"First things first, he's thorough. The way he mimics the Stalker's MO is almost perfect — but not quite. There are small differences, which suggests he doesn't have full access to the original case files, or maybe he wasn't directly involved in the original investigation. However, he's done his homework."

"You think someone's feeding him the information?"

She studied him. "You mean someone from your office?"

"Maybe." He shrugged.

Jo let out a slow breath. "Could be. It's hard to know for sure."

"I'm still not sure whether this is a true copycat or an opportunist using the Stalker's MO to kill Lucy Andrews. We haven't had any more murders." He quickly touched the wooden kitchen table, even though he wasn't usually superstitious.

"You won't know that for sure until it happens, but my report is based on the assumption that he is a true copycat."

"Okay." Rob drew the word out. Jo knew her stuff, and as much as he hoped to hell this was a one-off, part of him wasn't convinced.

"So what kind of person becomes a copycat killer?" he asked. Thank goodness Jack was too young to understand what they were talking about.

"A serial killer is driven by their own compulsions — an internal need that builds over time. But a copycat? That's more about external validation. They're not just killing, they're mimicking someone else, usually someone they see as superior."

"He's after attention?" Rob tried to make sense of it.

"Exactly. He's insecure in his own abilities, so he piggybacks on the fame of the original killer. Copycats often fixate on the notoriety of their 'idol', trying to replicate their crimes to get the same level of recognition."

"So, he's not driven by a compulsion to kill, but by a need for notoriety?"

"Right." Jo nodded. "For the copycat, it's about stepping into the shoes of someone infamous. There's a certain thrill in recreating a murder that's already made headlines. He's not confident enough to create his own legacy, so he steals someone else's."

"By replicating his kills?" Rob asked.

"Or in this case, his kill. Like you said, you've only got one murder so far, so he might not be a full-blown serial killer. You're right in thinking he could just be an obsessed wannabe. The first victim is often a test run to see if they can pull it off."

Rob thought about what Mallory had said. "And if he's copying Burridge, he won't stop at one, will he?"

Jo shifted slightly, her tone serious. "Not if he's truly following the pattern. Copycats tend to escalate — they want to outdo their 'idol', push further. He's likely still fine-tuning his process. If he feels like he's succeeded, he'll be emboldened to keep going."

Rob lowered his voice. "What kind of person am I looking for here?"

"Someone highly meticulous," she began, leaning back in her chair. "His ability to closely replicate Burridge's crimes demonstrates a methodical, almost obsessive nature."

That made sense.

"He's emotionally unstable. Despite his deliberate nature, there's an underlying volatility. His need for external validation and attention indicates deep-seated insecurities."

Rob nodded, feeling the tension in his jaw.

"He's probably employed in a nondescript job that doesn't draw attention to him, possibly something solitary. Data entry, IT, something like that."

"So, a loner?" Rob asked. He'd been down this road before, several times. Most killers fit a similar profile. Loners, insecure, socially inept.

"Not necessarily, but it's likely, yes. His vivid fantasies in which he's the criminal mastermind compensate for his unremarkable day-to-day existence."

"Doesn't sound so scary when you put it like that."

She pursed her lips. "No, but he's capable of extreme violence. Look what he did to Lucy, and he'll seek to emulate Burridge's other crimes too. Like I said, he may even escalate as he gains confidence."

"I hope to God this isn't going to get worse," Rob murmured, scraping the bowl. Jack had almost finished.

"Once he tastes the thrill, he'll want more," Jo warned. "His need for attention will grow, as will his desire to push the boundaries. He might even start deviating from Burridge's methods, making it harder to predict his next move."

Shit. That was all they needed. At least a straightforward copycat was predictable. You knew what their MO was ahead of time and could use that to outwit them. A copycat gone rogue was another kettle of fish.

"So what you're saying is we have to catch this guy now, before he gains momentum."

"Exactly."

"What about physical attributes?" he asked. "What kind of man are we looking for?" He didn't mention the shadowy CCTV image.

"I'd say late twenties or early thirties. Old enough to have followed the original Stalker case. He'd have a history of social isolation, few close relationships or meaningful achievements. Insecure, power hungry and attention seeking. That's it, in a nutshell."

Rob pondered this for a moment while he cleaned Jack's face, and lifted him out of his chair. That could fit the physical description of the man in the black hoodie. He'd looked like a prowler, young enough to move stealthily and fade into the shadows along the foreshore.

Suddenly he didn't want to talk about it anymore. "I'll take Jack up and play with him for a bit before bed."

"Sure, thanks. He'd love that."

Trigger, not wanting to be left out, got up and followed them. Through the coloured glass panes in the front door, Rob could still see the huddle of reporters. Surely they wouldn't camp out there all night. The news cycle must be pretty dry if they'd resorted to this.

All three of them padded upstairs.

"Oh, I forgot about this." Jo reached for the envelope Mallory and Sylvia had brought in from the night before.

Rob turned on the landing. "Who's it from?"

"Don't know. Looks like it was hand-delivered. No stamp." She ripped it open and pulled out a card. "Oh, it's an engagement card."

"What?" He froze.

She glanced up, puzzled. "It's handwritten, but not signed."

Rob went cold. He descended the stairs, still clutching Jack in his arms. "Let me see the writing."

She showed it to him. On the front was a bouquet of red roses. Inside, the message *Congratulations!* with a single 'x' below. No name.

Rob felt the walls close in around him and he struggled to breathe. He'd seen that writing before.

"What's wrong?" Jo frowned. "Are you okay?"

His voice was a hoarse whisper. "No, I'm not. Jo, I think that card is from the killer."

"The killer?" Jo stared at him like he'd grown horns.

"Yeah, Lucy Andrews received one before she was murdered. Same handwriting. No name."

"Holy shit." She set the card down carefully on the sideboard. "Get it analysed for fingerprints."

"I will." He handed Jack to her, who was gazing at the card like he wanted to play with it or put it in his mouth. Rob got a plastic bag from the kitchen and carefully inserted the card, including the envelope, into it.

"Why send it here?" Jo shifted Jack to the other hip. "What's he trying to say?"

"It's a message, all right," Rob said grimly. "No, not a message. A warning."

Jo exhaled shakily. "Are we in danger, Rob?"

He felt weak and breathless, like someone had sucker-punched him in the gut. "We could be. Remember what happened to Yvette?"

Jo nodded. She'd been SIO on the original investigation.

Her complexion paled. It took a lot to spook Jo, but Rob could tell she was freaked out by this. "Now *I'm* your fiancée."

Jack started wriggling, so they went into the living room and put him down on the floor. Immediately, he toddled over to Trigger and started playing with his tail. Jo sank onto the sofa, while Rob perched on the armrest.

"This is bad." He raked a hand through his hair.

"He's made it personal," Jo whispered. "He's messing with you."

"It's not Burridge." Rob was aware it sounded like he was trying to convince himself.

"It doesn't matter," Jo said. "Whoever it is is copying Burridge's MO. It's like dealing with the Stalker all over again."

Rob exhaled loudly. "Yvette was the final step. He murdered three women before he got to her."

"So we have time?"

"I don't know. Do we?" He stared at her. The last thing he wanted to do was put his family in the firing line. "If this psycho is coming after you, then we might have to put some contingencies in place." He hesitated. "It may be time to think about leaving town."

CHAPTER 23

The next day, things got substantially worse.

"Raza Ashraf is here," Jenny hissed as Rob walked into the office.

He handed her the plastic bag containing the envelope. "The Mayor is the least of my problems right now."

She glanced down at the card. "What's this?"

He told her. "It was hand-delivered to my house. I think it's the same writing."

"Shit," she whispered, and took the bagged card into the incident room to compare it to the others.

Rob followed, although he didn't have to double-check. He remembered the writing. A flowing cursive, a practised hand. Someone used to writing a lot.

She stared at the two lying side by side. "We'll have to get it analysed, but I'd say it's a match."

He gave a stoic nod. "The killer has made this personal."

"He's jumped a few steps, hasn't he? Yvette was only targeted after the other three victims in the Julie Andrews case."

"Yes, but he always did his homework. Burridge stalked his victims for weeks before he killed them. He found out their routines, where they'd be, what the easiest point to target them would be. In Lucy's case, he sent her this card before she died."

"I'll call her parents and see if they can remember exactly when she received it."

Rob nodded. "If nothing else, it'll give us a time frame. If he's sticking to Burridge's MO, we'll know how long we've got until he targets his next victim, and eventually Jo." He croaked her name. The thought of anything happening to her or Jack made him physically ill.

"What are you going to do?" Jenny asked.

"I've told her we need to think about getting her out of town for a while. Out of the country would be better, but I doubt she'll go."

"At least get some security outside your place," Jenny said. "Talk to Mayhew. Maybe we can get Uniform to set up a watch."

"It's an engagement card," he said doubtfully. "I'm not sure she'll go for it."

"Still, it's worth a shot."

He nodded. Jenny was right. He couldn't leave Jo unprotected, not now they knew the killer had her in his sights.

Fuck. He needed a lead. Needed to hunt down this bastard and stop him in his tracks before he killed again.

"We don't have much time — a matter of days, maybe."

Jenny's shoulders slumped. "Crap. We don't have a whole lot to go on. So far, none of our leads have checked out. Burridge's mother is still our strongest possibility."

"We may have to circumvent procedure in that case," he said slowly.

"What? Go in illegally, you mean?" Her voice dropped to a whisper. "You know if we do that, we can't use the proceeds from the search in the prosecution. None of it will be admissible."

"I know, but I don't see what choice we have. Now fucking Ashraf is involved, we're going to be under more pressure than ever. No judge is going to grant us a warrant for a sweet old lady."

"Sweet, my arse," Jenny muttered. "She's a delusional old bat."

"Still, if we want to find out how the killer planted that evidence, we need to look through the stuff boxed in her spare room. It's got to be from there."

Jenny bit her lip. "What do you suggest?"

Rob thought for a moment. "It's a derelict old place. What's to say a petty criminal or homeless person might not break in?"

Jenny frowned. "What are you saying?"

"They might not even need to break in, just attempt to. She'd call the cops to report it. She'd have to."

"You mean stage an attempted break-in?" Jenny's voice was a hoarse whisper.

"Why not? Then we intercept the call from Dispatch."

A long moment passed where Jenny just stared at him. Then, she gave a slow nod.

It was crossing the line, no doubt about that. If anyone found out, he'd be hung out to dry. His career would be over. So would Jenny's, and probably Mayhew's. Three more corrupt cops cast out, annihilated in the media, bringing the Met into disrepute, adding to its already crippled reputation.

Rob thought about his family, about Jo and all she'd been through in the last few years. He thought about the next victim, planning her big day, excited about starting a new life with her husband-to-be, oblivious to the fact that a psycho killer was planning her murder. All of it, taken away in the blink of an eye.

He hesitated, then said, "Forget it, it's too dicey."

She shook her head. "I think it's worth the risk."

"Are you sure?"

She gave a tight nod.

He exhaled. "Okay, then. I know someone who can help."

CHAPTER 24

"About this leak," Rob said, once the rest of the team had filtered into the incident room. Through the blinds, he could see Mayhew talking to Ashraf, her hands on her hips. By the rigid stance of her body, she didn't look happy. He twisted them closed, blocking the two from his line of sight. "I've thought of a way to find out for sure if it's coming from this department."

They all stared at him.

"How?" Celeste and Trent chorused.

"Well, it's obviously not one of us." Rob eyed them all individually. He was a hundred per cent confident that none of his team would hand over classified information to a stranger, or even someone close to them. They knew the risks, and this wasn't the first time they'd been down this road. The media was like an annoying dog, constantly yapping at their heels. "Which means someone else is accessing those files."

"You're going to set a trap!" Harry's eyes gleamed.

"Something like that." Rob leaned forward and they huddled around the boardroom table. All eyes were on him. "I suggest we fabricate additional information about the original investigation. Something outrageous that we claim we held back from the media. We slip it into the files on the system and we wait to see if it hits the press."

"You think the killer is feeding information to the media?" Trent asked.

"How else did they get access to those images?"

"It could be someone other than the killer," Jenny pointed out.

"I called the reporter who wrote that article," Will said, his features set. "But they said the image came in the post, with no sender's address."

"Anonymous. That makes sense." Rob thought of the engagement card. "Our killer likes to remain in the shadows."

"I also checked the database," Will continued. "We're the only ones who've accessed any information. Oh, and Mayhew, of course."

"She checks everything," Rob said, with a slight roll of his eyes.

"So if it hits the press, we'll know the killer got hold of it somehow?" Trent concluded.

Celeste put her hands flat on the table. "It also means the killer might use it when he murders his next victim."

Rob stiffened. "I hope we apprehend him before that happens. But if we don't, he may copy it, yes. Even though it wasn't part of the original MO."

"It'll have to be something unusual," Harry pointed out. "Anything obvious and it'll have already been photographed and documented."

"Agreed."

Jenny leapt up. "Oh! I've had an idea. What about flowers? A dead rose, or rose petals maybe. It's kind of dark but romantic. You know, if we're trying to make it seem like something the Surrey Stalker would have done."

Harry narrowed his eyes. "That's so creepy. How did you come up with that?"

"Err, sorry, guv, but I was thinking about that engagement card you received," Jenny said sheepishly.

They all studied Rob, puzzled expressions etched on their faces. He brought them up to date on the latest development.

Trent stared at him in awe. "Aren't you scared?"

Rob glanced at him but didn't reply.

Trent cleared his throat, his cheeks bright red. "Sorry, forget I said that."

Jenny continued, warming to her idea. "We could say a dead rose, or rose petals were found next to Sara Bakshi's body in Richmond Park, but we held it back from the press."

"Excellent idea. Rose petals are more subtle." Rob clicked his fingers. "Let's do that asap. Will?" He glanced at the tech whiz, who nodded.

"Any particular colour?"

"Dark is more ominous," Jenny said thoughtfully, "but I actually think pink would be creepier, almost like he's celebrating."

Will nodded, got up and left the room.

* * *

A knock on the door pulled Rob from the meeting. He knew it was Mayhew before he'd even opened the door.

"We're in the middle of something." He didn't want to face the Mayor, who he knew was itching for an excuse to get rid of him. After the embarrassment Rob had inflicted on him during a previous investigation, where he'd pretty much accused him of money laundering, the Mayor had been gunning for Rob. It wouldn't take much to push him over the edge.

"I need to talk to you," she hissed.

He peered behind her at the office.

"He's gone," she added.

Rob exhaled. "Thank God."

Mayhew frowned, then gestured for him to follow her. Instead of her office, they headed for the door.

"Where are we going?" Rob looked over his shoulder. He had a ton of work to do, a trap to set and a man to call about a break-in.

"I need a coffee." She marched down one flight of stairs to the canteen.

Rob followed. He knew the feeling. In a way, he felt sorry for Mayhew. She was constantly putting out fires, not through any fault of her own. It was a thankless job, being superintendent, and he didn't envy her one little bit.

Once they were seated, she nodded at him. "You're not having one?"

"Can't stomach the canteen stuff."

"Beggars can't be choosers." She took a sip, then studied him from across the cheap plastic table. There weren't many others about, only a sergeant from Galbraith's team reading a report in the corner and a young officer texting on his phone, both with their heads down. "Listen, I don't know if you've seen the papers today—"

"I purposely didn't look," he cut in. "They're camped out on my lawn."

"Shit, really?" She blew a stray hair out of her face. "Can't say I'm surprised. Most of the articles I read were questioning whether we got the right man five years ago."

"Bloody hell," he growled.

"Your name came up more than once." She took another gulp and pulled a face. "Questioning your motives in killing him."

Rob gave a resigned sigh. He'd known that would happen. "Not much we can do about it."

"We can bloody well catch the man who killed Lucy Andrews. He's making us look bad."

"I know, we're trying."

She leaned forward, her fiery red hair almost falling into her coffee. "Please tell me you have a lead?"

"We have a development." He told her about the engagement card that had been hand-delivered to his house.

"Are you sure it's from the perp?" She turned even paler, if that was possible, and a flash of concern crossed her normally icy blue eyes.

"Pretty sure. Lucy Andrews received one before she was killed. We've compared the handwriting. It's identical."

"Christ, Rob. What the fuck is this guy playing at?"

"He's coming after my family."

Mayhew's gaze bore into his. "You want protection? We can arrange for a squad car to be stationed outside your house."

He hadn't needed to ask her, but still he hesitated; that was even more of an invasion. But then again, it might spook the reporters and deter anyone thinking of paying them an unwanted visit. "That might be a good idea — just until we catch this bastard."

She nodded. "I'll arrange it. Any prints on the card?"

"Will has sent it to the lab for analysis. We'll get the results in a day or two."

"Expedite it," she snapped, then hissed out a breath. "The Mayor is beside himself. As you know, he's no fan of this department. Thinks we're all a bunch of cowboys. He's had numerous complaints from the community about the Stalker being back. Women are scared. Feminist groups are demanding answers. Obviously, he's also worried we got the wrong guy."

"We didn't," Rob gritted out.

"We know that, but he doesn't. There was no trial. The internal investigation into Burridge's death wasn't subject to public scrutiny. You can see how it looks."

"We can't let the community or the sodding Mayor dictate how we conduct our investigation." He avoided her gaze. "We're following protocol. Chasing down leads is our only hope of catching this guy. We're working the case. It takes time."

"Time, unfortunately, is something we don't have. God forbid there's another murder." She dropped her head into her hands.

Rob held his tongue. Now wasn't the time to mention Jo's report. In light of the card they'd received, it seemed probable there would be another murder, and, unless they acted quickly, he wasn't sure how they were going to prevent it.

"We need to make sure the Stalker case is airtight." She looked up. "Questions are going to be asked, and I'll have to answer them. I need to know that everything you and your team did back then was above board — and that there is absolutely no fecking doubt that man whose head you caved in with a rock deserved it."

Rob resented her tone, but he got that she was stressed. They all were. "He did."

"I need proof, Rob."

He spread his hands in the air. "With all due respect, ma'am, we don't have time for this — you said so yourself."

Her mouth morphed into a straight line. "Make time. This is important. Otherwise I can put Galbraith or Linden on it."

Her passive-aggressive streak was never far away. No way did he want another team looking into the original investigation. It was hard enough to keep a lid on the information now, especially with the leak.

"We'll do it. My team knows the case best." He thought for a moment. "I could bring Jo in. She was SIO on that investigation."

Mayhew narrowed her gaze. "Do it. She can bullet-proof that case while you concentrate on catching this perp."

He knew her head was on the block over this. The whole department's was. "I'll speak to her."

"Good." She got up, leaving her coffee behind.

"You not finishing that?" he asked.

She shook her head. "You were right. It's undrinkable."

* * *

After the little pow-wow with Mayhew, Rob went outside to get some fresh air. He walked around the block and popped into one of the many nondescript phone shops on Putney High Street.

The entire street was buzzing with anticipation for the upcoming boat race. A massive banner, strung high between two lampposts, proudly announced the event, its bold letters rippling slightly in the breeze. Shop windows along the street had been transformed, filled with rowing displays — oars crossed like swords, crew uniforms draped on mannequins and posters celebrating past victories.

Using cash, he bought a prepaid mobile off the shelf. It was cheap and nasty, with next to no functionality other than the ability to call and text, but it would do the trick.

With ten pounds on the SIM card, he called a number from the contact list on his normal phone. It rang for a while, then a voice said, "Hello?"

Rob hesitated. He was about to cross a line he couldn't come back from.

Not ever.

Still, if he wanted to get into Monica Burridge's house, he didn't have much choice.

He waited for a lorry to drive past, tyres rumbling over the tarmac.

"Hello?" the voice said again, followed by a frustrated curse.

Rob took a deep breath. "Hello, Dad."

* * *

"It's set up for Friday night," Rob murmured as he and Jenny stepped out of the MIT building. The day had dragged on, and the sky was now a deep indigo, with a handful of stars struggling to break through the dusk.

Jenny gave a quick, wary nod. "Can we really trust him?"

"Yeah." Rob's father had called back, as promised, with a date and time. "He's just a small-time crook, in it for the jewellery. My contact told him the collection's upstairs in the master bedroom, and that the old woman'll be out."

"Isn't she going to be there?" Jenny's eyes widened, a flicker of doubt crossing her face.

"Yeah, but he won't know that. Once he realises she's still in the house, he'll leg it. With any luck, that'll be enough to spook her into calling 999."

"Why didn't your contact tell him to throw a stone through the window or something?"

"Because if he gets nicked, we don't want him telling the cops he was paid to stage a burglary. He's got to think it's the real thing."

Jenny gnawed on her lower lip. "I hope it works," she whispered, her voice barely audible over the faint hum of distant traffic.

He scratched his chin, trying not to think of all the things that could go wrong. They were taking a hell of a risk doing this. The only consolation was that the thief had been told about the job from a reliable source, by way of Rob's father, who'd made sure nothing could be traced back to him. "So do I."

"Will planted the fake report in the database," Jenny added. A damp mist clung to the air, settling over the car park in a hazy film, the cool evening breeze meeting the remnants of the day's warmth.

"Good, although it'll probably take a few days to filter through."

"You really think the leak is coming from the department?"

"It's got to be. There's no other way the killer could have known about the rings — or been able to feed information to the press."

"Anonymous sources." Jenny rolled her eyes.

"I'd better be off." Rob unlocked his car and opened the door. "I've probably got the press arguing with the police outside my house now."

"It'll be good to see Jo back in the office," Jenny said with a smile.

Rob grunted. "I don't know whether to send her and Jack somewhere safe or bring her in to help work the case." He was worried about leaving Jack at home with Tanya, with only one officer to protect them.

"It's a tough call, but if I know Jo, she won't back away from this."

Rob grimaced. That's exactly what he was afraid of.

CHAPTER 25

Jo followed Rob through the glass doors of the Major Investigation Team offices, the hum of familiar voices and the shuffle of paperwork already in full swing. She glanced around, sensing the undercurrent of tension running through the room.

Will was hunched over his desk, reviewing something on his screen. Celeste was on the phone, scribbling furiously on a notepad. Mayhew was pacing the length of her office, her brow furrowed, deep in conversation with someone on speakerphone. Everyone was on edge.

"I've set you up in Incident Room One." Rob led her past the shamble of desks to the glass-walled rooms standing in a row on one side of the open-plan office. "We're using Two and Linden's team is in Three."

"That's perfect." Jo knew Rob was giving her the incident room for the privacy. With the surround blinds and secure lock, nobody could get in and compromise the evidence, or snoop at what they were doing. She'd be able to work uninterrupted there, answerable only to Rob and Superintendent Mayhew. Rob had a somewhat rocky relationship with his superior, but Jo deeply admired her. There were few female officers who had risen through the ranks as she had.

Speaking of whom, Mayhew spotted her, ended her call and came out of the office to greet her. "Nice to see you again, Jo. I trust you've got everything you need?"

"Yes, Rob's given me full access to the investigation."

"Let me know if you need anything else."

"Thank you, ma'am."

"Please, call me Felicity."

Out of the corner of her eye, Jo saw Rob raise an eyebrow. Jo relented with a smile. "Okay, Felicity."

"She likes you," Rob said as they walked into the room and closed the door.

"I like her too." Jo set her laptop down on the table. The room was cool, the air conditioning on low, enough to rid the room of the stuffiness often found in enclosed spaces. There were no windows overlooking the streets, no prints on the walls, only a whiteboard on a wheely-stand at the front of the boardroom table, a dedicated printer and a trolley in the corner containing flasks of tea and coffee, mugs and a tin of biscuits.

"You've got all the access codes," Rob told her, pulling out a chair so she could sit down. "Will has reactivated your old login, so you're good to go. Need anything else?"

"Nope, I'm good." She flashed him a smile and took the proffered seat. "I'd better get started. There's a lot to get through." She was effectively building a case against them, scrutinising the evidence, not only to ensure it was solid, but to find any cracks that might be exploited by the media or legal powers.

Rob gave her a quick peck on the cheek, then left her to it.

Jo opened her laptop, a surge of adrenaline kicking in.

Damn, she'd missed this.

The rush of a new case, the intrigue of the puzzle, the anticipation of what she'd uncover or whether she'd get her man. Not that this was an actual manhunt — not for her, anyway — but she was still looking for answers, proving they'd got the right guy.

Her task was to pick apart a case everyone thought was closed — a case that had haunted Rob for years. The outcome of which would now be under intense scrutiny.

Five names, five victims, their lives ended brutally. Her job was to relive each case, look for cracks, for the places where they might have overlooked something.

There was a lot to get through — she'd be studying old photos and evidence reports. It was going to be one heck of a day. Luckily Tanya had agreed to stay late, and with Trigger guarding them, the police officer outside and the press still camped out on the kerb, she didn't think the killer would try to make contact.

If anything, he was after *her*, not Jack. She was the fiancée. She was the one at risk.

Like Yvette had been.

A chill threatened to overcome her, but she ignored it. She was done being a victim. After the attack last year, she wasn't going to let the fear take hold. This time she'd come out fighting. They were going to take the perp down before he got to her. She knew Rob, and he always got his man. This way, she was doing her bit to help.

The problem was the Stalker case had never been airtight.

"Let's start with you." She pulled up the police report on Julie Andrews. Bridget Kane's murder had set the whole thing in motion, but if there was any case where the cracks could seriously hurt the department — and Rob's reputation — it was the most recent ones.

Julie and Sara.

She wasn't even sure the press knew about the Stalker's previous victims. Still, they might dig them up. The photographs in the media had been leaked, according to Rob, so who knew what they could get their hands on. The department couldn't afford to take any chances.

Julie's face stared back at her, bruised, battered and blotchy. Eyes swollen shut, nose filled with blood, mouth covered with duct tape.

"What a way to go," she whispered.

The media would focus on these victims, the ones whose families still wanted answers. These were the cases that had real forensic links to Simon Burridge.

Julie's case had been their strongest, the linchpin of their investigation. They'd found Simon Burridge in the vicinity of the National Archives just hours before Julie's murder. There had been blurry CCTV footage of a man wearing a hoodie leaving the scene, consistent with the description they had for the Surrey Stalker.

Jo opened the footage, grainy as it was, and hit play. She watched the figure make his way down the street beside Kew Retail Park in his signature hoodie. It was hardly a perfect match, but they'd had little else at the time.

Unfortunately, it was all circumstantial. Even though Burridge's phone placed him in the area, a skilled lawyer could argue that mere proximity wasn't enough.

Jo sat back in her chair and stared at the shadow. The problem wasn't whether Burridge had done it — they *knew* he had. They needed to prove it in the court of public opinion. With Burridge dead — no trial to wrap things up in a neat little bow and no confession to secure — everything hinged on circumstantial evidence, phone data and spotty CCTV footage.

Next, she clicked open Sara Bakshi's case file. The cause of death was strangulation, just like Julie, but this time, a partial print had been recovered at the scene. She pulled up the forensic report containing the fingerprint analysis. A sixty to seventy per cent match. The forensic team had confirmed it was likely Burridge's print, but there was still that margin of error.

Jo sighed. The press loved partial prints — loved to question them, tear them apart. These days, fingerprint evidence was seldom enough by itself, especially with that level of accuracy. It wasn't enough to definitively prove Simon Burridge was the killer. If only they'd had an eyewitness or a secondary verification. That would have made their case a whole lot stronger.

She opened the report on Bridget Kane, the Stalker's first victim. While reading, she ate a sandwich she'd brought with her and sipped a cup of coffee from her flask. Rob had warned her the stuff they served here wasn't worth the caffeine rush.

Bridget's photo, young and full of life, stared back at her. Her murder had started everything, and yet, it was the case with the most questions.

Her body had been found near the shore, but the evidence suggested she'd been killed somewhere else. Forensic reports mentioned grass stains on her jacket, which had initially pointed to a meadow. And then, of course, Ben Studley's boot. His car. His proximity to the victim. All of these had made him an easy target for suspicion. Studley had been arrested and spent six long years in prison, until they'd come along.

Problem was, they hadn't proved it was Burridge either. Sure, he was linked to Bridget, a fling, a one-night stand, but that was hardly watertight.

Jo glanced at her watch. She'd been so ingrained in what she'd been doing, time had sped by. How was it already five o'clock?

Feeling stiff and slightly dazed, Jo left her stuff in the incident room and went to find Rob. He was still at his desk, hunched over his screen, focused on a map of Putney.

He turned towards her. He looked tired, dark shadows lining his usually alert eyes, and his jaw was tense and covered in stubble. "You okay?"

She pulled out a nearby chair and sank down. "Yeah, I think I'm done."

"What did you find?"

"It's not good. The links between Simon Burridge and Julie and Sara . . . they're mostly circumstantial. We've got partial fingerprints, dodgy CCTV and phone records that put him in the area of Julie's murder, but they don't definitively prove he was the killer."

Rob's expression darkened. "What about Sara?"

"Same again. There's the partial print, but those have been proven unreliable."

"Shit." He gave her a look that made her want to take him into her arms and hug him.

"The press are going to have a field day with this, aren't they?"

"They could pull it apart, yes. Do they know about the previous victims? Bridget, and the others?"

He shook his head. "Not yet."

"Well, let's hope they never do, because those are even more tenuous. Bridget's case, being the first, is the linchpin of the investigation, and if they go back that far, they'll realise there was nothing proving Burridge killed her."

Rob cursed, and she could feel his frustration. "We're just going to have to find this guy, then."

Jo nodded. "It's the only way to prove he's a copycat. Figure out how he obtained the information about the original case and get a confession out of him. That's your only hope."

He sighed. "Okay. Thanks, Jo."

"I'll write up a report based on my findings tomorrow and send it over to Mayhew."

He gave a tired nod. "I'll be home as soon as I can."

"No rush. We're fine. I spoke to Tanya and we still have a crowd on our driveway. Doesn't look like they're going anywhere soon."

"It's a deterrent, I suppose."

She bent over and kissed him on the cheek. "Go easy on yourself. You're only human, Rob."

He reached for her hand and gave it a squeeze. "Let me walk you out."

"I'll just get my things."

She walked back to the room, feeling his despair radiate across the office after her.

CHAPTER 26

The killer sat in the corner of the café, the murmur of conversations around him nothing but background noise. His coffee sat untouched, growing cold, as his eyes scanned the newspaper spread out in front of him. A headline leapt off the page: *NEW EVIDENCE LINKS MURDERS — IS THE KILLER STILL OUT THERE?* His lips curled into a slow, satisfied smile. Perfect.

Thanks to him, the press had finally made the connection. The two cases, previously dismissed as unrelated, were now plastered across every front page, sparking a media frenzy. The insinuations were clear: had the police caught the wrong man? Of course they had. They'd bungled the investigation, locked up some nobody while he was still free to roam, to kill.

He tapped a finger against the newspaper, feeling a surge of pride. *They're starting to wake up, starting to realise.* The thrill of outsmarting them all was intoxicating. He could imagine the panic rippling through the police department, the desperate scrambling for answers. And Rob — he'd be looking the fool, the golden-boy detective with his nose buried so deep in his files, he'd missed what was right in front of him.

"Idiot," the killer whispered under his breath, his eyes narrowing at the thought of Rob's smug face turning pale when he realised how badly he'd messed up. *You think you're so clever, but you've no idea what's coming.*

He folded the paper carefully, tucking it under his arm as he stood. Tonight would be another step in his game. They hadn't seen anything yet. He'd make sure the next one left no doubt, no questions about whether the killer was still out there. He wanted them to know. He wanted Rob to know.

His mind flashed back to the woman under the bridge, her face turning purple beneath his grip. The thrill, the power — he could still feel it coursing through his veins. The terror in her eyes had been exquisite, and the way she'd fought, futile and desperate, had given him everything he needed. But that was just the beginning. Tonight, someone else would meet the same fate.

He pushed open the café door, stepping out into the bustling street, his heartbeat already quickening with anticipation. The sun was sinking. Evening was descending, and with it came the perfect cover.

He knew his next target, had been watching her for days. She was predictable, just like the others. Her routine, her habits, all laid bare for him to exploit. She'd be jogging tonight, like clockwork, running through the park at dusk. Alone, always alone. He had studied her every move, memorised the paths she took, the blind spots where no one could see or hear.

He could already picture the moment she realised something was wrong, the split second when her jog turned into a fight for survival. The excitement thrummed in his chest, a slow, building pulse of adrenaline. He wouldn't rush this one. He'd take his time, savour it. Each kill was better than the last, each more thrilling than the one before. They were learning, piece by piece, but he was always one step ahead.

As he walked, the crowd around him bustled along, oblivious to the predator in their midst. He blended in seamlessly, just another face in the throng. No one looked at him twice. That was the beauty of it. He was invisible until it was too late.

Tonight, the park would be his hunting ground once more. He had everything planned — the route, the timing, the perfect spot where he'd make his move. By the time they found her, the media would explode again, and the police would be forced to admit the truth: they had the wrong man all along, and the real killer was still out there, taunting them.

Rob would be humiliated. That was the best part. He could imagine him staring at the crime scene, piecing together the clues, realising he'd been played. *Too slow, too late.* Rob was supposed to be the sharp one, the one who got the job done, but all he'd done was chase shadows while the killer roamed free, right under his nose.

The killer's smile widened as he crossed the street, his pace increasing with excitement. The park was just ahead, the trees casting long shadows in the fading light. He could already hear the faint rustle of the wind through the leaves, the quiet that would soon be shattered by the sound of footsteps, then gasps, and, finally, silence.

He was just getting started. Tonight, another would fall and the game would escalate. They hadn't caught him because they weren't smart enough. But soon they'd realise he wasn't just lurking in the dark — he was the darkness itself. And he wasn't done yet.

Not by a long shot.

CHAPTER 27

The gravel path through Richmond Park stretched ahead, bathed in the soft amber light of dusk. Lena Jakubowski pushed herself forward, her feet pounding the well-trodden trail. The cool April air filled her lungs, fresh and invigorating, yet she couldn't get rid of the deep sense of unease in her chest. She focused on her stride, feeling the rhythmic beat of her trainers against the ground, syncing with the music flowing through her earbuds. It was a temporary escape, a way to drown out the chaos swirling in her mind.

Her thoughts, however, were impossible to completely outrun.

Felix.

She could see his face clearly in her mind, that look he'd given her yesterday. Detached. Cold. The Felix she knew, the Felix she loved, had been slipping away from her ever since they'd got engaged.

Lena glanced down at the ring on her finger, its sparkle muted in the fading light. A symbol of love that now felt like a burden. Her heart ached with uncertainty. Was it her? Was she the reason he had changed, or was there someone else?

She had tried to shake the suspicion, but it clung to her, gnawing at her relentlessly. Felix was distant, evasive.

When he was home, he barely spoke to her, his mind clearly somewhere else — or on someone else. She'd tried to brush it off, telling herself it was the stress of the wedding, the overwhelming weight of commitment, but deep down, she knew better.

She had watched his every move, even followed him once or twice. Both times, he had managed to slip away, disappearing into the crowd as if he knew she was there. He was good at that — too good.

Her pace quickened, driven by a fresh surge of frustration. The breeze tugged at her loose ponytail, strands of hair whipping across her face, but she didn't care. She wanted to outrun her own thoughts, the doubts that had kept her awake for weeks.

Felix hadn't always been like this. Once upon a time, he had been attentive, loving. The man who'd knelt down and asked her to be his wife had been different. But something had changed, something she couldn't pinpoint, and the fear of losing him consumed her.

Her vision blurred, and she blinked back the tears threatening to spill. Her feet pounded along the shadowy path, the ancient oaks towering above like silent arbiters, judging her.

Richmond Park was vast, sprawling in every direction, the landscape shifting from open fields to dense clusters of trees. It was both beautiful and isolated, which is why she loved it so much. A sanctuary where she could be free — just not from her thoughts.

Her chest tightened as she recalled yesterday's argument. She had confronted Felix about her suspicions, cornered him in their flat after yet another evening where he'd come home late. His reaction had shocked her — anger, not denial. He'd lashed out, accusing her of being paranoid, of smothering him. It was as though the Felix she once knew had been replaced with a stranger, someone capable of cruelty she hadn't imagined.

Maybe she should leave him. The idea, once unthinkable, now lingered in her mind like a shadow. But breaking off an engagement wasn't something to be taken lightly and, despite everything, she still loved him. Didn't she?

She wiped the perspiration from her forehead, forcing herself to focus on the present. Her legs burned from the effort, but the physical strain was a welcome distraction from her emotional turmoil. As she rounded a bend in the path, the trees thickened, their branches forming a canopy overhead, filtering the last rays of sunlight. The park was quieter now, the usual evening crowd thinning as dusk settled. Only a few distant figures remained, jogging or walking their dogs, but none of them paid her any attention.

She pressed harder, her feet barely touching the ground as she powered through, desperate to outrun her thoughts, if only for a moment.

And then — a sharp, jarring pain across her throat.

The world tilted as she stumbled, her hands instinctively flying to her neck. Something had struck her, hard, and she gasped for air, her breath coming in strangled bursts. Her vision swam as she tried to stay upright, but her legs buckled beneath her, sending her crashing to the ground. The stick had come out of nowhere.

Dazed and gasping, she lay there, her mind struggling to process what had just happened. Her throat burned, a raw, searing pain radiating through her body. She couldn't speak, couldn't cry out. The music from her earbuds continued to play, oblivious to the violence of the moment.

Her thoughts blurred. She tried to move, but her body felt heavy, her limbs unresponsive. Somewhere, in the fog of her mind, she was aware of movement — a presence, dark and silent, lurking just beyond her field of vision. A shadow slipped through the trees, purposeful and menacing.

Her heartbeat thundered in her ears as rough hands grabbed her arms, pulling her off the path. She wanted to scream, to thrash, to fight, but her body betrayed her, weakened by the blow to her throat. Her vision flickered, and all she could hear was the rhythmic pounding of her pulse as she was dragged into the undergrowth.

The trees loomed closer now, their branches twisting like claws overhead, shrouding her in darkness. The last sliver of sunlight disappeared behind the horizon, and the park seemed to hold its breath.

No one saw. No one heard.

Lena's mind screamed in desperation, but her body remained limp and unresponsive. She was vaguely aware of the gravel scraping against her legs, the chill of the evening air biting at her skin, but it all seemed distant and disconnected.

As the shadows swallowed her, she heard music beating in one ear, and blood pumping in the other. Instinctively, she knew it would be the last soundtrack she ever heard.

CHAPTER 28

Rob had just got home when he got the call. What with Jo's findings and no headway in the case, it had been a shitty day. Rubbing his tired eyes, he hung up the phone and looked at Jo.

"Another body. Richmond Park." The description felt like déjà vu: strangulation, bruising, sexual assault.

"Oh God. Really?" She stared at him, her blue eyes clouding. It wasn't wholly unexpected, but the news still came as a shock.

"I thought we had more time," he murmured. A latenight dog walker had found her while walking home past Cambrian Gate, near a pond, a quiet part of the park. Eerily quiet, and almost the exact spot where Sara Bakshi had been found five years earlier.

"He's following the Stalker's MO to a T," she said as he got up off the sofa. "It's not going to be pretty."

"No." That was one thing he could count on. It was never pretty. Grabbing his jacket off the hook by the door, he kissed her goodbye and strode out into the night. The small group of reporters left on the drive looked up excitedly.

"Has something happened?" asked the *Times* reporter, an eager journalist who Rob recognised from past cases. He stuck to the Major Investigation Team like glue. Barney Something, his name was.

"Nothing to get worked up about." Rob got into his car.

Still, the journalists all exchanged looks and immediately pulled out their phones. It wouldn't be long before they rocked up at the crime scene.

Pulling away from the kerb, Rob put his foot down and sped towards Richmond Gate. The illuminated Star and Garter building cast a welcoming glow at the top of the hill, but he didn't have time to appreciate it. Swinging left, he drove up to the black wrought-iron gates that closed at sunset. A park ranger was stationed outside, his breath clouding the cold air. Rob showed his ID, and the ranger manually opened the gates to let him through.

"Don't let the reporters in," Rob snarled. The ranger nodded, nervously scanning the street like he was expecting a cavalry.

Rob's phone rang just as he pulled up to the roundabout where several other squad cars were parked, their blue lights pulsing ominously off the dark trees.

"Liz?"

"I just heard. Do you need me there?" Liz Kramer, the pathologist, wasn't one for small talk. This was a courtesy call to ask if her expertise was required — or if someone more junior would do.

"It's him, Liz," he replied, his voice hollow. "It's the same bastard as before."

"Right. I'll be with you in thirty minutes. Look after her for me."

"Will do." He knew the drill, unfortunately, all too well.

He swallowed the growing sense of dread as he strode through the deepening darkness to the huddle of police officers and park rangers. They had formed a loose circle around the victim. Early twenties, from what he could see. Slender frame — about five foot seven — wearing leggings and a pale blue sweatshirt. Her leggings were bunched around her ankles, exposing her lower half.

"Back off, please," Rob snapped, holding up his warrant card. "I'm the SIO on this case, and I need you to move away from the victim. Let's erect a perimeter at ten metres out, extending all the way back to the path. Now!" he bellowed when nobody moved.

They were in shock, he understood that. But that was no excuse for shoddy police work. More importantly, he needed to preserve her dignity and the integrity of the crime scene. He couldn't cover her until Liz got here, but he could prevent more prying eyes.

The park rangers wouldn't have seen anything like this before. Their pale faces contrasted starkly with their khaki uniforms. The Parks Police, technically part of the Royal Parks Operational Command Unit, were only stationed in the park during office hours. They would have been notified by the rangers and scrambled to get here, judging by their crumpled uniforms and skew-whiff ties.

"I'm sorry. It won't be long," he said as he pulled on sterile coveralls and overshoes provided by one of the scenes of crime officers who'd just arrived. Only once fully prepped did he step forward to inspect the body.

Her face was swollen from bruising, and there was a thick, vivid contusion across her throat. She'd been struck by something — a branch, a pipe or some other hard object. The imprint was similar to what he had seen with Sara Bakshi. This woman wore a silver chain with a pendant. The killer had left it in place, though the silver glinted almost mockingly against the dark purple bruising. There was one earbud still in her ear, but the other was missing. He glanced around, not seeing it immediately. It was likely back on the path.

Rob called over one of the SOCOs. "We'll need to sweep this whole area and the path — search for the other earbud, personal belongings, anything."

He continued studying the scene, noting the absence of any mobile phone or wallet on her person. She may have dropped them during the attack. Slowly, Rob stood and retraced her likely steps back towards the path. She must have been jogging when she was ambushed, caught off guard by a blow to the throat. As he suspected, the second earbud lay in the long grass by the path.

Satisfied, he returned to the perimeter and waited beside the body for Liz.

When she arrived, she was all business, already dressed in coveralls and carrying her silver case of equipment. "Evening, Rob."

"Liz." He nodded.

She bent down and began her examination, working methodically from the victim's head down to her feet. When she reached the neck, Liz looked up. "Obvious contusion. Likely caused by a branch or other blunt object."

Rob gave a stiff nod. "Nothing obvious around here. Looks like he took whatever he struck her with away with him."

"She's been strangled as well," Liz continued, "judging by the marks on the sides of her neck. But I doubt it took much after the initial blow."

Rob clenched his fists, trying not to imagine the woman's last moments.

Liz's gloved hand touched the necklace. "Inscription reads: *Lena, love Felix.*"

"Felix. Her partner?" Rob speculated, scanning her hands. No rings. Other than the necklace, there were no signs of jewellery.

Liz paused again, examining her lower body. He heard her take a steadying breath. "She's been sexually assaulted, but he likely used a condom. There's lubricant present, but no semen."

Rob grimaced. No DNA from that, then. He hesitated. "What about—?"

She glanced up. "I won't know that until I get her back to the lab."

He nodded.

"Bruising on the thighs and calves," Liz continued, looking back down at the body, "consistent with an assault."

Just like Sara.

Liz glanced up at him. "Help me turn her over?"

Rob crouched beside her, and together they gently rolled the victim onto her stomach. Rob's breath caught in his throat. She was lying on a blanket of rose petals.

CHAPTER 29

Rob stood beside the whiteboard, which now had Lena's picture pinned next to Lucy Andrews', as the team filed into the incident room. He'd sent them all a text message this morning notifying them that there was a second victim.

Jenny took off her jacket and slung it over the back of the chair. "Why didn't you call me?"

"It was late, so I handled it. Liz came out too. No need for any more of us to be there."

"What about the fiancé? Did you trace him?" Celeste asked.

"Yeah, the victim's fingerprints identified her as Lena Jakubowski. She lived with her fiancé, Felix Patterson."

"She was on the system?" Jenny asked, surprised.

"Minor collision when she was eighteen," Rob explained. "No fatalities."

"Lucky," Jenny murmured, her eyes drifting back to the whiteboard.

Rob grimaced. "The family liaison officer I sent round said Patterson was in no state to be questioned. His mother drove up from Brighton to stay with him. We'll pay him a visit after the briefing."

"So, it was him," Trent whispered. "The same perpetrator?"

"Looks like it." Rob turned to the crime scene photograph of Lena. She would have been pretty once — blonde hair in a ponytail, wide eyes and high cheekbones. "The MO is identical to Sara Bakshi, the woman Burridge murdered after Julie. Hit in the throat, strangled and raped. It looks like the rape, in this case, was post-mortem."

"Jesus," whispered Will, dropping his gaze.

"How did he find her?" Jenny asked. "I mean, it's not exactly easy to find an engaged woman who jogs through Richmond Park. What are the chances?"

It was something Rob had pondered most of the night. He took a deep breath. "I don't know. Strictly speaking, it's not the same route as before, but still . . ."

"It's creepy," Celeste whispered. "Like history repeating itself."

"He's a copycat nutjob," Rob growled. "Not a ghost. Burridge is dead and buried, and this guy thinks he can take over where that psycho left off. Well, we're not going to let that happen."

Trent nodded in agreement. "Maybe he waited until he saw a woman who fit the profile running in the park. There are loads of joggers there."

"But engaged?" Celeste challenged. "That's a stretch."

"We need to talk to the fiancé," Rob said. "He might be able to give us an idea of how she was targeted."

"If he's up to it," Jenny muttered.

"What about the . . . you know?" Will bit his lip. Nobody wanted to mention the rings.

"Liz Kramer will let us know after the post-mortem." Rob paused, looking at each of them in turn. "There was something else."

"What?" Jenny leaned forward.

"You remember the false report we stuck into the file?"

"The petals?" Will nodded.

"Well, guess what? The killer had placed some underneath the body."

"No freaking way!" blurted out Jenny.

"Seriously?" Will's eyes widened.

"Yep. The killer somehow found out about it and thought it was part of the original murder, so he re-enacted it."

Jenny exhaled loudly. "That confirms he has access to our files."

"But how?" asked Celeste.

"Is he hacking in?" Harry turned to Will.

"Not that I can see," Will replied. "I've asked IT to take a closer look, but as far as I can tell, nobody other than our team has accessed those files in the last two days."

"So they're either using our login details, or they've found a way to cover their tracks," Harry surmised.

Will frowned. "I'll chase IT."

"You do that." Rob turned to Trent. "You and Celeste go and question the grieving fiancé. We need to figure out how the killer targeted Lena. It can't be as random as just watching the park for a runner who fit the profile. Celeste, you're right — there's no way he'd know she was engaged, which suggests prior knowledge or a hell of a lot of prep work."

Celeste glanced at Trent but nodded. "Yes, guv."

"I'm going to speak to Mayhew. By now, she'll have heard of the second murder."

"You're too late," hissed Jenny, as a slender shadow with a red tinge appeared at the door. The handle turned, but the door was locked. "I'll get it."

Jenny unlocked the door and breezed past Mayhew, whose poker face was cracking with the strain. The rest of the team slipped out, disappearing back to their desks. Only Rob remained, standing next to the dismal photograph of Lena Jakubowski.

"So, we have a bona fide serial killer on our hands." Her gaze fell on the board and she walked around the table until she was standing in front of it. "What a tragic waste of a life."

Rob nodded.

"Who was she?"

"Lena Jakubowski."

"Eastern European?"

"Originally, yeah. Came to this country when she was six. Educated here. Her mother died several years ago, and her father lives in Poland."

"No one to mourn her," Mayhew murmured. Rob frowned — she was acting oddly. Maybe the pressure had finally got to her.

"You okay, ma'am?"

Immediately, her shoulders straightened. "Yes, of course. I suppose I was hoping there wouldn't be another murder. Stupid, really."

"I was too," he admitted reluctantly.

She gave a small nod. "Well, now we've got a shitstorm on our hands. Any leads?"

"Not yet, but it's early days. Liz Kramer's scheduled the PM for this afternoon, so we'll know more then. DC Parker and PC Trent have gone to talk to the fiancé, and we're looking into the victim's background, trying to figure out how he targeted her."

Mayhew pursed her lips thoughtfully. "Any DNA?"

He guessed what she was thinking. A link to Simon Burridge. "Not yet, but Forensics will take a few days."

She gave a resigned nod. "Okay, keep me posted."

He hesitated. "There's something else, ma'am."

She narrowed her eyes. "What?"

"It appears we have a leak in the department." He went on to explain about the petals they'd found at the crime scene.

"Holy Mary," she blurted out. "Who the hell is it? We can't have classified documents being hacked and fed to the press — or used by the bloody killer." She ran a shaky hand through her hair. "Christ, imagine what the Assistant Commissioner will say. He'll use that to shut us down."

For once, Rob felt her pain.

"We're working on it," he said. "Nobody else knows. Only my team and you. Let's keep it that way, and it never has to come out."

She hissed out a breath, opened her mouth to speak, but no words came. Instead, she nodded, turned on her heel and marched back to her office.

"That woman is on the edge," Rob said to nobody in particular, staring after her.

* * *

The team met for a further update later that afternoon.

"Lena worked for an estate agent in East Sheen," Harry informed them. "Her colleagues were shocked to hear of her death. She was generally well liked, but more than one agent said she had a very competitive nature."

"House sales can be a cut-throat business," Celeste said matter-of-factly. At Rob's arched eyebrow, she added, "My sister is in property."

"What did the fiancé say?" Rob asked her.

She glanced at Trent. "Not much, he was in a bad way."

"Which is to be expected," Trent added, hurriedly.

"They'd been together for seven years but engaged for one," Celeste continued, glancing down at her notes. "The wedding was supposed to be next month."

Rob nodded. "Any leads?"

She shrugged. "I'm not sure. He broke down when we asked him about their relationship. Said they'd been arguing a lot lately."

"Really? What about?" Rob tilted his head.

"Money troubles," Trent said, continuing the explanation. "He's being made redundant at the end of the month. He wanted to postpone the wedding, but he didn't know how to tell Lena."

Rob's gaze narrowed. "What does he do for a living?"

"He works for a security firm, but they've gone into administration."

"That's not good."

Will cleared his throat. "According to his bank records, the house is heavily mortgaged, and they've missed a few repayments."

"It's possible he kept this from Lena," Trent added.

"Ouch." Jenny winced.

"He appeared stressed," Celeste said thoughtfully, "and obviously distraught. He couldn't tell us whether Lena had been acting strangely because he'd been so worried about his finances and the state of their relationship, but she hadn't mentioned anyone following her or anything out of the ordinary occurring."

"Except she was running more than usual," Trent pointed out.

Celeste nodded. "Yes, he said it was how she let off steam."

"Interesting." Rob turned to study her photograph. "Did she run alone?"

Trent looked up. "Actually, she was part of a running club. They went out twice a week and did park runs together every Saturday. Her fiancé said she never missed one."

Rob clicked his fingers. "Maybe that's how the killer found her. The running club."

"If he was a member, he'd know she was engaged. After that, all he had to do was pick his moment," Jenny breathed, her eyes shining.

"It would have been a long shot," Will said cautiously. "I mean, if he joined the club, he wasn't guaranteed to find someone who was engaged."

"Maybe he was a member of more than one running club," Rob suggested. "That way he could scout around."

"A non-participant?" Harry asked. "I mean, there's only so much running one can do."

"True, he wouldn't necessarily be very active, especially if he belonged to more than one running club."

"You two, find out when the club meets and go and talk to them. We need to interview all the members. Harry, you call around the other clubs in the vicinity of Richmond Park. We can't drag our heels on this one. Mayhew is about to have a nervous breakdown."

All three nodded.

"What's next?" Jenny asked once the others had left the room.

Rob met her gaze. "You and I have a break-in to attend tonight."

"It's going ahead?" She glanced nervously at the door.

He gave a firm nod. "It's definitely on."

CHAPTER 30

PC Trent didn't know what to make of Celeste. She seemed like a nice person, but every now and then she'd throw in a barb that caught him off guard. Since she was one of the longest-serving members on DCI Miller's team, he wouldn't have thought his presence on the MIT was a threat to her. Other than DS Bird, she was the only one to have been there since the very beginning. Since the Surrey Stalker case.

He was also slightly envious of that. What a way to learn the ropes. A prolific serial killer case that had rocked West London, ending in a deadly showdown on Wimbledon Common. It was nearly as exciting as the Debbie Morris disappearance last year, and that had been the most exciting thing to happen to him in his entire career. Life, even.

"How's the house-hunting going?" Celeste asked as he drove the squad car to the Richmond Athletic Club, where the team was meeting before their evening run. Not all the members would be there, but the stalwarts would, including the founder, Joy Masterson, and they would be the ones who knew everyone.

He sighed. "Rentals in this area are exorbitant. I don't know how anyone can afford to live here."

She grinned. "We don't. Most of us live in neighbouring boroughs. Have you tried Wandsworth? It's a little cheaper than Putney."

"I'll take a look. Thanks." There was a pause, then he said, "Do you think it's the same guy?"

She frowned. "Of course not. Burridge is dead. I even took you to the Common and showed you where it happened."

"I know the guvnor killed Burridge, but was he the real Stalker?"

Celeste nodded. "We tied him to the other victims. He was the only common denominator. It *had* to be him."

"The newspapers are saying—"

"The newspapers are wrong," she snapped.

He shut up. Best not go there. Jenny and Celeste both seemed adamant they'd got the right guy, and they were the ones working the case back then.

A few moments later, they pulled into the car park for the athletic ground. Two well-kept rugby pitches stretched out in front of them, with a squat, white clubhouse off to the side. "That's where they meet," Celeste said.

It was a typical clubhouse with wooden floors, team photographs on the walls and a well-stocked bar running down one side. The running group was there, warming up. Most were in shorts and T-shirts, and there was a plethora of water bottles, running packs and mobile phones on the table.

"Hello, everyone," Celeste said, before Trent had a chance to open his mouth. "Thank you for seeing us."

"Can we make this quick?" a lithe woman in a luminous yellow T-shirt asked, coming forward. "We'd like to get going before it gets dark."

"We'll be as quick as we can, madam," Celeste said.

"Joy Masterson. We spoke on the phone." The woman with a resting frowny face shoved out a hand, which Celeste shook. Trent didn't think she looked very joyful.

"Pleased to meet you." Celeste looked around at the other members. "As you know, Lena Jakubowski was murdered in Richmond Park yesterday evening."

"Shocking," whispered a grey-haired woman with the body of a thirty-year-old. "In Richmond Park too."

"I can't believe she's gone," said a tanned middle-aged man in Nike running trainers.

Celeste let the murmuring stop. "Do any of you know anyone who would want to kill her?"

A chorus of "No, of course not" echoed around the room.

Celeste nodded. "Okay, then can you tell me who her friends were in this group, the people who'd know her best?"

There was a short pause where everyone looked at one another. A slender man with dusty blond hair stepped forward. He had sincere eyes and a concerned frown. "I knew Lena. We used to run together most Saturdays."

"At the park run?" Trent cut in.

He nodded.

"And you are?" Celeste asked.

"Rupert. Rupert Lawson."

"Rupert, had Lena been upset at all these last few weeks? Did she mention anyone harassing her? Stalking her? That kind of thing?"

The man thought for a moment, then shook his head. "No, I don't think so. I mean, she was having some relationship problems, but she never mentioned a stalker."

"You mean with her fiancé, Felix?"

"Yeah. Not that she told me much about it, only that he'd been acting strangely."

Celeste nodded and glanced at Trent. He got the impression she didn't quite know where to take the questioning after that.

"How was he acting strangely?" Trent asked. He was used to this from questioning the good citizens of Marlow about bike thefts and the occasional break-in. Nothing like this, mind you, but he was good with people.

Rupert hesitated. "I don't want to say anything out of turn."

"You wouldn't be. If there was something going on in his life that contributed to Lena's death, we need to investigate it."

"I don't think it had anything to do with her death," Rupert said, "but she suspected Felix might be having an affair. He'd been working late, coming home after she'd gone to bed, not communicating with her, that sort of thing."

An affair. Wow.

He met Celeste's gaze. That was something they'd have to look into.

"Did Lena say if she knew who he was—"

"No," Rupert interjected. "She didn't know for sure. She just said his behaviour was erratic, and he wasn't the man she fell in love with."

That wasn't good. "Okay. Thank you, Rupert." That was certainly a lead, but not in the direction they wanted to go. Still, he knew it was important to keep an open mind, and not try to twist the evidence and the testimonies of others to fit your own narrative.

Celeste was frowning at a list on her phone, a list of members given to her by the unjoyful Joy Masterson. "There appear to be a few members missing this evening."

"Oh yes," Joy said. "Not everyone runs every session. We have a substantial group, but it's usually only the core members who attend most of the sessions."

"Who are the most recent joiners?" Trent asked.

Celeste raised an eyebrow but didn't cut in.

"Kyle Buckland," said Rupert. "He joined a couple of months back, but I've only seen him on one run."

"Did he show much interest in Lena?" Trent asked.

Rupert frowned. "Not particularly. Why?"

"No reason. Anyone else?" Trent continued.

A few people shook their heads. "Not since last year," Joy said.

"Do you think Kyle had something to do with her death?" the grey-haired woman asked.

"No, it's just something we have to ask." Celeste forced a smile. "I'm going to need Kyle's details," she added to Joy, who nodded.

"I'll give you what I've got on him, but can it keep until later? We'd like to get going now." There were several murmurs of agreement.

"I'm afraid not," Celeste said. "If you could get it now, that would be great. We'll wait."

There were a few groans, and Joy heaved a frustrated sigh but stomped off to the locker room. A couple of minutes later she was back, with a A4-sized black notebook. She turned to the most recent page and ran her finger down a list.

Trent raised an eyebrow. Clearly, the Richmond Running Club had not embraced technology.

"Here it is." She turned the book around.

Celeste punched the details into her phone, then nodded. "Thank you, Joy. That's very helpful."

The woman turned to her flock. "Let's saddle up, guys. Time to head out."

"They take it very seriously, don't they?" muttered Trent as the group jogged past them out of the clubhouse.

Celeste smiled. "This Kyle sounds promising. One session and he didn't come back."

"It would have been enough to scout for an engaged woman," Trent said, excitement building in his stomach. He loved this bit — finding leads to follow up on.

He grinned to himself as he climbed into the squad car. The guvnor would be pleased.

CHAPTER 31

"I hope he's home," Celeste said as they approached the block of flats in Isleworth where Kyle Buckland lived. They'd called the office and told the guvnor what they were doing. He'd approved, even complimenting them on their good work.

Ever polite, Trent stood back to let her enter the building. "Should be, this time of day."

They walked along a draughty corridor.

"This is him." Celeste halted outside flat number seven and knocked the door. The building had an austere, seventies feel, its walls pockmarked with wear. There was no view, with most of the flats facing away from the river. She didn't like it, but as Trent had noted earlier, property was expensive in this part of the borough.

Trent had done well at the athletic club. Despite herself, she'd been impressed. Embarrassed too, that she'd faltered in her line of questioning, but she'd seriously just gone blank. Luckily, he'd stepped in and taken over until she'd regained her composure. The nice thing was, he hadn't mentioned it at all.

She felt a pang of guilt that she'd been so hard on him.

The door opened and a lithe man stood there.

"Kyle Buckland?" Celeste asked, studying him. His dark hair was damp and dishevelled, and he wore a loose T-shirt over a pair of workout shorts. There was also the faint, manly odour of sweat.

"Who wants to know?"

She straightened to her full height, but he still towered over her. So did Trent, but he was so nice, it didn't feel intimidating. "I'm DC Parker and this is my colleague, PC Trent. We're from the Putney Major Investigation Team. Do you mind if we ask you a few questions?"

Kyle eyed them with suspicion. "What's this about?"

"It concerns a young woman from your running club who was murdered in Richmond Park yesterday." Celeste watched him closely.

"Bloody hell, really? Who?" He blinked several times in a row, his shock seemingly genuine.

"Lena Jakubowski," she replied.

"Oh my God." He ran a large hand over his damp hair. "Lena's dead?"

Was he acting surprised? She couldn't tell.

"Yes, do you mind if we come in?"

"Er, sure, but I don't see why you'd think I'd know anything." He gestured for them to come in. Was that a flicker of defensiveness? She looked at Trent, who gave a teeny nod, then turned his gaze back to Kyle.

"We're talking to everyone who knew her," he said diplomatically.

Buckland stood legs apart, arms folded. He had toned biceps, like he lifted weights. "Yes, I knew her, but not well. We never met up outside the running group."

"You recently joined, didn't you?" Celeste asked, as if confirming.

A nod. "Yeah, I've been wanting to get fitter, maybe do a few park runs, but . . . I haven't been going regularly. Work and all that."

"What do you do?" She thought he looked pretty fit already.

"I work for the *Richmond and Twickenham Times*."

"You're a reporter?" Celeste raised an eyebrow, noticing Trent's gaze sharpen beside her.

"Yeah. Is that a problem?"

"Er, no. Of course not." But it meant he likely had access to sources, police contacts and a working knowledge of major crimes in the area.

"You said you didn't know Lena outside of the running group?" Trent repeated, steering the questioning back to the victim.

"No. I only met her a couple of times."

"When was that, exactly?" Trent pressed.

Buckland thought for a moment. "Twice at the club, and once at a Saturday park run in Richmond Park. Look, I don't see—"

"Were you aware she was engaged to be married?" Celeste interjected, watching his reaction carefully.

He shook his head. "No, I didn't know that. That's awful."

She still couldn't tell if he was lying.

"I'm sorry to have to ask this, Mr Buckland, but where were you yesterday evening between five and eight o'clock?" The victim's body had been found by a dog walker at around 8.20 p.m., after the park gates had closed. The post-mortem would give a more precise time of death, but for now, they were working with that window.

"Cycling home from work," he said without hesitation. "I leave the office around six thirty and get back here by seven, give or take."

"Can anyone confirm that?" She watched his face closely.

He looked slightly taken aback. "You mean, was anyone in the office when I left?"

"Yes, were any of your colleagues there?"

His brow furrowed. "Yeah, a couple of people."

"We'll need their names," Celeste said.

He gave a hesitant nod.

"What about when you got home?" Trent added. "Anyone see you get back?"

He shifted position. "I don't think so. I locked my bike in the downstairs shed and came up to my flat. I live alone, as you can see."

"You didn't see anyone downstairs?" Trent asked. "A neighbour, someone else in the bike shed?"

"No, I'm sorry. I didn't speak to anyone else." He glanced between them, then wiped his forehead with the back of his hand. Nervous, or sweaty from his workout?

"Do you know a woman called Lucy Andrews?" Trent asked suddenly. Good question. She wished she'd thought to ask that herself.

Buckland's expression shifted, caught off guard. "The woman who died at Putney Wharf?"

"So you do know her?" Celeste arched her eyebrows.

"I only know of her because I covered it for the paper."

"You did?" Her eyes widened.

"Yeah. That *is* my job." He stared at them, slightly bewildered, slightly adamant. It looked genuine. "It's been in all the newspapers."

She couldn't refute that.

There was nothing here to arouse suspicion. Nothing they could arrest him for, no red flags they could use to bring him in for questioning. He couldn't prove he'd been cycling home when the attack took place, but that didn't mean he was guilty. It just meant they had to disprove it, if they wanted to catch him out.

Celeste looked up at him. "Okay, Mr Buckland. Thanks for your time. We'll be in touch."

Once they were back in the squad car, she turned to Trent. "What do you think?"

"Hard to say. Buckland seemed genuinely shocked to hear about Lena, but he couldn't give us an alibi for the time of the murder."

"True." She started the engine, pulling out onto the A316 towards Richmond. The traffic was crawling, worsened by roadworks that had been dragging on for months. Rain drizzled down, casting a grey haze over the streets. "We'll have to confirm what time he left with his colleagues."

"There might be some CCTV footage of him leaving the office or along the route home," Trent said.

"Unless he stopped at Richmond Park, did what he needed to, and then cycled back to Isleworth," she murmured, thinking out loud. "He may have known she was engaged, despite what he claimed."

"I'm not sure I believe him either," Trent agreed. "It'd be easy enough to enter the park after hours on a bike. Pedestrian gates stay open late."

"Easy to slip away unnoticed too," she added quietly.

Trent stared out of the window at the rain. He seemed deep in thought.

"He fits the description of the shady man we saw on the CCTV footage," Celeste added, warming to their theory.

Trent shrugged. "That could have been anyone, really. The image wasn't clear. I don't think we can use that."

"Still, if nobody saw him get home, nobody can substantiate his alibi."

"True."

"Also, he's a journalist."

Trent glanced across at her. "Yes, I thought that was interesting too. You think he could be the leak?"

"I'm not sure how, but he could have contacts in the Met," Celeste reasoned. "I mean, they all do, don't they?"

"I don't know. I haven't had much experience with reporters."

They inched around Richmond Manor Circus, where Celeste peeled off. She accelerated as she drove up Kew Road towards the town centre. "It might be quicker this way."

It wasn't. Upper Richmond Road was just as gridlocked, and it was half an hour later by the time they made it back to the office. They told Rob what they'd discovered.

"This Buckland is a definite person of interest," Rob said. "Get him on the board. I want a full background check.

If he's our man, we should see links between him, Lena, Lucy and maybe even the Stalker case." He looked at Jenny. "See if he worked on the original investigation for the *Richmond and Twickenham Times*."

Jenny nodded.

"Trent, check all CCTV around the park's pedestrian gates from last night. See if we can catch him leaving on his bike."

Trent nodded.

"And Will," Rob continued, "go through his phone records, bank statements and any travel data we can access."

"On it," Will replied, already rolling back to his desk.

They all got to work.

"If there's anything dodgy in his past, I want to know," Rob said.

"You think this could be our man?" Celeste asked, her pulse racing. This was *their* lead, and hopefully it was a good one. Imagine if they'd ended up finding the killer.

"Can't assume anything at this stage." Rob headed towards Mayhew's office. Halfway there, he turned. "Can't rule it out either. Good job today, you two."

Trent flashed Celeste a smile, and she couldn't help but grin back.

CHAPTER 32

The call came in just after four o'clock that afternoon.

"Rob, it's Liz."

He held his breath. "Yes?"

"I've sent you the post-mortem report, but before you ask, it's the same."

He nodded wearily, even though Liz couldn't see him. It wasn't like it was unexpected, so why did he still feel a wave of dread wash over him?

"I'm sorry, Rob. I wish it was better news."

"It's not your fault."

She moved on. "I've sent her necklace along with the ring to my lab techs to test for DNA and prints. I'll let you know as soon as I can."

"Thanks, Liz. Oh, remember, nobody is to release the information about the ring. It's imperative that doesn't hit the media."

"Understood." Her clipped, no-nonsense tone was reassuring. "You can trust my team. Talk soon."

He hoped she was right.

"*Evening Standard*'s on line three," DCI Linden called across the office, once he'd hung up. "They're asking for an official response."

Rob scowled. The *Evening Standard*? A prickle of dread crept over his scalp.

Official response to what?

He picked up the phone. "DCI Miller speaking."

The voice on the other end was curt, unmistakably a journalist's — a mixture of smug and urgent, like they'd just hit the front-page jackpot. "Detective Chief Inspector, can you comment on the letter from the Surrey Stalker? It's running in today's *Standard*. He's claiming responsibility for the recent murders — and provided details about the victims."

Rob's blood ran cold.

"He also asked if you found the rings. What does he mean by that?"

Rob struggled to keep his voice steady. "You've got the letter there?"

"Yeah, we received it this morning."

"It's evidence in an active investigation. I'll be right over."

He slammed the phone down, not bothering with pleasantries, and shot a look at his team. "Everyone. Briefing. Now."

They piled into the incident room, Jenny and Will exchanging worried glances, while PC Trent gazed at Rob wide-eyed. Linden stared after them, shrugged, then went back to his desk. The usual hum of chatter had fallen into a tense silence.

"The press know about the rings," Rob hissed, his voice low, barely controlled.

"How?" Jenny gasped, her hand flying to her mouth. She knew what a disaster that was. They were about to get crucified.

"That was the *Standard* on the phone. They claim they've received a letter from the killer."

"What?" gasped everyone.

"He's taken responsibility for the killings and asked if we'd found the rings."

"Holy shit," whispered Celeste, who never swore.

"We need to see that letter," Jenny said, jumping up. "I'll head over there now."

"I'm coming with you." Rob turned to the others. "Get a copy of the *Standard* now and analyse that article, look for anything that might tell us who the hell he is."

"Mayhew's going to be livid," Harry whispered.

That was the least of their problems. Once this gathered momentum, the department was as good as dead.

Jaw set, Rob followed Jenny out of the room.

* * *

When they reached the newspaper's office, Rob flashed his badge at the security desk. "Which floor for the editor-in-chief?"

"Third," came the reply. "But you can't—"

Rob didn't hear any more, as he and Jenny took the stairs to the third floor, their footsteps echoing in the stairwell. Rob burst through the double doors into the crammed, open-plan office and glanced around.

"Over there." Jenny pointed to a mezzanine floor accessible only by a short flight of stairs. On it, they could see three rooms, two offices and a boardroom.

They marched across the sprawling office, weaving between cluttered desks, ignoring the curious glances of reporters and staff members. Up the stairs and into the office marked PHILIP RAYBURN: EDITOR-IN-CHIEF.

Not bothering to knock, Rob flung open the door and marched inside. Jenny followed. A man in a navy suit sat waiting, a crisp copy of the *Evening Standard* spread out on his desk. Rob's eyes went straight to the headline: *SURREY STALKER STRIKES AGAIN*.

His stomach twisted.

Rayburn didn't waste time on introductions. "The letter arrived this morning, no return address. We have no reason to believe it's not genuine. We knew the public would want to see it."

Rob just managed to keep his voice even. "I need to log it into evidence." They'd have to get their lab techs to analyse it for fingerprints or DNA. Unlikely, but they might get lucky.

Jenny stepped forward, donning a pair of gloves before taking it from Rayburn and slipping it into an evidence bag. Once that was done, and the letter had been preserved, she handed it to Rob, who took a long, hard look at the handwriting.

It was the same slated scrawl as the two handwritten cards. He glanced across at Jenny and knew she was thinking the same thing. It wasn't a long letter, but it packed a punch.

To the Editor of the Evening Standard,

They thought they silenced me five years ago. Wimbledon Common, a so-called "heroic" battle in the woods. Detective Miller's little fairytale ending.

But he was wrong. Instead of the Surrey Stalker, he killed an innocent man, while I slipped away.

Lucy Andrews. Lena Jakubowski. Yes, that was me. I had to show the police just how wrong they were.

Did they find the rings? Each one placed with care, my special signature. Does the public know you lied to them?

This isn't over, Detective. The chase has just begun, and I promise you, this time there will be no mistakes, no convenient endings.

Only the chase, and you'll never catch me.
—The Surrey Stalker

"What rings, Detective Chief Inspector?" Rayburn asked softly, his probing gaze fixed on Rob's face.

Rob took a deep breath. "That detail was purposely held back from the press," he said cautiously. "It's a detail only the killer would know."

Rayburn's eyes widened slightly. "Then this really is from him? It's really the Surrey Stalker?"

"No," Rob snapped. "The Stalker is dead. This is someone trying to emulate him."

"A copycat?" Rayburn's eyebrows arched.

Rob shrugged. "I can't say anything more, only this isn't Burridge. I want that on the record." He gestured to the headline on the newspaper spread out on the editor's desk. "*That* is misinformation."

"*That* has already gone out." Rayburn shrugged, not a shred of remorse. "Our investigators are working on uncovering the truth. You'll understand if we don't just take your word for it."

Rob sighed. "Your investigators don't have access to all the information."

"We have our sources."

Rob knew he wouldn't get anywhere with Rayburn. He'd print what he wanted, regardless of what Rob said. He'd have to get a court injunction to prevent anything from coming out, and nobody was going to support that idea. Least of all the Mayor. Besides, he had more important things to do than stand here arguing with this idiot.

"How did the letter arrive?" He changed tack.

Rayburn didn't flinch. "It came in the morning's post."

Jenny turned the packet around and looked at the envelope. "There's no stamp or postmark."

Rob fixed his gaze on the editor. "How would it get into the main post since it must have been hand-delivered?"

"You'll have to ask Nigel in the post room," Rayburn said. "We get a lot of letters from the public."

"I'd like to speak to him," Rob said. "Can you call him in here?"

Rayburn nodded and picked up his desk phone. He asked to be put through to the post room and issued the request to the person on the other end of the line. A moment later, he said, "He's on his way."

A few minutes later, a portly man in his late fifties trudged into the editor's office. He wore a fraying cardigan over his shirt, and his balding head glistened under the fluorescent office lights.

He blinked at Rob and Jenny, his mouth twisting into a nervous half-smile as he glanced at the editor for reassurance.

Rob wasted no time. "Nigel, I'm Detective Chief Inspector Miller. I need to ask you a few questions about a letter that came through your post room this morning." He held up the evidence packet, watching Nigel for a reaction.

Nigel squinted at the envelope inside, then shrugged. "We get hundreds of letters every day. Not sure I remember that one."

Rob's gaze sharpened. "There's no stamp or postmark, which means it was probably hand-delivered. Any idea how it made its way into your morning post?"

Nigel scratched the back of his head. "Well, sir, people drop things off all the time. We've got a box just outside the main entrance where folks can leave mail. Someone from the post room collects everything early in the morning and brings it inside. Don't usually pay attention to who put what where."

Jenny stepped in, her voice calm but probing. "Who collected the post this morning?"

"As it turns out, I did. Bob — he's the other post room clerk — was late this morning, so I went down and got it."

Rob pressed on. "Was anyone unusual hanging around the post room or the drop box? Anyone watching as you collected it?"

Nigel squinted, as if trying to recall, then shook his head. "I don't think so. Sometimes we get the odd person dropping things off directly, but it's usually letters from local businesses or readers sending in tips. No one suspicious, if that's what you mean."

Rob let out a controlled sigh. "You sure you didn't notice anyone lurking about outside?"

Nigel's face creased in concentration, then relaxed into a shrug. "No, sir. I just grabbed the whole pile, brought it to the sorting table, and that's that. Didn't notice anyone outside."

Jenny exchanged a frustrated look with Rob. The envelope had been mixed into the morning's pile like any ordinary letter, leaving them with nothing to go on.

Rob sighed, but he had one more question. "Did you, or anyone you know, make copies of this letter before it reached the editor?"

Nigel shook his head, his face earnest. "No, sir. That would be against office policy. Once I bring the post up, I leave it on the table for the editorial team. They do the sorting. I didn't copy anything, and neither would Bob. He's not one for tampering."

Rob gave Nigel a long look, searching for any hint of dishonesty, but the man's gaze remained wide-eyed and blank.

"All right." Rob could feel the pressure of the day weighing on him. "If you think of anything else, or if you receive any more letters like this, let us know immediately."

Nigel gave a vigorous nod, visibly relieved to be dismissed. "Yes, sir. I'll keep an eye out."

He shuffled out of the room, leaving them alone with the editor.

"You happy now?" Rayburn said.

Rob ignored him. The letter had slipped into the newspaper's post room with infuriating ease, leaving no trail for them to follow. He only hoped Forensics or the expert analyst he'd call in to study the letter would be able to give them a lead.

CHAPTER 33

The team pored over a copy of the letter. Rob had made several before he'd sent it away for analysis.

"I've got Jo coming in tomorrow, along with a handwriting expert to see if we can glean anything from the letter itself," Rob said. "And the forensic techs are looking for fingerprints, trace DNA, saliva, skin cells, that sort of thing."

"I'm sure he's too careful for that," Jenny said.

Rob agreed with her, but sometimes killers got sloppy. Even the most meticulous organisers occasionally overlooked details. Maybe they'd get lucky.

"What have we got on Buckland?" Rob asked. He knew the team had been busy digging up what they could on the runner.

"His colleagues confirmed he left work around six o'clock on the night of Lena's murder," Celeste said, sounding almost disappointed. "According to his statement, nobody saw him arrive home, so we can't confirm that. He could have stopped at the park on his way back. It's out of his way, but not by much."

Rob nodded. "Okay, what about his background check?"

"Came up clear," Harry said. "No record, no convictions."

"Okay, so he's clean. What about his phone records? Where does that put him the night of the murder?"

"Inconclusive," Will said. "He pinged a phone tower in Isleworth around seven thirty, which proves he was home by then, or at least his phone was. He also pinged earlier in the day in Isleworth, like he said, but I didn't get anything in the vicinity of Richmond Park during the time frame in question."

"Doesn't mean he wasn't there," Celeste murmured. "Just means his phone was off."

Rob confirmed his agreement with a nod. "Okay. Thanks, Will. Financial records?"

"Nothing out of the ordinary. He earns an average salary, pays his taxes, doesn't have any other income sources as far as I can tell. On paper, everything's above board."

"Doesn't owe any money? What about credit card debt?"

"Nothing like that. He doesn't have a credit card, and he pays his bills on time. He doesn't have many expenses, other than the usual utilities, rent and council tax, which is quite high, but then Isleworth is in the Hounslow borough."

Trent grunted.

Rob pursed his lips. "He doesn't own his own home?"

"Nope. Rents, and has done for years."

"Hmm..." Rob frowned. Buckland didn't really fit the profile of a socially defunct loner with resentful tendencies. He seemed clean, stable and orderly. "Any links with Lucy Andrews?"

Trent shook his head. "Nothing I could find. Justin King didn't recognise his name or photograph. Neither did Lucy's parents."

"Okay. Thanks, Trent."

"I'm still going through the newspaper articles in the *Richmond and Twickenham Times* from the Stalker case," Harry said. "So far, I haven't seen anything with Buckland's byline. Are we sure he was working there back then?"

Celeste nodded. "Yep, he was. I checked. He started there six years ago, according to his editor."

"Keep looking," Rob said.

Harry gave a quick nod. "Will do, guv."

"Trent, any sign of him on CCTV in the vicinity of the park yesterday evening?"

"Not yet. The only camera on the Richmond side is on Queen's Road, and it's nowhere near either of the two pedestrian gates. On the Kingston side there is another one, but it's unlikely he came in that way. Same goes for the Roehampton side." He bit his lip. "The Star and Garter have a security camera aimed at the main gate on Richmond Hill, but they haven't sent the feed through yet."

"Chase them," Rob ordered.

Trent nodded and made a quick note on his iPad.

"Okay, that's it. Let's keep digging. I need something concrete if I'm going to bring Buckland in for questioning."

The team filed out. Unfortunately, Mayhew intercepted him before he could make it back to his desk.

"Rob, my office." Her voice was a vice.

Shit.

He took a deep breath as he followed her through the office.

Linden shot him a sympathetic grimace as he passed the seasoned SIO's desk. Like Rob, Linden preferred to sit in the bullpen with his team. He hadn't been around during the Stalker case, but he'd seen the papers — who hadn't? — and he knew Rob was already walking a fine line with the Superintendent.

"I've got a meeting at Scotland Yard this evening," was the first thing she told him. "Please tell me you've got something?"

She hadn't mentioned the article in the *Evening Standard*, but he could see a copy on her desk.

"We're working on it."

"That's not what I want to hear, Rob."

He raised an eyebrow. She rarely used his first name these days. Either she was feeling insecure, or she was appealing to his better side. Both options were disconcerting.

"This article could be the death of us."

"Of me, you mean."

She shrugged. "My career is unfortunately tied to yours. You go down, I go down."

That's what you get for being the boss.

He pressed his lips together, then sighed. "Look, I know it's a blow, and we still have no idea how he found out about the rose petals, but IT is looking into the hacking angle, and we've gone offline. From now on, all new information on this investigation will be stored in a manilla folder that is never going to leave my sight. That's all we can do to prevent any further leaks."

She heaved a sigh. "That's something, I suppose. If it's a hack, it implies sketchy firewalls, which is hardly our fault."

He gave a tight nod.

"Are you any closer to finding out who did this?"

"Lena Jakubowski's murder has led to a person of interest." He told her about Buckland. "But we're still looking into it. So far, we can't place him in the park at the time of death."

"He's a journalist, you say?"

"*Richmond and Twickenham Times.*"

"So he could have tipped off the media about the other details? The crime scene photographs, the link between the two cases?"

"It's a possibility."

"Bring him in," she said, with a flick of her head. "I want to hear what he has to say."

Rob held his tongue. He felt it was premature, but he understood she wanted to be able to tell her superiors they had a person of interest.

"I'll get Uniform to pick him up."

"Keep me posted. Anything to report, and you message me. I don't care how late it is."

"Of course, ma'am."

She rolled her eyes. "Thank you, DCI Miller. That will be all."

CHAPTER 34

Mayhew climbed into the Uber. It was raining again — bloody April showers — and she didn't want to get her new suede jacket wet. She also couldn't stomach the rail network today, not after the meeting she'd just had with the Assistant Commissioner, Matthew Gray.

The smug bastard loved making her feel inadequate. Ever since he'd been outed as an adulterer and a liar in that Marlow fiasco last year, he'd been absolutely beastly to her. Not even the good graces of the Police Commissioner would be able to save her if this case went down the shitter.

"This is not looking good for you, Felicity," he'd said.

No kidding.

"We're doing everything we can, Assistant Commissioner." Now she was doing a Rob, refusing to call him by his first name. "You have to admit that being hacked is out of our control. It's a department-wide danger that should be addressed at the highest level. Everyone could be at risk."

"Except nobody else's files appear to have been pilfered," he'd said flatly. She'd resisted the urge to pick up the stapler on his desk and hurl it at his face.

"Because it's our case he's interested in," she'd retorted. "We're dealing with a very sophisticated criminal here. He's meticulously mimicking the Stalker's MO from five years ago."

"Which should make him easier to catch," Gray had challenged.

Felicity had grimaced.

"Unless, of course . . ." He'd cocked his head and studied her across his oversized desk. "Unless you got the wrong man five years ago."

She had cleared her throat. "Firstly, I wasn't with the department five years ago, as you know. Secondly, DCI Miller and his team are confident they got the right man. This is not the Stalker. Simon Burridge is dead. This is a copycat — possibly linked to the original murders. We are exploring several angles and are questioning a person of interest as we speak."

She had felt herself getting angry and blew a hair out of her face in a futile attempt to calm down. Her face got all blotchy and pink when she got worked up, which clashed with her red hair. Damn Irish genes. Damn Irish temper.

Matthew had left her with a warning. "I hope you've found your man, Felicity. I don't mind telling you, the Police Commissioner is under pressure from the Mayor to do something about your department, and there's talk about shutting Miller's team down."

Somehow, she'd managed not to react and had left with most of her dignity intact. Now she wanted to go home, pour herself a glass of wine, and lie in the bath for an hour, unwinding.

Her phone beeped.

You free tonight?

Bloody Tom. She wasn't in the mood. Last time had left her feeling rather sordid, and a little embarrassed. Especially since he'd "surprised" her at the office, and one of her senior investigating officers had seen them together in the coffee shop.

One thing she'd been adamant about was that her workplace was off-limits — she didn't have time for distractions during the day. No, their little fling had run its course. She wouldn't be seeing Tom again.

Ignoring the message, she focused instead on her future. Even if Rob got his man, would the department survive this? It could be the final nail in the proverbial coffin.

What then? What if they wanted to close her down? Or at least get rid of Rob and his team?

It would be a crying shame, that's for sure. The SIO closed cases. He may not be the most popular detective on the block, and he sure as shit ruffled some feathers, but he was beyond reproach. Incorruptible, determined to a fault, and relentless in his pursuit of justice. Nobody was exempt from the law in his eyes. Not even the powers that be, and that made him a liability.

That made her a liability.

Sighing, she did a quick email search on her phone to see if she still had the job offer from the National Crime Agency. It had been a while ago now, but it might be worth getting in touch — before her reputation was completely destroyed. She hated abandoning ship, but if it was sinking, she couldn't afford to go down with it.

Locating the email, she made a mental note to reach out to them when this was over. In the meantime, while London traffic had them crawling up King's Road towards Putney Bridge, she thought about what Rob had said about going offline. Had they really been hacked? If so, that was a serious data breach.

Yet another hammer blow. They just kept on coming. She didn't know how much longer she could keep fending them off.

CHAPTER 35

"Do we have time for this?" Jenny glanced at her phone. They were in the interview suites at Putney Police Department, where Kyle Buckland had been brought in for questioning.

"Not really," Rob replied. "Let's hope he's forthcoming, otherwise we'll have to let him go and try again tomorrow."

"If he's guilty, that could give him a chance to run," Jenny warned.

Rob knew that, but they didn't have much choice. Mayhew had insisted, and she was under enough pressure as it was. He wasn't sure when he'd started caring about her, but if they were going to survive this case, he needed her onside.

"Let's get a move on," he growled, striding towards the interview room.

Kyle Buckland stood up as Rob entered, followed by Jenny. He'd been prepped, cautioned and informed the session was being recorded. That cut out any need for formalities and saved them precious time.

"I'm DCI Miller." Rob extended a hand. "This is DS Bird. You understand you're not under arrest. We just need to ask you some questions about Lena Jakubowski."

Buckland gave a nervous nod and sank back into the hard, wooden chair. "I told the other two detectives everything I knew earlier this afternoon," he said.

"I know, and that's why you're here," Rob replied. "We have some follow-ups."

"Oh, okay." Buckland's gaze flickered from Rob to Jenny.

"How well did you know Lena Jakubowski?"

"Not well. I only met her a couple of times — twice at a training session and once during a park run."

"What did you think of her?" Rob asked casually.

"I thought she was nice." Buckland shifted in his seat.

Rob slid a photograph of Lucy Andrews across the table. "What about this woman? Did you know her?"

Buckland stared at the photo for a long time before answering. "I know who she is."

"Who?" Rob prompted.

"That's Lucy Andrews, the woman who was murdered at Putney Bridge last week. I recognise her from the newspaper — and my own articles."

"You work for the *Richmond and Twickenham Times*?" Rob asked.

Buckland nodded.

"For how long?"

"Nearly six years now."

"Do you like it there?" Rob's tone was neutral, but his eyes didn't leave Buckland's face.

Buckland looked momentarily thrown. "Yes, I suppose so."

"You suppose?"

"I mean, it's not the *Sunday Times* or the *Guardian*, but it's decent work. I get to stay local."

Rob seized the opportunity. "How long have you lived in this area?"

"A little under ten years."

"Why did you move here?" he pressed.

"I visited with friends once. It looked nice — safe and quiet. I liked that."

"You're originally from South London, aren't you?" Rob said.

"Yeah."

"Except you moved here after your girlfriend at the time, Megan Carr, called the police over a domestic dispute." Harry had dug up the police warning only after Buckland's name had surfaced in connection with Lena.

Buckland swallowed. "That wasn't my fault."

"Why don't you tell us what happened?"

"It's a long story and irrelevant."

"We'll decide that," Rob said, his voice even.

Buckland sighed. "I was dating this woman, Megan. She was . . . wild. Get-off-your-tits-on-coke wild. One night she went off, started kicking and scratching. I tried to push her away, but she kept coming. I slapped her across the face to calm her down. It didn't work."

Rob kept his expression neutral. "So you're saying you were the victim?"

"Yes, exactly. She was batshit crazy. A neighbour called the cops, but by then, she'd calmed down enough to lie to them, saying I'd attacked her."

"Why didn't you give your side of the story?"

"I did, but they didn't care. They could smell the pot from a mile away. They gave me a warning, told her it was going no further, and left. I was spooked and moved out the next morning. Haven't looked back since."

Rob exhaled. "All right, let's move on. You were working on the Putney Bridge case?"

"Of course. It's on our patch — that's front-page news."

"What about the Surrey Stalker case five years ago?"

He nodded. "I remember it. Very similar to this one. I couldn't believe it when I found out one of the Stalker's victims was Lucy Andrews' sister. How bizarre is that?"

"Bizarre indeed," Rob replied. "You think it's a coincidence?"

"It can't be," Buckland said. "What are the chances that two sisters are killed the same way, five years apart? And now Lena." He shook his head. "Either the Stalker is back, or someone wants everyone to think he is."

Rob glanced at Jenny. Buckland had hit the nail on the head, but Rob still wasn't convinced the journalist was involved.

"Which do you think it is?" Rob asked. "The Stalker or a copycat?"

Buckland hesitated. "I don't know enough about the original case. I know the Stalker was killed." He paused, his eyes widening. "Wait, that was you, wasn't it?"

Rob nodded.

"Oh wow. I mean, I knew, but I hadn't made the connection." Buckland shifted uncomfortably in his chair.

"Well, obviously it's a copycat," he said, then gave Rob an appraising look. "You were there. What do you think?"

Typical journalist, turning the tables mid-interrogation. It was almost admirable.

"I can't discuss it," Rob replied coolly.

Buckland gave a resigned nod. "So what do you want from me?"

Rob leaned forward, his gaze hardening. "We'd like to know why your phone shows you were at work at five thirty yesterday evening, and in Isleworth at seven thirty. But it only takes twenty minutes to cycle home, even in heavy traffic. So, what took two hours?"

Buckland didn't answer immediately.

"Kyle, where were you for an hour and forty minutes?"

"How do you know I only got home at seven thirty?" he whispered.

Rob's stare didn't waver. "Your phone pinged a phone tower at seven thirty, and it does that every few minutes. There were no location updates between five thirty and seven thirty. If you'd been cycling, it would've pinged towers along the route."

Buckland bit his lip.

"Did you stop off at Richmond Park?"

His eyes widened. "Jesus, no. Of course not."

"So why turn your phone off, Kyle?"

Buckland shook his head, defensive. "I didn't want it distracting me while I cycled home."

Rob wasn't convinced. "You sure? Last chance to come clean."

"I've got nothing to hide. I didn't kill Lena."

Rob studied him, noting the anxiety etched on Buckland's face. He was hiding something, but Rob wasn't entirely sure what. "If you had anything to do with her death, it'd be a lot easier to admit it now," he pressed.

Buckland's jaw tightened. "I didn't."

Jenny glanced at her phone, then nudged Rob under the table. Time was slipping away. They needed to get to Monica Burridge's house to intercept the expected "break-in". It was nearly eleven.

Rob stared at Buckland across the table. He looked tired, maybe disturbed — but resolute. Making a decision, Rob said, "Kyle, I'm going to hold you overnight. We'll have another chat tomorrow."

"But why? I told you, I didn't do anything."

"We have enough grounds," Rob replied. "You have a history of domestic violence, you can't account for your whereabouts the night of Lena's murder, and you have prior knowledge of the Surrey Stalker case. You can see how it looks."

"No way. I can't believe this. I explained about the domestic thing. And Lena — she was in my running group. Besides, it's my job to cover local homicides!"

"Then tell us where you were last night, and you can go," Jenny said, standing up. Her voice was softer, almost sympathetic — the good cop to Rob's bad.

Buckland hesitated.

Definitely hiding something.

He sighed. "I turned my phone off."

"Have it your way." Rob opened the door. "We're keeping him in," he told the officer waiting outside, who nodded.

"I'm innocent!" Buckland called after them, but Rob kept walking, Jenny following close behind.

"We'd better hurry," she said as they exited the building.

"Let's take my car," Rob replied, veering towards his vehicle. "We don't want the thief to know we're coming."

CHAPTER 36

The call came through to the Control Centre at precisely 11.23 p.m.

"Unit required for a possible forced entry at Tidewatch House, Mortlake High Street."

Rob's radio crackled to life. He exchanged a look with Jenny, then picked up the handset. "This is DCI Miller, in the vicinity. Responding to the break-in."

"Copy that, DCI Miller," the controller replied. "Do you require assistance?"

"I'll let you know."

He pulled up outside Monica Burridge's house, lights flashing, but siren silent. No need to wake the whole neighbourhood — especially as the intruder was likely long gone. He scanned the street, the surrounding houses, the shadows. Nothing out of place.

The door creaked open, revealing Monica Burridge, frail and pale in a long dressing gown. Her white hair hung loose, framing her gaunt face. She clutched the door frame, her breaths coming in shallow gasps. "I was reading when I heard glass breaking," she wheezed. "It came from the kitchen. When I got there, there was glass everywhere."

She coughed, a harsh, rattling sound. Rob shot a concerned look at Jenny, who stepped forward, placing a gentle hand on Monica's shoulder.

"Are you all right, Mrs Burridge?"

Monica nodded weakly, then motioned for them to follow her down the hallway to her library. Jenny threw Rob a pointed look and followed, leaving him alone in the corridor.

"I'll check the rest of the house," Rob said, but instead of heading towards the kitchen, he made for the stairs. With Monica out of sight, he raced up two at a time, darted across the wooden landing, and sneaked down the corridor towards the spare room.

Switching the light on, he looked around. It was crammed with boxes of all sizes. Where to start?

He didn't have much time. None of the boxes were labelled, so he started at one corner, deciding to work his way across the room. He pulled out his pocket knife, sliced through the duct tape on the nearest box, and peeled back the flaps.

The first box was stuffed with women's clothes — old blouses, cardigans, dresses.

Not Simon's.

He moved on to the next box, which was filled with Christmas decorations, dusty tinsel and plastic ornaments.

He was halfway across the room when he found a box with men's items. Could these have belonged to Simon? He pulled out a white shirt, a blazer that smelled of mothballs and a pair of smart trousers. Holding up the blazer, he scanned the collar for hairs but couldn't find any. He rifled through the box and pulled out a few dress shirts, more trousers and a pair of large work shoes. No toiletries or cosmetics, no hairbrushes or toothbrushes. Not a comb in sight.

Gritting his teeth, he moved to the next box. This one was more promising. There was a stuffed toy, but the tag was still attached. New. Maybe a gift for someone? A present that was never given. A party unattended and long forgotten.

He picked out several notebooks, flicking through them. An old cookbook, gardening notes, a ledger of some sort dated 1976. Nothing of value.

He was about to move on when he heard Jenny's voice calling from below.

"Rob, come quickly."

He poked his head over the railing. "What is it?"

"Monica, she can't breathe. It's bad — I've had to call an ambulance. They're on their way."

Damn it.

"Is she conscious?"

"Barely. Her pulse is weak. She doesn't have long."

"All right. I'll be down in a minute."

"Hurry," Jenny hissed, vanishing back into the library.

Rob glanced back at the boxes, his heart pounding.

Where are the keepsakes she mentioned?

He opened another, hoping for a last-minute stroke of luck — more glassware, unused cutlery, crockery.

Useless.

Outside, he heard the approaching wail of an ambulance siren.

Time's up.

Swearing under his breath, he turned off the light and slipped out of the room, pulling the door closed behind him. He made his way down the stairs just as the paramedics arrived.

"She's in here," he said, guiding them to the library.

* * *

Rob arrived at the office with Jo just after nine o'clock the following morning. He was tired after last night's shenanigans, and more than a little frustrated that his search had been cut short.

Mrs Burridge was in critical care at Kingston Hospital, and the staff weren't optimistic. It seemed the break-in had triggered a major coughing fit that she'd been unable to recover from without medical intervention.

He felt bad about that.

What else could go wrong?

"We're just waiting on the language expert," Jenny told them, leading the way to the incident room. Mayhew was already there, sitting at the head of the table.

"Ma'am," Rob greeted her, while Jo stopped to chat. He left the two women to talk and made his way to the whiteboard, turning it around so everyone could see the blow-up of the letter the *Evening Standard* had received.

The team filtered in and took their seats, each glancing at the board in turn. A hush fell over the group. Finally, Jenny walked in with a man in his early forties, wearing spectacles too large for his face, his tiny beady eyes gleaming behind them. With his puffy cheeks and overbite, he reminded Rob of a squirrel.

"Thanks for coming in, Dr Reinecker," he said.

The man pressed his hands together and nodded. "Happy to be able to assist."

You haven't assisted yet, Rob thought, then tried to shift his sour mood. It wouldn't help matters and would just rub off on his team.

Taking a deep breath, he turned to Jo. "Right, this is the letter from the killer. You've both had time to study it, and I'd like your professional opinions, please. Any insights that will help us understand him better."

So we can catch the fucker.

Jo nodded at Dr Reinecker to go first. He gave a thin smile and nodded at the board. "The language in this letter is precise and deliberate," he began, his voice floating easily across the soundproof boardroom. "The writer is educated or, at the very least, well read. His vocabulary is straightforward, without slang or overtly complex words, but his phrasing is precise. For example, he uses 'a so-called heroic battle' and 'Detective Miller's little fairytale ending', which implies a certain sophistication and familiarity with irony. He's likely intelligent, potentially self-taught, and has a good command of English."

Jo was nodding, agreeing with everything he said.

He went on, "The letter avoids spelling or grammatical errors, implying the writer is not only educated but also meticulous."

"Jo?" She was his litmus test. With a degree in psychology and a long career in law enforcement, he trusted her judgement above all others.

"I agree with Dr Reinecker. Every sentence feels calculated, designed to provoke, which suggests someone who pays attention to detail — a trait often seen in serial killers who enjoy taunting police. The Zodiac Killer, for example. His structured, almost rhythmic sentences indicate he's likely to plan carefully rather than act impulsively."

"Well said." Reinecker nodded approvingly. Jo had clearly impressed him.

"What else?" Rob asked.

Reinecker pointed to the whiteboard. "He addresses the *Evening Standard* formally, 'To the Editor', which could suggest a desire to be seen as professional or official. This formality gives the impression that he considers himself on the same level as law enforcement or the media."

"He's arrogant." Jo turned towards him. "He refers to the events of five years ago as a 'fairytale ending', implying disdain for the way we — the police — presented the original investigation."

Rob found he was clenching his jaw and forced himself to relax. The rest of the team were hanging on to every word, including Mayhew, whose icy gaze remained fixed on the letter as the two experts discussed it.

"Furthermore, his rhetorical question 'Did they find the rings?' is a classic manipulation tactic." Jo met Rob's gaze. "It positions him as having knowledge we don't, making him appear omniscient. The question about whether the public knows they were 'lied to' reveals a desire to erode trust in the police, which could suggest a personal vendetta against law enforcement or a thrill in creating chaos."

"You think he's doing all of this for a sick thrill?" Rob asked.

"No, but he likes creating confusion. He sees himself as smarter than us. Not only does he mock your actions, Rob, but he uses words like 'innocent man' and 'convenient endings' to imply he's always been in control. It's a common trait among killers who like to taunt the police."

Reinecker cleared his throat. "I agree with Ms Maguire. The mocking tone towards you, DCI Miller, suggests personal animosity or perhaps an inflated sense of his own importance in your life, hinting that he might even feel wronged or overlooked by your department. This kind of language could indicate he wants to be recognised for his 'work'."

"Well, we know that. It's why he's recreating the crimes."

Reinecker flushed. "I'm just telling you what I surmised from the letter."

Rob exhaled. "Sorry, please continue."

Reinecker pushed his glasses up his nose. "The reference to 'the rings . . . placed with care, my special signature' suggests he's fastidious and ritualistic."

Jo cut in. "This detail aligns with the behaviour of serial killers who insert unique, repetitive elements into their crimes as a form of signature, as we know Burridge did."

"What does this letter tell us about his background?" Mayhew asked, from the back.

Reinecker turned to her. "The person who wrote this letter is likely well educated or has developed a good vocabulary through reading. He might not have a higher degree, but he has at least a secondary-school level of education and may have been exposed to books, media or philosophy that have contributed to his calculated, mocking tone. His measured structure and subtle wordplay suggest he could have a background in writing or public communication, or he may simply be someone who has studied language enough to craft his message carefully."

"Like a journalist?" Mayhew's gaze narrowed.

He touched the rim of his glasses. "Exactly."

Mayhew got to her feet. "Have you still got Buckland in custody?"

Rob turned to face her. "Yes, but we haven't charged him yet."

"If he doesn't give us his alibi for the night of Lena Jakubowski's murder, charge him. We don't have time to play games. Either he has an alibi or he doesn't, in which case, he's under arrest. Is that clear?" Her tone was frosty.

Rob gave a terse nod. "Yes, ma'am."

CHAPTER 37

Felicity connected to the live feed from the interrogation room at Putney Police Department and sat back to watch DCI Miller and his sidekick, the ever-present DS Bird, question Kyle Buckland for the second time.

She studied the lithe but dishevelled man facing them across the table. He didn't look like a serial killer, a man capable of beating, strangling and raping two women in as many weeks, but appearances could be deceiving. He was fit — she could tell that much just by looking at him, with his strong arms and sinewy legs. Average height, dark hair, angular features. He could be the man in the grainy CCTV image.

She hoped he bloody was. They needed to make this whole mess go away. Hopefully, DCI Miller would annihilate him, and he'd crack and confess.

Kyle Buckland would achieve his infamy, though not to the same extent as Burridge. They would issue a press release stating they'd caught the killer and that he was nothing more than a wannabe. She'd be back in the Commissioner's good graces, and her career, as well as that of the department, would be salvaged.

Her fantasy fizzled out as the interview began. Rob got all the preliminaries out of the way and reminded the suspect he was still under caution.

"Why am I still here?" Buckland demanded. "I told you I had nothing to do with Lena's death."

Rob leaned forward. His back was to the camera, but Felicity could imagine the steely gaze he was directing at the suspect right now.

"If that's true, give us your alibi." His voice was low, almost threatening.

The slightest hesitation. "I already told you, I was cycling home."

Rob shook his head. "You know, it's almost impossible to hide anything these days. With modern technology, cameras and satellites, even when you go off-grid, it's noticeable. That's why we know you're lying, Kyle. Your mobile phone was on all day. Would you like to see?"

Kyle nodded, and Jenny slid a piece of paper across the table to him. The suspect glanced down.

"Those are all the times it pinged the phone tower near your work. Every few minutes for the whole day, until five thirty. Then, nothing for two hours, until it comes back on again at seven thirty, but this time from a phone tower in Isleworth."

Kyle said nothing, but Felicity was sure he paled.

"Now, I know you said you turned it off, but we checked the data for every other day of the week. Do you know how many times you turned your phone off in the last two months?"

Kyle shook his head.

"Not once."

Felicity arched her eyebrows.

"Not once in eight weeks — that's forty workdays — did you switch off your mobile phone. That includes all the times you cycled to and from the office. So my question to you is: why did you switch off your phone the evening Lena Jakubowski was murdered?"

Felicity found she was holding her breath, waiting for an answer. *Damn, he was good.*

Kyle closed his eyes.

Gotcha, Felicity thought. *Come on . . . Confess.*

There was a short silence as Rob faced the suspect. Up until this point, DS Bird had said nothing, letting Rob take the lead.

She spoke now, her voice soft. "Kyle, if there's something you want to tell us, now is the time."

"It's not what you think," he croaked, glancing up at her.

"It doesn't matter what it is," she coaxed, "but if it gives you an alibi, we need to know. Then you can go home."

He nodded, as if considering it.

"This is not the time to be protecting anyone," Rob said, his voice much harder than his sergeant's. "You could go to prison for murder, Kyle."

Protecting? What was he on about?

Felicity scowled at the screen. *Bloody hell.* He was her top SIO and he never told her anything. Clearly, something else was going on here that she wasn't privy to.

"I could lose my job," Kyle whispered.

"You could lose your freedom if you don't talk," Rob rebutted.

A shaky breath.

"Okay, fine. I turned off my phone because I was with someone. Someone from work. We're . . . having an affair."

Felicity shook her head. *What?*

"Who were you with, Kyle?" Rob asked.

"Are you going to speak to them?" His gaze was pleading.

"Yes, I'm afraid we'll have to verify your alibi."

"Oh God." He glanced down at his hands.

"We'll be discreet," DS Bird said. "We won't come to the office. Nobody will know we've spoken to them."

He sucked in a breath. "I was with Randal Simms. We've been flirting with each other for a while now, but that evening, when I turned off my phone, that was when we first — you know . . ."

"Slept together?" asked Rob.

Felicity balked. He'd known all along it was something like this, hadn't he? Even when she'd been praying for a confession, he'd known Buckland wasn't their man.

"Having a relationship is not a crime," Rob remarked dryly. "Why hide it? You could have prevented all this." He waved a hand over the table.

"Because Geraldine Simms is the editor of the *Richmond and Twickenham Times*," he said quietly. "Randal is her son."

Oh, for fuck's sake. Felicity slammed her laptop shut. She didn't need to hear any more. Kyle Buckland was a dead end. He wasn't the killer. He was just an employee screwing his boss's son, afraid to lose his job.

They were no closer to finding the monster than they had been an hour ago.

She was still simmering when her phone buzzed. Glancing down, she saw it was Tom. She'd ghosted his last two messages, but he was getting bolshy now.

If you don't want to see me anymore, just say so.

Okay, fine. I don't want to see you anymore, she wrote back, but then paused.

Shit. That was cruel. They'd had fun. It had just reached its natural end.

Deleting her text, she wrote: *Sorry, just busy at work. Can't handle anything else right now.*

Before she could think any more about it, she hit send.

There, done. She felt better for coming clean, and it wasn't a lie. With the situation the way it was, the last thing she needed was a fledgling relationship and all the pressure that went with that. Not that Tom would ever have been a real boyfriend. He wasn't her type.

What *was* her type?

The steadfast, determined face of DCI Rob Miller appeared in front of her, and she wondered what kind of partner he'd make. DCI Jo Maguire seemed happy. They'd met at work, apparently. On the Stalker case, as it was.

Felicity huffed. Well, Jo Maguire must have something she didn't, because she couldn't even get him to call her by her first name. Sighing, she opened her computer and got back to work.

CHAPTER 38

Rob got back to his desk, only to be bombarded with questions.

"I was sure it was him," Trent said, coming over. "How did you know?"

Rob shrugged. "I knew he was hiding something, but I didn't know what. I was pretty sure he wasn't the killer, though."

"Why not?" Harry asked. "I must admit, I was convinced too."

"He didn't fit the profile, for one."

"He was a journalist," Celeste pointed out, her face glum. Rob knew it was because her lead had turned into nothing.

"True, but that was the only bit that fit. Everything else was wrong. His demeanour, his reactions to our questions about Lena and Lucy — his role in the original investigation was minor at best. Then there was the fact that he was unmarried, lived alone in his forties, no kids."

"That only proves he's a loner," Will said.

"Or gay," Jenny replied with a faint smile.

She'd known what he'd been thinking prior to the interview. They'd played it perfectly, taking turns to intimidate and coax Buckland into divulging his alibi — and he was happy with the outcome. Now they just had to do the follow-up to confirm it, but, as Jenny had said, they'd be discreet, and Kyle could go back to his normal life.

One thing Rob hated more than bureaucratic nonsense was being forced to arrest an innocent man just to save face. That was never something he would knowingly do, and if that made him unpopular, so be it. Mayhew would just have to suck it up. No point doing this job if you're going to lock up the wrong person.

"What about the domestic violence incident?" Celeste asked.

"That was a long time ago and probably self-defence. I don't condone what he did, but I think he was provoked. I ran his ex's name and found several run-ins with the police over the years. She's the one with the pattern of violence, not him."

Celeste sighed. "So we're back to square one."

"We've eliminated another suspect," Jenny said, trying to keep up morale. Rob appreciated the effort. Spirits were sagging under the weight of another setback.

"How's Monica Burridge?" he asked. Her condition had been gnawing at him.

"She's stable," Jenny replied. "Out of critical care and moved to a general ward."

Thank God. At least he wouldn't have her death on his conscience as well as her son's.

"Any word from SOCO on the forensics or that letter?" Rob asked.

"I chased them up this morning," Will replied. "Nothing from Richmond Park. Her phone's still missing, so the killer must have taken it with him."

This told Rob that the killer was being fed information, not gathering it first-hand. If he were, he'd know that both Julie Andrews' and Sara Bakshi's phones were left at the scene. Someone — likely an insider — was leaking to him. A co-worker? A hacker?

He raked a hand through his hair in frustration. "What's IT said about the system break?"

"They're still trying to find it. It looks like the hacker used a staff login, because there are no signs of an actual breach."

Harry frowned. "Can't they see whose computer it's coming from?"

"Apparently not. The system doesn't record individual IP addresses, just login information, and we all use the department login. It could be anyone."

"That needs to change," Rob muttered.

"I've already put in a change request," Will said, grimacing. "Not that it helps us now."

"I've got the security footage from the Star and Garter," Trent said, optimistically. "I'm about to review it."

"Let me know if you spot anything unusual." Rob turned back to his desk. He half expected Mayhew to give him a bollocking for his handling of the Kyle Buckland interview, but she remained in her office. He could see her working on her laptop, head bowed, face illuminated by her screen. She was deep in concentration, and if she had watched it — which he knew she would have, because it was Mayhew — she had decided not to say anything. Thank goodness for small mercies.

His phone buzzed on his desk. He glanced at it — an unrecognised number. Frowning, he opened the message and his blood ran cold.

"Fuck," he hissed.

Jenny looked over, alarmed. "What is it?"

He turned the screen. The image was of Jo, Jack and Trigger in the park — a candid shot of Jo with her arms out, waiting for Jack to toddle towards her, Trigger beside them, tongue lolling happily. The moment was serene, carefree — completely unaware they were being watched.

Jenny gasped. "Who sent this?"

"Burner phone," he growled, handing her the device.

"Will," she said, "trace this number now." She read it out, and Will's fingers flew over his keyboard. He knew from Jenny's tone that this was serious.

"I'm calling it." Rob hit dial. It went straight to voicemail — the phone was off. He doubted it would ever be switched on again.

"I need to reach Jo." Hands shaking, he dialled her number. It rang out. He swore and tried again. "Come on, pick up!"

It went to voicemail again.

"I'll send Uniform to your house." Jenny was already dialling from her desk phone. Moments later, she was instructing a local unit to check on Jo and Jack.

Rob's stomach churned. He got to his feet, ready to run out the door, when his phone rang. It was Jo.

Heart pounding, he answered, "Jo? Are you guys okay?"

"Yes, I'm fine. Sorry, I was feeding Jack his lunch. What's wrong? You sound weird."

Rob exhaled, the tension easing as he fell back into his chair.

She was fine.

They were all fine.

Giving Jenny a thumbs-up, he quickly briefed Jo on the photo he'd just received. "Sending it to you now."

After a pause, she said, "This was taken the day that man offered to take our picture, remember? In fact, I'll bet that was him. It fits the profile that he'd want to contact his next victim before . . ." She petered off.

"Jesus, Jo," he erupted. "What did this guy look like?"

There was a pause as she thought about it. "Five eleven, dark hair, average build, in his forties."

"Can you remember anything else about him? Distinctive marks, accent, language?"

"Come to think of it, he was quite well spoken. Not posh, but he seemed intelligent. He did fit the profile of the letter writer."

Christ. She'd met with the killer. Face to face.

"Eye colour?" he pressed.

"Didn't notice. He was . . . unremarkable, really."

Unremarkable, but bold. Exposing himself like that. Then, holding back until the right time to let his presence in their lives be known.

Sick bastard.

"Would you be able to sit with a sketch artist?" he asked.

"I can try."

"Good. Jo, listen to me. It's not safe for you and Jack at the house. I'm sending round a police escort, and I want you to go to a hotel. Anywhere but there. I'm going to post officers outside the door and make sure you're safe until this bastard is behind bars."

He couldn't shake the memory of Yvette's abduction. It had been a week or so after Sara Bakshi's death, but maybe this killer was escalating, or maybe he just didn't want to wait that long. Whatever the reason, Rob wasn't going to take any more chances.

"He's doing this on purpose, Rob," Jo said, her voice steady. "He's toying with you. You know that?"

"No, I don't know that," he replied. "Yvette was abducted and nearly killed. I'm not going to let the same thing happen to you."

Not again.

He didn't need to say it. She knew.

"Okay," she agreed softly. "I'll pack a few things, and we'll wait for the police escort. What about Trigger?"

"Call Mrs Winterbottom. Ask her if she'll take him until this is over — and tell Tanya to stay away too. I don't want her caught up in this."

"Will do. Try not to worry, Rob. We'll be okay. Go catch this psycho. We'll see you tonight."

Try not to worry? Rob paced up and down, unable to sit still. He was beside himself.

The worst part was he couldn't leave the office, not now they had a description. Not now they knew he'd made contact. Suddenly, there was a lot more work to be done. They had another location. Old Deer Park. A date, and a time.

They needed CCTV footage, motor vehicle information, a witness appeal. As soon as Jo had sat with the sketch artist, they'd circulate his picture.

The hunter had become the hunted.

"Briefing!" he yelled.

CHAPTER 39

"You know, this looks a bit like that physiotherapist that was leaving Monica Burridge's place when we first arrived — minus the glasses." Jenny tilted her head as she studied the artist's sketch.

Jo and Jack were safely ensconced in a hotel in Central London, surrounded by police officers, and for the first time since he'd got the ominous message, Rob felt able to relax.

"You think?" He thought back to the first time they'd gone to see Burridge's mother. "I suppose so. Hair's a different colour but the features are similar.

"Easy to dye your hair," Harry said.

"Find him," Rob ordered. "I want him brought in for questioning. Bring in the care worker too, while you're at it. I want to talk to her on the record." He was done playing nice.

"On it." Jenny swivelled back to her desk.

"You've got a sketch?" Mayhew strode towards them as fast as her tight skirt and heels would allow.

"Yeah, the artist has just left the hotel. Jo says this is a pretty good likeness of the man in the park." He handed it to her before turning to Trent, who was trying to get his attention.

"Sir, I've found something on the security camera outside the Star and Garter. I think it's him."

"Seriously?" Rob went to peer over Trent's shoulder.

Mayhew set the sketch down on his desk. "Circulate this," she ordered, before stalking back to her office. Strange that she didn't stay to check the security footage. It wasn't like her to walk away from a lead, the control freak that she was.

"What do you think?" Trent whispered.

He stared at the paused image on the screen. It was dark, which meant visibility wasn't good, but he could clearly see a hooded figure wheeling a bicycle through the park gates. The timestamp read 6.17 p.m.

"The timing fits." He straightened up, bumping into Harry and Celeste, both of whom had leaned over him so they could also see. They shuffled back.

"Sorry, guv," Harry muttered.

Celeste, who'd had some experience with CCTV footage said, "Can you zoom in on the bike? We might be able to tell what make it is."

Trent did what he could, but it didn't make a great deal of difference. "That's as far as it'll enhance," he said through gritted teeth.

"He's wearing gloves." Rob studied the hand on the gate. "He's the right size too. Five eleven, average build. This could well be our killer."

Trent sucked in an excited breath.

"Can you see when he left?" Rob asked.

"No. I started at seven thirty and worked backwards, until I found this. There's nothing after that."

"He must have left a different way," Rob surmised. "Makes sense. Going in, his back is to the camera, and it's early enough that there are several cyclists and walkers still in the park. It's not going to raise suspicion. Coming out, however, once it's completely dark, that would be suspect."

"You think he knew about this camera?" Trent breathed, his eyes wide.

"Maybe. I wouldn't put it past him. He's arrogant enough to taunt us with this. He'll know it won't stand up in court."

Trent's shoulders slumped.

"Still, very well done." Rob thumped him on the back. "We're making progress, and it all paints a picture of his movements."

Trent gave a relieved grin. "I was wondering if any of the houses near the other pedestrian gates have private surveillance. I mean, it is Richmond."

"Good idea. Get Uniform to do a door-to-door. You never know."

Not for the first time, Rob was glad he'd brought Trent on. The young PC was proving extremely useful. He was keen to learn, and his ideas were good.

"Guv — Paul Oswald, the physiotherapist, has disappeared," Jenny said, putting down the phone. "He didn't turn up for work today, and there's nobody at his home address. The officer on site says the place looks deserted."

"Shit." Rob banged his fist down on the desk. "If he's the copycat—" His voice caught with emotion.

Goddammit. They'd seen him, he was right there, and he'd outwitted them. Now he was in the wind.

"That's how he got Simon's DNA," Jenny whispered. "He was inside her house. He had access to Simon's belongings."

"I don't know how," Rob growled. "I searched that spare room and didn't find anything."

Jenny shrugged. "Shall I put out an APB?"

"Yes, I want that man found. Can we pull his details?" He turned to Will, eyebrow arched.

"I'm on the DVLA website as we speak," Will replied. "Then I'll call his company and get any information they have on him."

Rob gave an impatient nod.

"Guv, Oksana Petrenko is downstairs." Celeste was holding her phone in her hand. "Shall I get security to send her up?"

"I'll go down and get her."

He strode from the room. He always thought better when he was moving.

The killer had made contact several times, first when he and Jenny had attended the house. That had been accidental, as there was no way he'd have known they were coming. After that, he'd deliberately approached Jo in the park. That made his blood boil. The maniac had taken Jo's phone, used it to snap a photograph of her.

Of his family.

He clenched his fists as he marched down the stairs. Then, he'd sent them that engagement card, just like Lucy Andrews.

Then came the text message. Will hadn't been able to trace it. The phone had remained off — probably destroyed already. The copycat might be a risk taker, but he wasn't stupid. Everything was calculated, timed to perfection. Even the information to the press had been drip-fed to have maximum impact.

Rob hissed out a breath.

The killer had been planning this for some time. That much was obvious.

But why?

Why choose Julie's sister? Why Lena? Only to mimic the Stalker's MO?

Why toy with them like this?

To what end?

Was there a personal connection?

He was still pondering the endless list of questions when he saw Oksana standing in the lobby.

"How well do you know Monica's physiotherapist?" Rob asked, when they were seated in the interview room and Jenny had joined them.

"I don't know him," she replied, her expression defiant. "He usually come when I am not there."

"When's that?"

"Tuesday and Thursday," she replied. "I only see him two times before."

"When was that?" he asked.

"The day I see you, and one time before. I don't remember exactly."

"Did he ever speak to you?"

She thought for a moment. "I think he say hello or something like this."

So, basic communication. Oswald was keeping it to a minimum.

"Did you see him treat Mrs Burridge?" Jenny asked.

She nodded. "Yes, I show him to the library, and he do some exercises with her."

"Did you watch?"

"No, I leave them in the library."

Rob thought for a moment. "Oksana, can you describe him?"

She hesitated. "Why? You also see him."

"I know, but I don't remember," he lied.

She gnawed on her lower lip, thinking. "He have brown hair." She pointed at Rob's. "Brown eyes."

"Any marks or tattoos?"

She shook her head. "Oh, he had a . . ." She pointed to her chin.

Rob frowned. "A dimple? He had a dimple in his chin?"

She nodded.

That was something. The carer didn't know much more than that, so Rob let her go and thanked her for her time. As soon as she'd left, he pulled out his phone and called Jo.

She answered straight away. Rob asked her if the man she'd spoken to in the park had a dimple in his chin.

"Oh yes," she said, without hesitation. "Now that you mention it, he did. Sorry, I completely forgot about that."

He sucked in a breath. Same guy.

"You know who he is, don't you?" she said softly.

"Not yet, but we're getting closer."

He said goodbye and found Will, who'd been researching Oswald. "What did the agency say?"

Will pushed his chair away from his desk and looked up at Rob. "Here's the thing. Oswald joined them at the start of this year, but when I showed them the sketch, they said it wasn't him."

"What?" Rob scratched his head.

"The Paul Oswald that works there looks like this." Will angled his screen to show Rob a photograph of a muscular man with light brown, almost blond hair and a disarming smile. This guy was far better looking than the man they'd met at the house.

"So, who did we see?" Jenny asked, sliding over.

Will crossed his arms over his chest. "I don't know, but it wasn't Paul Oswald."

Rob slanted his gaze. "Are we to understand that the killer was going to see Mrs Burridge under the pretence of being someone from the agency?"

"Seems like it," Jenny replied. "That way, if anyone checked, they'd find that a Paul Oswald does work there."

"He's smart," breathed Harry, who'd also joined the conversation.

"It's one way of getting into her house," Will commented.

"Okay, so how did he know whose name to steal?" Rob looked at Will.

"Someone similar in appearance?" Jenny suggested.

"Except they aren't really." Harry peered at the sketch again.

Celeste came over. "Maybe there was nobody else," she said.

Will brought up the agency website and clicked on *ABOUT US*. "You're right."

They all squinted at his computer. The group of physiotherapists were a mixed bag. Some were older, some younger, a mix of different racial groups.

"Paul Oswald is the only white male in the same age group as the killer," Will said.

CHAPTER 40

Mayhew walked into the crowded wine bar and headed straight for the bar. "Shot of tequila, please." It came, and she threw it back, relishing the burn and the warmth that followed. She needed it to steel her nerves.

Was she crazy meeting a man she suspected of being a serial killer?

Undeniably, but what else could she do? She had to be sure.

When she'd seen that sketch, she'd nearly fainted. It looked just like Tom, apart from the eyes. They were darker in the sketch, but he could have worn contact lenses.

After that, things had started tumbling into place.

The way they'd met. Here. In this very wine bar. A chance meeting, she'd thought, but now she wasn't so sure. It wouldn't be hard to follow her, figure out where her local watering hole was and arrange to bump into her — literally.

Oh, I'm so sorry! I'm Tom. Let me buy you a drink to apologise.

It had been as easy as that.

She shook her head, hot tears prickling her eyes, but she blinked them away.

Then there were the leaked documents. She'd taken the case files home, left them in her living room when he'd come over for sex. How thick could she be? She ought to have known better. She was a fecking superintendent, for God's sake.

She gulped over the lump in her throat and ordered a bottle of Sauvignon Blanc. Not that she planned to drink it, but she had to act normal. If she only ordered a glass, he might suspect something was up. Everything had to be the same.

As it was, she'd told him she was too busy for a relationship, and then the very next day, she'd messaged him to meet for a drink.

It's been a hell of a week. Fancy a drink?

Then she'd waited, heart hammering in her chest. His reply had been mercifully swift.

Sure. See you at eight.

Perfect.

She hadn't been entirely stupid, though. She'd invited her sister to join them. But first . . .

She glanced up as Tom walked in. He raised a hand in greeting, then headed to the bar. This was their Friday evening routine, their dance, except it wouldn't end with him coming back to her place. She watched as he ordered a beer and made his way over to her table.

He pulled out a chair and sat down. "I was glad to get your text," he said. "I didn't think you wanted to see me again."

"Sorry, I've been so busy at work," she said. "There's this case. It's very stressful."

"I understand. It can't be easy doing what you do for a living."

Understatement of the year.

"No, but let's not talk about that. Tell me about your day. I'm sure it must have been better than mine." How did she sound so normal? This was surreal, like she was in a stage play, and everyone around them was the cast.

"Oh, you know." He shrugged. "It was okay."

He'd told her he worked for a recruitment agency, but he rarely spoke about his work. Another sign she'd ignored, because she'd been too caught up in her own world to care about his.

"Sounds like you need a drink too." She smiled, and hoped he didn't see straight through her little charade. Out of the corner of her eye, she saw her sister, Faith, walk into the bar. Hopefully, she'd remember what Felicity had asked her to do.

Enter stage left.

"You going to watch the boat race this weekend?" Felicity asked. She'd purposely chosen a table in the middle of the bar, so there were plenty of people around them. It was noisy and loud, as she'd known it would be tonight.

Faith held her slim clutch bag in her hand as she made her way to the table. In the outside pocket was her phone, the top of it sticking out. It wasn't obvious, but the camera was on. She was filming Tom, as per Felicity's request.

"Felicity!"

She got to her feet, as did Tom. He was perfectly in shot.

"Faith, fancy seeing you here!" She turned to her date. "Tom, this is my sister, Faith. Faith, this is my . . . Tom."

How should she describe him? Her shag? Her booty call? The psycho killer murdering women in West London?

How would Faith react if she knew? Her sister was neurotic enough as it was. Felicity was hit by a pang of guilt for dragging her into this. She had young kids. She lived alone, recently divorced.

But she had to know.

It might not be him, she told herself. She might be blowing this completely out of proportion, letting her paranoia run wild. Yet deep down, she knew.

It was him.

It explained . . . everything.

* * *

Even though it was Saturday, Felicity knew Rob's entire team would be in the office. They didn't stop when they were working a case. She'd long since given up wondering if they had better halves or families to go home to. Their dedication to the job was admirable — although she suspected it had more to do with their intrepid senior investigating officer, rather than the department as a whole.

She arrived early, before anyone else. On her desk was a perfect printout of Tom's head and shoulders. It hadn't taken her long to go through Faith's video and select a suitable screenshot. She'd printed it out in full colour, and now she was waiting for Rob to arrive.

Last night had ended rather abruptly. Faith had joined them, curious about Tom, and the conversation had shifted to the school run, subject choices and cheating husbands. Tom hadn't lasted long after that. He'd made up some excuse about an early start and left.

Felicity, wanting to keep up appearances, had texted him when she got home apologising for her sister's intrusion, saying she didn't know she was going to be there. She didn't get a reply.

Feeling his eyes on her, she turned the photograph over so she couldn't keep looking at it. Practising her yogic breathing, she paced up and down her office, until she saw Rob walk in.

Finally.

DS Bird was with him, and the rest of the team would be arriving shortly. They were like a flock of birds, always together. Even Trent, who had to drive in from Marlow every morning, seemed to arrive at the same time as the others.

Leaving her office, she approached his desk.

He glanced up. "You're in early." He must have seen something in her face, as he added, "Are you okay?"

DS Bird stared at her, then blinked and turned away. What was up with her?

"I need to speak to you." Her voice was a low rasp.

With a nod, he followed her into her office. "What's up?"

"How's Jo?"

She couldn't come right out and ask, even though she was dying to. Even though that was the *only* thing on her mind. Had been since last night. She hadn't slept, just stared at the picture for hours, comparing it to the sketch.

Close. Too close.

"She's fine, thanks. She and Jack are both fine. I've got twenty-four-hour security at the hotel. He won't be able to get to them there."

"I'm glad." She ran a shaky hand through her hair.

"Are you sure you're okay?"

"Yeah, why?"

"Well, your jumper is on inside out and you're wearing slippers."

She looked down.

It was true. On both counts.

"Oh God." What must he think of her?

To be fair, her nerves were shot. What did it matter what anyone thought, anyway? When it came out she'd been sleeping with the copycat killer, that she'd been the one leaking classified documents to him, her career was over.

She'd never live this down. They'd want her out.

She'd be lucky if she got another job anywhere in law enforcement after this.

"Felicity?"

The use of her first name wrenched her out of her stupor. He *never* called her that. "Yes, sorry. I'm fine, but I've got something I need to show you."

Reaching over her desk, she picked up the upside-down photograph and handed it to him.

"Is this him?"

CHAPTER 41

Rob stared at the photograph. "How did you get this?"

Mayhew's legs seemed to give way, and she collapsed onto the edge of the desk. "It's him, isn't it?" she whispered.

"This is the man we saw outside Monica Burridge's house, yes — the one who posed as her physiotherapist."

"Oh Lord." She'd gone white.

"I don't know if this is the man Jo saw in the park, but I'll ask her."

Mayhew gave a faint nod, her gaze unfocused.

What the hell was going on? He'd never seen her look so . . . disturbed.

Taking out his phone, he snapped a quick photo of the printout and sent it to Jo. "We'll know in a moment," he said. "Do you need some water or something?"

She shook her head.

Moments later, his phone buzzed.

He glanced at the screen. "Jo confirms it's the same man." Looking up, he said, "Now, tell me — how did you get this? Do you know him?"

Mayhew looked like she might faint.

"Yes," she murmured, her voice so quiet he almost didn't hear her. "He's . . . he's the man you saw me with in the coffee shop the other day. He's the man I've been seeing."

Rob stared at her. "You're having a relationship with this man?"

"Not a relationship, exactly." She sighed, her shoulders slumping. "It was just . . . sex."

Rob drew in a sharp breath. "Let me get this straight. The man we now suspect of being the copycat killer is also your lover?"

She nodded miserably. "I'm sorry. I didn't know. It was only when I saw the sketch that it hit me."

She looked so broken that, despite everything, he felt sorry for her.

"You're the leak," he whispered, as the pieces slotted together.

"I didn't know." Tears were falling freely down her face.

In all the time she'd been here, he'd never known Mayhew to cry. Luckily, she wasn't wearing any make-up to smudge.

"All right." He took a deep breath, forcing himself to stay calm as he tried to process this new information. Guiding her over to the two armchairs by the small coffee table at the far end of her office, he said, "Sit down and start from the beginning. How did you meet him?"

Slowly, painfully, Mayhew shared her story. They'd met at a wine bar in Putney. He'd introduced himself as Tom. One thing had led to another, and they'd ended up in bed. Every time, it had been at her place. Frustratingly, she didn't even know where he lived.

They'd met five times now, not including this last time. She'd brought work files home, never suspecting he'd go through them while she was sleeping. Not all of them, though — there were gaps in his research. Like the phones that were left at Julie's and Sara's murder scenes, while he had taken Lena's with him.

"What's his last name?" he asked.

She blinked and gave a despairing shrug. "I never asked."

"We'll trace his number, although I suspect it's a prepaid burner."

"It might still be on. It's the only way I can get hold of him."

"Let's hope so. We're also going to need to analyse the text messages between you. Does he have your work phone?"

"No, it's my private phone." She let out a weary sigh. "This is beyond embarrassing, but I suppose I deserve it."

"No, you don't." Rob glanced at her tear-stained face. She was taking this hard, but he couldn't blame her. She'd made a terrible mistake, and now she was going to pay for it, probably with her career. "He used you. Seduced you to get information. Luckily for him, he didn't have to pump you for details. He had access to your files. That was enough."

She closed her eyes. "I can't believe I was so bloody stupid."

"What's done is done," he said matter-of-factly. "But if we play our cards right, this might be just what we need to catch him. He doesn't suspect you know, does he?"

"I—I don't think so."

"Last night, you act any differently?"

"No, of course not. I knew not to. In fact, my sister arrived, so Tom left early. He made up some bullshit excuse and went home. It wasn't me."

"Okay, that's good." Rob didn't even know she had a sister.

"What are you thinking?" She wiped her face with her sleeve.

"I'm wishing I paid more attention to who you were with at the coffee shop," he said.

She sniffed. "He asked about you."

"He did?"

"Asked who you were. I said you were one of my senior investigating officers."

"He would have known who I was anyway," Rob said, belying his inner turmoil. "It's not hard to find me online. There are a dozen articles with my picture in them, and we know he's done his research."

"I suppose."

He nodded to the printout now lying on the coffee table. "Now we have positive ID that this man is our killer, can we send a search team round to Monica Burridge's house?"

She nodded. "With the physiotherapist, Jo's testimony and mine, I think we have enough justification."

"Great. I was thinking we could issue a press release. Get a little of our own back."

She gasped. "You can't release that photograph. He'll know it's me."

"I wasn't planning to. That would just send him underground, and we want him out in the open, so we can catch him."

"What will you say?"

"That we have confirmation that this is a copycat killer, not the Surrey Stalker. We'll destroy the carefully crafted image he's tried to portray. We'll say we know who he is and have instigated a nationwide manhunt. We have DNA evidence found at the crime scene and, once we catch him, we'll be able to use it to put him away for good."

"We don't have DNA evidence, do we?" Her blue eyes scanned his face, looking for answers. "I thought the crime scene was clean."

"No, but he doesn't know that. He'll think he's slipped up. The only way to know for sure will be to get hold of you."

Her eyes widened. "He won't need to. He knows where I live."

Rob broke into a slow grin. "Then that's how we'll catch him."

CHAPTER 42

Rob herded the team into the incident room and broke the news about Mayhew.

They all stared at him, stunned into silence. Eventually, Jenny said, "That's why she came in looking like she'd rolled out of bed."

"She was in shock," Rob said, not wanting to talk ill of her. He'd seen first-hand how broken she'd been by the revelation.

"It was a brave thing that she did," Celeste murmured. "To confront him on her own and get that photograph."

"It was a stupid idea," Rob said. "If she'd come clean yesterday, we might have been able to catch him. Set up a sting operation. Yet she decided to handle it herself."

"I suppose she wanted to know for sure," Trent said kindly. "I mean, that sketch was all she had to go on."

"True. I'll give her that much." He looked around the room. "Be that as it may, we now have a situation that we have to handle very carefully. This is our chance. Tom doesn't know that we know he's the killer. That gives us the advantage."

"What do you propose?" Jenny asked, her eyes gleaming. He felt it too — the adrenaline rush, the thrill of the chase. Now they had the killer in their sights and were homing in.

"We set a trap. First, I'm going to issue a press release." He told them what he'd discussed with Mayhew, and they were all in agreement.

"Perhaps you can get Jo to craft it for you," Jenny suggested. "She'll know how to push his buttons."

"That's a good idea. Jo will be up for that."

"What trap?" Will asked. "How are we going to get him?"

"That depends on the article," Rob replied. "We're going to make him so worried he's made a mistake, that he'll question everything. In fact, he'll be so concerned, he'll try to arrange a meeting with Mayhew to see what she knows."

"That could be risky," Harry cautioned. "He'll have to coerce it out of her."

"Yes, but it won't get that far," Rob said confidently, "because we'll be waiting for him."

The rest of the morning flew by. Rob spoke to Jo, who wrote a carefully constructed press release designed to crush the killer's reputation and make him panic that he'd left some DNA behind at Lena Jakubowski's crime scene.

Next, he got hold of Vicky Bainbridge and explained to her exactly what he wanted. The press release would go out to all the major publications. In addition, he was going to issue a statement.

The film crews were there within the hour. Rob didn't bother with Scotland Yard — he delivered the update on the steps of Putney Police Station, less than a mile from the MIT headquarters.

"Good morning, everyone. Thank you for being here. Today, I want to provide an update on our investigation into the recent homicides at Putney Wharf and Richmond Park.

"Firstly, I'd like to clarify that we believe these incidents to be the work of an individual attempting to mimic the crimes attributed to the Surrey Stalker. Let me be clear: the original Surrey Stalker is no longer a threat, and we are now focused on apprehending this copycat.

"Recent forensic discoveries have provided us with valuable new leads, including DNA evidence, that we're confident will aid us in identifying this individual. Our investigative teams are pursuing every available resource, and we're working around the clock to bring this case to a swift and successful conclusion.

"To the public, I want to assure you that we are committed to your safety. We ask that you remain vigilant and report anything unusual or suspicious that may assist us in this investigation.

"Thank you."

Rob stepped back from the microphone, nodded to the reporters assembled below the steps and headed back into the building.

* * *

The killer's eyes bored into the screen, fingers clenched around the remote as the footage replayed. Rob Miller, smug and composed, stood on the steps of the station, flanked by uniformed officers, the Metropolitan Police crest glinting in the morning light behind him. Every word Rob spoke was like a fresh slap in the face.

"*We are now focused on apprehending this copycat,*" Miller had said, calm and confident. The cameras had zoomed in on him, capturing the faintest hint of a smirk as he announced the case's latest developments. "*Valuable new leads, including DNA evidence . . .*"

The killer's jaw tightened, his breath quickening.

Copycat.

The word echoed in his mind, stabbing into him like a hot poker. It was meant to wound, to make him look small, insignificant. A sad, pathetic imitation. Miller had gone out there and torn down everything he'd worked so hard to build. The entire purpose of his mission — the meticulous recreations, the letters to the media, the trophies left just so — was now dismissed as the work of a mere wannabe.

How dare he.

He shot up from his chair, throwing the remote at the wall, where it shattered, pieces scattering across the floor. Blood pounded in his ears. Miller thought he was clever, thought he was safe, standing on those steps with the whole world watching. The killer's fingers twitched, itching to wrap around Miller's throat, to watch the smugness drain from his face as he realised, too late, what he'd unleashed.

All that careful planning, making the public question what really happened five years ago. All those efforts to show them that the so-called "heroic" Detective Miller hadn't stopped the Surrey Stalker, he'd just murdered an innocent man while the real Stalker slipped away.

He'd been so close to proving it — just one or two more bodies, and they would have seen it. They would have known Miller was a fraud.

But now?

Now the world thought *he* was nothing more than a shadow, a hollow imitation of something far greater. They thought he was some deluded fan, someone who could never live up to the legacy he'd tried to claim. They didn't understand.

Miller didn't understand.

"I'll show you," he hissed. His whole body vibrated with anger, every nerve on edge. All he could think about was Miller's downfall. "You think you're untouchable? You think you can humiliate me like this and walk away?"

He moved to his desk, grabbed a notebook and flipped through the pages with a frantic energy. Each page was filled with notes, plans, sketches of potential crime scenes, taunts he'd considered sending, ways to draw Miller closer. His finger traced over Miller's name, written over and over, crossed out and circled.

He'd wanted to do this slowly, to make the detective squirm, to leave him questioning everything he'd done, including himself, but patience was no longer an option. Miller had challenged him, thrown down the gauntlet in full view of the public.

Fine. If he wanted a confrontation, he'd get one.

The killer pressed his palms flat on the desk, breathing deeply. He would need to be careful. This couldn't be sloppy. Miller needed to understand that he wasn't dealing with some impulsive thug — he was facing a craftsman. Someone who had spent months preparing for this.

"No more games," he whispered, his lips curling into a cold smile. "This time, I'm coming for you, Miller. And when I'm finished, they'll see you for what you really are — a failure."

He stood still, the outline of his next steps already coming into focus. The idea of Miller finally realising he was outmatched made the anger melt into something darker, something close to pleasure.

"Soon," he murmured, almost tenderly. "I'll be coming for you soon."

With that, he grabbed a clean black hoodie from the bedroom, picked up his car keys and left the flat.

CHAPTER 43

Mayhew slipped out just before eleven, needing to escape the station's suffocating scrutiny. Rob and the team were poring over her phone messages — the humiliating exchanges with Tom. Knowing they'd seen every foolish, needy word was unbearable. She was their boss, for God's sake, and she'd been taken in by a killer, a man she'd let into her life, her bed.

It was shameful.

She'd dressed like a zombie this morning. How could she have gone in wearing her slippers? Thankfully, she'd found a pair of trainers in her office wardrobe and had managed to put her jumper on the right way round. But she still had to face the Assistant Commissioner later on a Zoom call, and she needed a plan. Rob's idea was a good one — a sting operation to make it look like she'd used herself as bait rather than being a victim. She'd found out who the killer was and turned the tables. That's what Rob was telling everyone.

He was saving her, and she was grateful. It gave her something to tell the powers that be, something to salvage her career — and the department's reputation.

If they caught him.

Her stomach twisted. *When* they caught him.

She hadn't eaten since the shock hit, and now her insides cramped with hunger. She needed air, a sandwich and the strongest coffee she could find.

Outside, the streets were teeming with people heading towards the riverbank. Rowdy groups of students in Oxford and Cambridge blues had started drinking early, their laughter spilling onto the streets, filling the air with excitement. Pub doors stood open, music and laughter emanating from inside.

Of course, today was the Oxford–Cambridge Boat Race. In all the chaos, she'd forgotten. This was her third year in Putney, and she'd still never been down to see it. Checking her watch, she saw it was almost midday. The women's race was at three, the men's at four. Doubtful she'd get away, given everything.

Her pulse kicked up a notch as she thought about what lay ahead. It all relied on Tom contacting her again. Hopefully, Faith's talk of children and adultery hadn't scared him off for good. She snorted softly as she weaved through the noisy throng on Putney High Street, heading towards Caffè Nero.

The place was packed, the line slow moving and filled with students in college scarves and hats. She was almost at the counter, digging into her bag for her wallet, when an arm slipped around her waist.

Startled, she turned.

Tom.

"Hello, Felicity." His voice was smooth, deceptively calm.

"Jesus, Tom." Her pulse spiked as she plastered on a casual smile, forcing herself to stay calm. "What are you doing here?"

His mouth curled into a creepy smile. "I wanted to see you. I think we need to have a little . . . talk."

The flicker of realisation burst into a flame.

He knows.

Pulse racing, she tried to play it cool. "About what?"

"Come with me." His grip tightened.

The barista called to her from the counter. "Can I get you anything?"

"No, nothing. Sorry." She backed away from the counter, her brain spinning. "There are a couple of empty seats. We can talk here."

His expression darkened. "I don't think so, and before you try anything, know that I have a knife pressed against your kidney. One wrong move, and it's over." A sharp prick at her side convinced her he wasn't kidding.

His grip on her arm was firm, and she considered shouting for help, but didn't want to spook him. If he escaped now, they'd never find him again.

If only she could get a message to Rob or a member of his team.

Frantically, she looked around, trying to get someone's attention. Why weren't they more observant? Couldn't they see she was in trouble?

The point of the knife pressed deeper into her side. Her breath caught. "Don't."

Together, they moved out into the street.

This was madness. How could he be kidnapping her in broad daylight, on a busy street on a Saturday morning?

"Tom, what are you doing?" She tried to twist out of his grip.

"I don't want to hurt you, Felicity, but I will."

She felt her skin break as the knife eased in. A searing pain filled her side, and she gasped.

"It's not deep," he said, "but if you don't do as you're told, it will be."

She felt a trickle of blood run down her side, under her jumper. Instinctively, she touched it. Her hand came away wet.

"Okay."

"Good girl." He led her around the corner to where his car was parked. Reaching out behind her, she pressed her hand against the wall, hoping to leave a bloody print. At least then, someone might report it. It was a long shot, but it was all she could think of in the moment.

Tom had parked on a yellow line, not that he cared. She looked around for a traffic warden, but there wasn't one in sight.

"Never around when you need them, eh?" He laughed, and she cringed. He was crazy, and she'd fallen right into his trap. How had she not seen this coming?

A policewoman. A super-bloody-intendent, and she'd been seduced by a knife-wielding serial killer. He raped and strangled women, and she'd had sex with him. The thought made her want to gag.

"Get in the car."

She hesitated. This was bad. At the back of her mind, she realised she might not come back from this. At the same time, if she made a run for it, he'd have no choice but to go underground, his cover blown. He might even leave the country. One wrong move now could ruin everything. If she wanted to be sure, she'd have to go with him.

If there was one last thing she was going to make sure of before she got fired, it was that the bastard paid for what he'd done. To those girls, to Rob, to her whole bloody department. The knife was still at her side, burning in its intensity.

"I'm warning you," he hissed. "Get in the car if you want to live."

Teeth gritted, Felicity climbed in.

CHAPTER 44

"Where's Mayhew?" Rob asked, turning away from her locked office. He'd wanted to give her an update on the suspect. His phone was off — no surprises there — but they'd managed to work out that he must live close to Putney, if not in Putney itself, judging by the time between text messages and the planned meetings at the wine bar.

Unfortunately, he kept his phone off most of the time, and the only location updates they could get were from a phone tower near Southside Shopping Centre in Wandsworth.

"I saw her leave about half an hour ago," said DCI Linden, who was catching up on some weekend paperwork. "Hey, is everything okay? She looked a little . . . unsettled."

"Tough case." Rob peered through the glass door. The blind was open, and he could see her handbag on her desk. She couldn't have gone far, then.

Linden gave a knowing nod. "I know you guys have come under heavy fire recently. Listen, if you need any help, just shout. I can put my team on standby."

"Thanks. Might take you up on that." Rob patted him on the shoulder as he headed back to his desk.

He tried Mayhew's work phone, but it went straight to voicemail. That was also strange. Still, maybe she'd popped out for a coffee or something and would be back soon.

"I've got her phone in my desk drawer," Will said, tapping his desk. "Just in case he tries to get in touch."

"He will," Rob replied confidently. After that public update and the press release, the killer would be fuming. He'd want to know how he'd messed up, and the best way to find out would be to question Mayhew. She was his only link to the department.

Will turned back to his screen. "On the bright side, at least we haven't been hacked."

"Not that it matters," Celeste said, "but Kyle Buckland's alibi checked out. His, er, lover confirmed they were together that evening."

"Thanks, Celeste." Rob rubbed his head. "Should we be worried about Mayhew? She went out half an hour ago and hasn't come back. Her handbag is still on her desk."

Jenny checked her watch. "Not yet. She was in such a state this morning — she probably just needed some time to regroup. A lot has happened."

"Yeah, she looked like a crazy woman," Harry murmured. "Those slippers, man."

"She *had* just discovered her boyfriend was a murdering rapist, to be fair," Jenny pointed out archly.

Harry gave a contrite frown. "Fair enough."

"There's no CCTV near that wine bar." Trent's shoulders sagged. "They have a private security camera, but it's been out of service for nearly a month, and they haven't bothered to get it fixed."

"Typical. He probably sabotaged it," Rob muttered.

Jenny nodded in agreement.

"I can't believe Mayhew didn't know the guy's last name, or where he lived," Celeste whispered. "I mean, she was dating the guy."

"She was *sleeping* with him," Harry corrected. "That's different."

"Let's not comment on the Superintendent's private life," Rob said. "She came clean, when it would have been a lot easier to keep silent. Let's give her credit for that."

They all nodded.

"Do you think she'll get the sack?" Jenny asked under her breath.

"I don't know, but it's not looking good." He hoped they could spin it so they all came out looking like the good guys in all of this, rather than a department that had inadvertently aided a criminal.

This was the second time they'd unknowingly handed classified information over to a killer. They needed to catch this bastard, and quick.

By noon, Rob was getting really worried. "She's still not back."

"I can try to trace her work mobile," Will offered.

"Don't bother — it's off."

Jenny frowned. "You say her handbag's on her desk?"

"Yeah, like she just dashed out for coffee."

"Maybe we should go and look for her," Trent suggested.

Rob was about to agree when his desk phone rang. "DCI Miller."

"Sir, this is Sergeant Cranley from Putney Police Station. We just got a report from Caffè Nero on the high street. They've found a bloody handprint on the wall outside. I don't know if it means anything to you, but I thought I'd pass it along, considering everything that's going on."

He meant the two murders.

"Thank you, Sergeant. Caffè Nero, you say?"

"Yes, sir. It's probably nothing, but—"

"You've been very helpful. We'll check it out." Rob hung up, then pursed his lips.

Was this significant?

It was the Oxford–Cambridge Boat Race today. There were tons of people milling about the high street. Caffè Nero was a prime location. The handprint could have been made by anyone.

"What is it?" Jenny asked.

He told her what the sergeant had said. "Think we should take a look?"

"Can't hurt," she said, getting up. "I could do with some fresh air."

They made their way through the swelling crowds towards Caffè Nero, jostling past groups of students and spectators, all heading down to the riverbank for the boat race. Rowing fans and university students alike filled the streets, some already chanting, waving flags or clutching half-empty pints as they joined the excitement.

"The women's race kicks off at three." Jenny nodded at the crowds. "Men's isn't until four."

"Half of them will be too plastered to see the finish line by then," Rob muttered, watching a group of young men stumble past, already singing a university chant.

Jenny laughed. "I'd be out there with them if I had a choice. Didn't you ever come down to watch it when you were younger?"

He shrugged. "Rowing wasn't exactly my thing. I'd watch it now, though, if I could find the time." In quieter moments, he enjoyed seeing the rowers practising on the Thames, the way they glided through the water with calm precision.

"Well, if we find Mayhew soon, maybe you can actually go today," she suggested, giving him a bright smile.

Rob forced a nod, but couldn't shake the gnawing feeling that something was terribly wrong. He hadn't seen or heard from Mayhew since that morning, and every passing moment increased his unease.

"She was convinced he didn't suspect anything," he said, almost to himself, as they reached the café.

"Rob, we don't know if this is connected to him," Jenny said softly. "There could be a completely reasonable explanation for her absence."

He knew she was right. Maybe he was jumping the gun — maybe Mayhew had gone straight back to the office after all. But the creeping dread wouldn't let up.

"That's it!" Jenny stopped in front of a dark, perfectly formed handprint on the wall. It was positioned at hip height, close to the corner.

"Could be paint." Rob stepped in for a closer look.

Jenny shook her head. "No, it's too dark and the texture's all wrong. Let's test it."

She reached into her bag and took out a sterile swab, rubbing it lightly over the edge of the print before dipping it into a small vial of solution. Within seconds, it turned bright blue.

"It's blood, all right," she confirmed, her voice taut.

Rob stared at the handprint. "It looks like someone slapped their hand against the wall deliberately. Maybe while they were turning the corner?" He mimicked the movement, pressing his own hand to the wall just above the stain.

"It could be a woman's handprint." Jenny tilted her head as she examined it. "The shape is narrow, more delicate than yours."

Rob pulled out his phone and snapped a close-up, capturing the clear whorls and loops on the fingertips. "I'll get Will to run this through the system. It might tell us who it belongs to."

He sent the photo to his tech whiz, then glanced up and down the street, trying to piece together what might have happened.

Jenny watched him closely. "What are you thinking?"

He frowned. "It's odd to find a bloody handprint here without any trail. No blood on the pavement or the opposite wall."

"Maybe they crossed the road or tried to get help at the station?"

"Worth checking." They made their way across to Putney Bridge tube station and approached the officer on duty in the information box. The man shook his head firmly.

"No, sir. Nobody came in here injured or looking for assistance. We'd have noticed."

"You're positive?" Rob pressed. "You didn't find any blood on the ground?"

The officer straightened. "No, sir. If one of the cleaning staff had found something, it would've been reported immediately."

Rob scratched his head. "All right. We've done what we can. Let's get back to the office."

They were halfway there when Rob's phone rang.

"DCI Miller."

"Guv, it's Will. I ran the print. Get this — it belongs to Superintendent Mayhew."

Rob froze. "You're certain?"

"What?" Jenny mouthed, as pedestrians circled around them, shooting annoyed glances in their direction.

"Positive match," Will said, his voice hesitant. "Guv, is she all right?"

Rob's chest tightened as the reality came crashing down. "No, Will. She's not. She's been abducted. He's got her."

CHAPTER 45

"We need that CCTV footage from outside the café, now," Rob snapped as soon as he got back to the office.

"On it," Will replied, not looking up.

"I can't believe she's been taken." Trent's normally ruddy face was drained of colour.

"This is serious," Harry muttered, tension in his voice.

Jenny looked at Rob, her expression grave. "We don't even know who 'he' really is," she said. "Apart from what we've gathered from Mayhew's messages, we don't have any verified information on him."

"We've got the photograph," Rob reminded her. He'd gambled on that press release rattling the killer, but he hadn't expected such a swift reaction. His plan had backfired, and now he had to fix it. "Update the APB with his description and circulate it to every law enforcement unit in the area."

Jenny hesitated. "What about the press?"

"Go ahead. Send it to Vicky and have her issue another press release. The sooner we catch this guy, the better." He clenched his jaw. "I'll speak to Linden, then we need to notify the Assistant Commissioner."

Linden's face was grim when he heard the news. "Are you certain? It's Saturday — she might've just gone home."

Rob shook his head. "We found her bloody handprint on a wall. Looks like she did it on purpose, hoping we'd find it."

"She's smart," Linden said approvingly, then grimaced. "But it sounds like she's injured. What do you think happened?"

"I don't know. He must have grabbed her when she went out for coffee. Knowing Mayhew, she'd have put up a fight, so he must have used force to get her to comply. Maybe a knife or some sort of concealed weapon. Nobody reported hearing a disturbance in the café, so she must have gone quietly."

Linden's mouth pressed into a hard line. "I'll call in my team. The more boots we have on the ground searching for her, the better."

Rob gave a grateful nod. "I'm going to call Matthew Gray. He needs to know."

Linden exhaled. "Yeah, he does."

* * *

Assistant Commissioner Gray did not take the news well. "What the hell is going on over there, Miller? First we've got these claims that the Surrey Stalker is still out there, that you lot bungled the initial investigation, and now your superintendent goes missing."

Not to mention the two recent murders.

"Are you sure she's been abducted, Miller?"

"Yes, sir. We found her bloody handprint on a wall where she was taken. She was leaving us a clue to follow."

There was a brief silence. "Is she all right?"

"I don't know, sir. We're doing everything we can to find her."

"Why Felicity?" he asked, surprising Rob with his use of her first name. Rob knew Mayhew was friendly with the Assistant Commissioner, but not that friendly. "Why'd he go for her?"

"Because she knew the killer, sir, and she cultivated a relationship to draw him out. We just didn't expect it to go this far."

"She used herself as bait?" Gray sounded incredulous.

"Yes, sir."

"For God's sake, she's your superintendent, not some detective constable doing grunt work."

"It had to be her, sir. She was the one with the connection to the killer — and because of that, we're now much closer to finding him."

Gray sighed. "If you say so. It's most unorthodox, and I'll be reprimanding her accordingly when she's found. In the meantime, I'll inform the Police Commissioner." He paused. "Who's in charge of your department in her absence?"

"She's only just gone missing, sir. We're hoping to find her before the end of the day." Damn idiot was already thinking about her replacement. Clearly, he had no faith in their department's abilities.

"Keep me posted, Detective Chief Inspector. I mean it. Any information on her location, and you let me know. We're all concerned for her safety."

Sure you are, Rob thought. "Will do, sir."

He hung up and Jenny beckoned him over. "Guv, we've got something."

Rob joined her behind Trent's desk. They were watching a CCTV shot from the high street, about fifty yards from Caffè Nero.

"Watch this," she said.

Trent pressed play, and the footage began to roll. Rob watched as Mayhew, accompanied by a man in a cap and dark hooded sweatshirt, exited the café.

"Looks like he's got her by the arm," Trent said, narrating as the video played.

They saw Mayhew gasp and double over. The man pulled her along the pavement towards the corner. She reached back, pressing her bloody hand against the wall before allowing herself to be led around the corner and into a side street.

"He stabbed her," Rob muttered. "Looks like it was on her left side."

"God, I hope she's okay," Jenny whispered.

"It couldn't have been too deep if he wanted to get her in the car," Rob said, frowning as he watched a slate-grey Toyota Prius — dull and unremarkable, with a faint dent on the rear bumper — pull away from the kerb. "Can you zoom in on that number plate?"

Trent zoomed in closer. The video pixelated, but they managed to make out the registration number.

"I'll run it." Will jotted it down and slid across the room to his computer.

A few moments later, he let out a yelp. "Guv, you'll never guess who the vehicle is registered to."

"Who?" Rob walked over to his desk.

"Jamie McNamara."

He frowned. "Jamie, as in Julie Andrews' ex-boyfriend?"

Will nodded, holding up a photograph of a UK driver's licence. "One and the same."

CHAPTER 46

"It can't be him. He's overseas," Celeste said, her eyes wide. "I checked myself."

"Middle East, wasn't it?" Rob narrowed his gaze.

She nodded. "The *Guardian* confirmed it. I spoke to the editor, who confirmed he's been over there since mid-March, and they don't know when he'll be back. The situation is ongoing."

"Get him on the phone for me," Rob barked, running a hand through his increasingly dishevelled hair.

"Is he our killer?" Trent asked, eyes wider than Celeste's. The news had come as a shock to the whole team. Jamie McNamara was a lead they'd shut down right at the beginning of the investigation. He hadn't been in the country when Lucy Andrews was murdered, and both his employer and his flatmate had backed that up.

"Go and visit the flatmate again." Rob turned to Trent. "Make sure he hasn't seen Jamie since he left. If you think he's lying, arrest him and bring him in. We'll question him here under caution."

"Yes, sir." Trent scrambled out of his chair and reached for his jacket.

"Harry, go with him," Rob said, as an afterthought. "Just in case Jamie is there. In which case, arrest him too."

Celeste looked downcast.

"It's not your fault," he said to her. "People lie all the time. Even newspaper editors."

She nodded, turning away to call the *Guardian*.

"Jenny, do you still have that contact at Border Force? We need to check the flight manifests to see whether Jamie McNamara re-entered the country in the last few weeks."

"Yes, I can give her a call, although she might insist we go through the official channels."

"See if you can expedite it. There's a missing person involved."

"I'll see what I can do."

"Thanks. If not, I'll call the Home Office." That should speed things up.

Jenny worked her magic, and her contact fast-tracked the request due to the serious nature of the investigation.

Not twenty minutes later, the contact called back. Jenny went very still, then thanked her and hung up.

"Well?"

She gave a bewildered nod. "He flew in on the third of April on an Emirates flight."

Rob breathed out, long and slow. "So, he is here."

"Then where is he staying?" Jenny asked.

"Guv, the editor of the *Guardian* is on line two," Celeste called across the room.

Rob picked up the phone. "I believe you have a reporter working for you called Jamie McNamara?"

The editor's voice was crisp. "Yes, he's currently on assignment in Lebanon. I've already told your constable this."

"And he's still reporting from there?" Rob pressed.

"He files biweekly articles for us, yes," the editor replied, a hint of irritation creeping into his tone.

Rob frowned. "How exactly do you receive this correspondence?"

"Via email, mostly," the editor replied. "Sometimes he calls in to confirm we've received it."

"So you've spoken to him?"

"Yes, several times," the editor affirmed. "As have members on the editorial team."

"And it's a Lebanese number he's calling from?"

"I wouldn't know," the editor admitted. "He calls on WhatsApp, using his mobile. Connectivity is patchy there, so it's been the best way to keep in touch."

A WhatsApp call wouldn't necessarily confirm Jamie's location. It was easy enough to disguise one's whereabouts that way. "Could he be filing his reports from here, just pretending to be in Lebanon?"

"No, that wouldn't make sense," the editor replied, sounding defensive. "His notes are incredibly detailed, and he even sends us soundbites."

Rob raised an eyebrow. "Soundbites?"

"Soundbites are short audio clips — quotes or local sounds — he uses to bring his stories to life. Street noise, voices, that kind of thing. He's sent a few from protests recently."

Rob leaned forward, scribbling a note to himself. "And when's the last time he sent one of these soundbites?"

"Let me think . . . I believe it was just last week, before his last article on the refugee crisis."

"Last week?" Rob repeated.

"Yes, is there a problem?" The editor sounded slightly defensive.

"We have a record from Border Force showing he entered the United Kingdom earlier this month, on the third of April."

There was a pause, and the editor's tone turned wary. "I . . . I honestly don't know why that would be. I'm telling you, we have no reason to doubt he's where he says he is. Maybe he left temporarily and returned. Freelancers do that sometimes for family emergencies."

Rob's voice hardened. "Then here's what we're going to need. I'll need copies of all recent correspondence with

Jamie — emails, article drafts, soundbites and records of any phone calls. And I'll need your staff to note exactly when they last heard from him."

The editor audibly swallowed. "Of course. But . . . can I ask why?"

Rob hesitated. "Jamie is a person of interest in a murder investigation, so we need to determine exactly where he is."

"Er, yes. I suppose under those circumstances . . . Which murder investigation would that be?"

Rob sighed to himself. Bloody journos, always after a story.

"I'm not at liberty to say," he replied curtly. "Thank you for your time. I'm going to hand you over to my constable, who will give you our details."

He transferred the call and nodded at Celeste, who picked up the phone on her desk.

"Seems he's still reporting out of Lebanon," Rob remarked to Jenny. "He must be fudging it."

"Otherwise he's getting someone to do the work for him," she said.

"What about his phone?" Will asked. "When we last checked where it had pinged, he was in Lebanon."

"Could he have faked that too?" Rob rubbed his chin. The stubble was beginning to itch.

"I guess so, although he'd need pretty sophisticated masking software for that."

"Check again," Rob ordered.

"I have. It still says he's in Lebanon, roaming on the cellular network over there."

He frowned. "How can that be?"

"Unless someone else has got his phone," Jenny murmured. "The same person who's writing the articles and sending the soundbites for him."

"That's a little far-fetched, isn't it? I mean, realistically, who would do that? They'd have to write in Jamie's style, well enough to convince an entire editorial team. It's more likely he's doing it from here, with second-hand intel."

Linden came over. "My team's on their way in. Let me know where you want them to look."

"Great, thanks. Let's get someone over to Mayhew's place, in case he's taken her back there. Check with her neighbours to see if they've seen her, and I believe she has a sister. Maybe she tried to contact her."

Linden nodded. Rob had briefed him on the suspect, but not the gritty details, just the broader picture — enough to know the man was dangerous and had had previous contact with Mayhew.

His phone buzzed. It was Harry. "Got anything?"

"Guv, the flatmate insists he hasn't seen Jamie since he left to go overseas. Swears he hasn't been home, but we're not sure if we believe him."

"Arrest him," Rob commanded. "Bring him in and Jenny will have a crack at him."

"Yes, sir."

Jenny's eyebrows arched. "Is that necessary, guv?"

Rob nodded. He was all out of patience. "He could be obstructing the investigation. I've just got a message to call Officer Hunt at Monica Burridge's house. They've found something." It had come in while he'd been speaking to the editor of the *Guardian*.

"They have?"

"Yep." He got to his feet. "I'm heading over there now. Stay in touch."

"I will."

It was nearly one thirty when Rob pulled out of the police car park and drove towards Putney High Street. Turning into it, he hit a wall of traffic.

Shit, the boat race!

The entire street was gridlocked. Goddammit, Lower Richmond would be impossible.

Switching on the siren, he turned towards Upper Richmond and bypassed the long line of vehicles crawling towards East Sheen. Once he got through the Roehampton

Lane junction, he turned right into White Hart Lane, towards the river.

It was a bright spring day and, for once, there wasn't a cloud in sight. The sun had come out for the rowers, and even here, he could see spectators crammed onto the wooden deck of the pub at the end of the road and spilling out onto the street. The river towpath would be packed as well, with barely room to move.

Despite the sunshine, Monica Burridge's house was as dark and oppressive as ever. Rob pulled into the gravel driveway and parked beside the SOCO van and a squad car. Scenes of crime officers were still working inside the property. Rob knew they'd be logging, photographing and carefully bagging each piece of evidence, to be catalogued back at the station. Only after the items were processed could his team examine them.

Rob rang the doorbell and a uniformed police officer answered. They'd been called to gain entry and guard the premises while the search was underway.

He flashed his ID. "DCI Miller. I ordered the search."

"Of course, sir. Come in." She held the door for him. "We're nearly done here, but Officer Hunt's waiting for you in the kitchen. There's something he wants to show you."

He caught the faint sound of coughing from down the hall. "Is Monica Burridge here?"

"Yes, sir. An ambulance brought her back earlier this morning. She's been discharged."

Rob was glad she was recovering, though he hoped her return wouldn't complicate things. As he entered the kitchen, he spotted Hunt, a tall, lean officer with a sharp gaze, still dressed in a protective suit but without the gloves or shoe coverings.

Hunt extended a hand in greeting. "Detective Chief Inspector, good to finally meet you in person."

Rob shook it. "Thanks for coordinating this search. What have you found so far?"

Hunt nodded towards the staircase. "We found a box of personal items that we suspect belonged to Simon Burridge.

There's a hidden compartment in Mrs Burridge's wardrobe — one of my team stumbled upon it. It was camouflaged with a fake panel at the back."

"Seriously?" Rob raised an eyebrow. He wouldn't have thought sick Mrs Burridge capable of that level of deception.

"Yeah," Hunt replied with a smirk. "Honestly, we nearly missed it, but then one of my officers realised it was hollow. After that, it didn't take long to remove it and find the items."

"Where are they?" he asked, trying not to appear too eager.

"Upstairs in the master bedroom. The team's just finishing up cataloguing everything before we take it away, but I thought you'd want a first look."

"Much appreciated." Rob took a protective suit from Hunt, slipping it on before heading upstairs.

In the master bedroom, two SOCOs were laying out the items on a large plastic sheet spread over the floor. Each object was being photographed, catalogued and bagged with studious care.

Rob approached. "Mind if I take a look?"

One of the SOCOs gave him a nod, stepping aside to let him see the array of items. Rob noted a photo album marked *Simon*, a small pencil case embroidered with the same name, a battered teddy bear with one eye missing, and a shaving kit, which included an old comb.

Bingo.

Rob gestured to the comb. "This one's important. Make sure it goes in for DNA analysis. I need any hair follicles, fibres or skin cells still on it."

"Understood, sir," one of the officers replied, carefully sealing the comb in an evidence bag.

Rob returned downstairs to find Hunt. This was exactly what he'd been after. This was how the killer had got hold of Burridge's DNA — a clever ploy that had made Rob question himself, that had made everyone question his team's integrity.

He scoffed. It had worked for a while, but now he knew the truth. The killer had failed. Except he still had Mayhew, and her time was running out.

"I appreciate the heads-up, Officer," he said, going back into the kitchen. "Please send me copies of all photographs taken here today."

"Absolutely, sir. This is your case — we'll get everything to you as soon as it's logged and transported."

As Hunt's team began to file out with the evidence boxes, Rob turned his attention to the library, where Mrs Burridge was still coughing. He found her seated in her armchair, wrapped in a thick blanket, a book resting on her lap.

"Apologies for the inconvenience, Mrs Burridge," he said, attempting a sympathetic tone. "The team's leaving now. You'll have the house to yourself again."

She looked up. "Where is your pretty sidekick, Detective?"

For a moment, he thought she meant Jo, but then realised she was talking about Jenny. Strange, he'd never thought of her in that way before, but he supposed she was, in a sporty, tomboyish way. To him, she was just Jenny, an excellent DS and a good mate.

"She didn't come with me today."

The sliding doors closed and a few moments later, they heard the SOCO van's tyres crunching on the gravel as it pulled out into the street.

"So you're here alone?"

Rob frowned, feeling uneasy. "Yes, I just wanted to check you were all right and thank you for allowing us access."

"It wasn't like I had a choice," she huffed. "They were already here when I got home. I've been told the lock will be fixed in due course."

"It will," he confirmed. "I'm sorry for your trouble."

She nodded thoughtfully. "Detective, before you go, there's someone here I think you should meet."

"Oh, who?" Rob frowned, scanning the room. There was nobody else here. He wondered if she'd lost the plot. Maybe she was hallucinating. He'd heard that could happen after a stint in hospital.

Monica's lips curled into a faint smile, one that didn't reach her eyes.

What the hell was going on?

She didn't answer, just held his gaze with a dark, knowing look that sent a shiver down his spine.

A floorboard creaked behind him.

Rob spun around, but before he could react, a sudden, blinding pain struck the back of his head. His vision swam, darkness clawing at the edges. The last thing he heard was Monica's calm, measured voice drifting through the deepening haze.

"Detective, meet the Surrey Stalker."

Everything went black.

CHAPTER 47

PC Trent arrived back at the office to find it almost deserted, save for Will, who was typing furiously at his computer.

He hung up his jacket. "Where is everyone?"

Will didn't look up. "Rob's gone to speak with the SOCO team at Monica Burridge's house. Apparently, they found a stash of Simon's personal belongings. Jenny and Celeste are at the custody suite, prepping for the interview with the flatmate, and Linden's coordinating the search for Superintendent Mayhew."

"Still no news?" Trent asked, hardly daring to hope.

Will shook his head. "She's not at her house, and the neighbours haven't seen her. Linden's put out an APB on Jamie McNamara's vehicle, so hopefully that will turn up something soon."

Trent sighed and sat down.

"You think the flatmate was lying?" Will stopped what he was doing and glanced up.

Trent rubbed the back of his neck. "I don't know. He's hiding something, but after what happened with Kyle Buckland, I'm not sure if it's relevant to this case."

"If anyone can get it out of him, it's Jenny."

Trent gave a half-smile. He trusted Jenny's instincts as an interrogator. Harry had taken the suspect in to book him and hand him over to her for questioning. "I guess I'll get started on the ANPR." He switched on his computer. His main focus was tracking McNamara's vehicle on the automatic number plate recognition system, hoping to trace its route and uncover Mayhew's location.

He liked the predictability of ANPR. Vehicles, unlike people, couldn't just disappear. Each time they passed an ANPR camera, a photograph of the number plate was taken and stored in a database that law enforcement could access.

The challenge, he knew, was that the cameras were primarily on A-roads and motorways, meaning a savvy driver could avoid detection by sticking to back roads or zigzagging through the suburbs. Not for long, however, because at some point, they'd have to hit a major route, and that's when the system would catch them.

Trent typed in McNamara's plate number and hit search. It didn't take long to return the first result. The plate had been picked up on Putney High Street earlier that day. He sniffed. That was expected — he'd have been surprised if there hadn't been a hit there.

Viewing the image, he saw the car was heading north, towards Putney Bridge, beyond which lay Fulham and Central London.

Why would he be heading that way? Surely it would make more sense to go south if you were trying to disappear. That way led into the Surrey countryside, with a hundred little villages to get lost in, and deep, dark woods in which to dump a body.

He shuddered and wished he hadn't thought about that.

He tried the camera on the A219, Fulham Palace Road, but didn't get any hits. The A308, also known as the New Kings Road, didn't return any results either. Strange. That meant the perpetrator hadn't crossed Putney Bridge but had stayed on this side of the river.

Trent pulled up a digital map of Putney. He was still relatively new here, so he didn't know the area as well as the others. Caffè Nero was there — he put his cursor on it and looked around. That meant McNamara would have had to turn onto Lacy, Weimar or Lower Richmond, the only options on the west side of the high street. On the east, there was Putney Bridge Road — a main road that might have a camera.

Yep, it did. Trent checked, holding his breath. Disappointingly, it didn't offer any hits either. Now what?

He glanced up. "I can't find any trace of the vehicle on any of the main roads out of Putney," he said. "He must have cut through the backstreets."

"Then he's in the wind," Will said. "Unless he tripped a speed camera."

That was a thought, although Trent suspected the killer would be way too careful for that. He checked anyway. Nothing. Sighing, he looked over at DCI Miller's desk.

"When's he due back?"

"Not sure. He's probably still at the house."

He was just about to get back to work when DCI Linden hurried over. "Where's Rob?"

"Not here," Will called. "What's up?"

"Celeste briefed me on the situation in Lebanon," he began. "You know, with that reporter."

"The one who's actually here," Trent said.

Linden nodded. "I got a friend in the Military Police to check McNamara's hotel, and guess what? There is someone staying there."

"There is?" chorused Trent and Will simultaneously.

"Yeah, he checked in under McNamara's name, showed his passport at the desk, the whole toot."

"What the hell?" Will got up. "How can that be?"

"On closer inspection, my friend was able to ascertain that it isn't Jamie McNamara staying there — it's his brother, Thomas."

"Holy shit," whispered Trent.

"He has a brother?" Will scratched his head. "I did not see that one coming."

"Half-brother, as it turns out," Linden said with a wry smile. "I looked into it. Thomas and Jamie share the same father. Two different mothers."

"That explains how he could write like his brother and submit articles under his name," Will mused. "They probably have a similar writing style and speaking voice."

"Close enough to fool the editorial team," Trent added.

"He really thought about this, didn't he?" Linden remarked. "I mean, this must have taken months to plan."

"He's had it out for the guvnor since the beginning," Will said, shaking his head. "None of us have been able to figure out why."

"Is he someone Rob's run into in the past?" Linden asked. "Maybe he put him away once or did something to offend him?"

Trent's respect for Linden grew. They'd all been so caught up in the case's details and the mimicry of the Surrey Stalker's MO that they hadn't stopped to think it might all be personal, a vendetta against Rob. Well, he hadn't anyway.

"I'll look at old case files," he said. "There might be something there."

Linden nodded. "In the meantime, I'll give Rob a call and update him." He darted back to his desk.

"I did run Jamie McNamara's name through the criminal database," Will said, "but there was nothing. He doesn't have a record."

"Right. Still, he may have been a person of interest or a witness."

Will nodded. "He might have, but nothing flagged for me."

"Mind if I take a look?" Trent asked. He didn't want to tread on any toes.

"Be my guest. You might want to do a broader search on HOLMES. I was only looking for past form."

Trent nodded and got to work.

Linden came back, looking troubled. "He's not answering. It went straight to voicemail. Is that normal?"

"No." Will glanced up. "Not in the middle of a case."

Trent's heart skipped a beat. "You think something's wrong?"

"We need to get a team out to Thomas McNamara's place," Linden said. "If they've swapped places, it makes sense that he could be staying there. He might have taken Superintendent Mayhew there. I'm going to call Specialist Firearms Command. Everyone okay with that?"

Trent marvelled at the way DCI Linden had seamlessly taken control of the investigation in Rob's absence. That was the sign of a true leader — stepping in when needed, with no fuss, just a calm confidence honed by years on the job. One day, he aimed to be like that.

"Yeah," Will said. "But we need to find Rob."

"I'll go to the house and check if he's there," Trent said. "It's not far away."

Will nodded. "Okay, I'll get hold of the others and see if they've heard from him."

"I'm going to Thomas McNamara's with SCO19," Linden said. "Stay in touch."

CHAPTER 48

Trent shivered as he pulled up beside Monica Burridge's house. The place was so darn creepy. From the car park he could hear a chorus of shouts and cheers from the riverbank. He glanced at his watch — ten past three. The women's race would be underway.

Rob's car wasn't here, which meant he'd left already. Still, he'd better check and find out when. He tried to get to the front door, then realised it wasn't in use. Nettles clawing at his trousers, he backtracked and went around to the rear of the property. A narrow porch gave way to a veritable wilderness of plants, trees and vegetation. It was like a jungle leading down to the river. In fact, he doubted you could even get to the river path from here.

The shouts were louder now, building to a frantic excitement as the crews approached. He couldn't see them, but he knew it was happening by the noise of the crowd. The back doors were ajar, but he knocked anyway. "Hello!"

There was no answer from inside the house. He slid the doors open wider and stepped inside. "Hello, Mrs Burridge? It's PC Trent from the Major Investigation Team. Are you all right?"

There was a thud, and the faint sound of coughing. He ventured further inside. "Mrs Burridge?"

The coughing got louder, and he heard a voice from the corridor. "Who's there?"

"It's PC Trent, madam. From the police."

"Oh." She wheezed a sigh a relief. "I thought it was that burglar back again."

"Burglar?"

"Yes, the break-in the other night. Didn't you know?"

"No, madam." He frowned. That was weird. He wondered if DCI Miller knew. A break-in might be significant, especially if the thief was after her son's DNA. "Who did you report it to?"

"Oh, your nice Detective Miller was here, and his colleague, the pretty, boyish one."

"DS Bird?" Now he was really confused. Neither of them had said anything to the rest of the team about a break-in. It hadn't been in any of the reports he'd read either.

"That's the one." She studied him with lined, slightly yellow eyes. "Now, what can I do for you, Constable?"

He refocused. "I'm looking for DCI Miller. I believe he was here earlier."

"Yes, they were all here." She smoothed her hair back with a trembling hand. "But he left after they did."

"When was that?"

"Oh, let me see. Maybe an hour ago. I didn't check the time."

Trent frowned. "Did he say anything before he left?"

"Only that he was sorry for the disturbance." She scoffed. "They took away my son's things, did you know that?"

He narrowed his eyes. "I did, madam. I'm sorry. I believe you hid them in the back of a wardrobe?"

"My ex-husband did that." She coughed again. "He tried to forget about him. But I never could."

That made sense.

Or did it?

He frowned. Building a false back to a cupboard was fairly extreme. Why not just get rid of the stuff, or box it up and stash it in the attic? Why hide it away?

He was about to ask her, when a spasm of coughing overtook her. "Are you all right, Mrs Burridge?"

When she could breathe again, she said, "I'm going to sit in my chair."

He walked after her into a room with floor-to-ceiling bookcases. An armchair positioned in the corner faced the wall of books. The room was dark, curtains drawn, with a shaded lamp offering a dim amber glow. Mrs Burridge sat down and pulled the blanket over her lap.

"Can I get you anything before I go?" he asked.

She shook her head. "I'm fine, thank you."

"Okay." He turned to leave. "The doors at the back were open when I got here. You should really keep those locked."

"Oh, I'm always forgetting to do that." She shook her head. "Those policemen must have left them open when they left."

"I'll close them for you on the way out." He left her to her books.

* * *

Back in the car, Trent called the office. Will picked up. "He's not here," Trent said. "Neither is his car. What should I do?"

"I'll trace his phone," Will said. "You'd better come back to the office. We need to call Jo. Maybe he's with her."

"I'll call her," he offered.

"Would you? Thanks." He could hear the relief in Will's voice.

Jo picked up straight away. She'd know it was the police by the withheld number. "Hello?"

"Jo, it's PC Trent."

"Hello, Constable," she said after a beat. "Is everything all right?"

His heart sank. DCI Miller wasn't with her.

"Um . . . Actually, ma'am, no it's not. It's the guvnor. He's — he's missing."

A pause.

"What do you mean missing?"

"He didn't come back to the office, and we're not sure where he is. We thought he might be with you."

Hoped.

"No, Constable. He's not with me. Have you traced his phone?"

"Will is doing that now."

"Okay." Another longer silence. "Should I be worried?"

Trent took a slow breath. "I don't know, ma'am," he said honestly. "What with the Superintendent missing as well, it doesn't look good."

"Mayhew's missing?"

Shit, she didn't know, and he probably shouldn't have said anything. Jo wasn't an active police officer anymore, she was a civilian.

"Trent, answer me."

He gulped. "She's been kidnapped, ma'am."

"I'm coming into the office."

"I'm not sure that's a good idea—" he began, but she'd already hung up.

Crap, now he'd be in the shit.

He berated himself all the way back to the office. The journey took longer than usual as he had to avoid Lonsdale Road and Lower Richmond, both of which ran parallel to the river and would be packed with traffic, media and corporate vehicles, and spectators.

Walking in, he was pleased to see Harry was back, but no sign of Jo. Jenny and Celeste must still be at Putney Police Station interrogating Jamie's flatmate.

"Any news from DCI Linden?" he asked Will, wondering how it went with the assault team.

"Nothing yet," Will replied. "Worse, the guv's phone is off. I can't trace it. He obviously wasn't with Jo?"

"No." Trent bit his lip. "I had to tell her. She said she's coming in."

Both Will and Harry stared at him.

"Is that allowed?" Harry finally asked.

Will shrugged. "I don't know."

With no SIO or superintendent, Trent didn't see who they could ask, either. Jo had been in before, so she obviously had clearance. Anyway, they had bigger problems right now. "Can you see where he was before it was turned off?"

"I traced it to Mortlake, in the vicinity of Monica Burridge's house, but nothing after that. It's like he just vanished."

"Well, he left the house," Trent told them. "His car's gone."

"Do you think something happened on the way back here?" Harry asked.

Will shook his head. "We'd have heard if he'd had a prang."

"What about Jenny?" Trent asked. "Has she heard anything?"

"She's interrogating the flatmate," Harry said.

"We'd better let her know." Will got up. "I'll go and get her. You guys stay here and man the phone lines."

Trent nodded, while Harry ran a hand through his hair. "First Mayhew, now Rob. It feels like the killer is picking us off one by one."

Trent shivered. It was beginning to look like that. "I'm sure he's fine," he said, but he didn't believe it himself. Rob had been missing for over an hour now, and Mayhew over four hours. This was not good.

Still, there were things he could do. He swung back to his computer and logged into HOLMES. Run a broader search, Will had said.

He typed in Jamie McNamara's name. The database whirred for a few seconds, then the results screen appeared.

Trent scanned the page.

Jamie McNamara was one of two sons of Patrick McNamara, a white-collar criminal who'd set up a Ponzi pension scheme and cheated his clients out of millions of pounds back in 2017. The other was Thomas McNamara, and there were pictures of both men attached.

Trent studied them. There were similarities, but they weren't identical by any means. Jamie was slender with dark brown hair and a hard, intense face, while his brother was heavy-set, with a square jaw and lighter hair. Still, the eyes were the same. Pale green, with a darker ring around them making them appear quite striking.

Trent closed the images and read on. McNamara senior had been tried and found guilty at Wandsworth court and sentenced to eight years' imprisonment, which Trent knew meant with good behaviour, he'd be out in four.

There was another attachment from HM Prison Service, which he opened. A letter, stamped with the official seal.

We regret to inform you that Patrick McNamara was stabbed multiple times in the prison yard and died of his injuries.

Trent sat back. Shit. Not even a month into his sentence, and the guy had been knifed. He'd bled out in the yard in front of a dozen other inmates, and medics hadn't been able to resuscitate him.

He closed the attachment and went back to the original crime report. At the bottom, he found what he'd been looking for.

DS Rob Miller had been the arresting officer.

CHAPTER 49

Rob woke up with a pounding headache. Monica Burridge, the creaking floorboard, the man behind him — it all came flooding back.

He'd been ambushed.

Groaning, he opened his eyes. The room swam before him. Where the hell was he? Dark, damp, with only a thin line of light seeping in from a small window high above. He was lying on a cold concrete floor, his hands and feet bound. The ceiling loomed in naked brickwork, and a fetid smell rose around him, a scent like . . . the river.

A basement.

Her basement?

His vision blurred, and he let his head drop back onto the floor.

Monica Burridge.

How could he have been so blind?

She was the mastermind. This was revenge. Revenge against him, against the department — for killing her son, Simon. Jamie McNamara was just a pawn in her sick, twisted game.

Monica had orchestrated the murders of Lucy Andrews and Lena Jakubowski. She'd studied the crime scenes, recreated every detail, arranged for her son's DNA to be planted on the bodies — but Jamie had been the one to kill them.

Why? What did Jamie McNamara have to gain? Why risk his career, his freedom, to do her bidding? He was still trying to piece it together when the door opened and they both came in.

"Look who's awake," Jamie smirked. Anger flashed through Rob, momentarily clearing his vision. If he got out of here, he'd wipe that smug grin right off the bastard's face.

Monica Burridge, leaning on a walking stick, shuffled over to him. "Walked right into that one, didn't you, Detective Miller?" He noted how she steadfastly refused to call him Detective Chief Inspector.

He gave her a curt nod, wincing at the pain in his skull. "Well played, Monica. I should've known it was you."

She let out a low cackle that turned into a hacking cough.

"How long have you been planning this?" he asked when she finally stopped.

"A while." Her gaze hardened. "Before I die, I wanted to make things right. I wanted justice for Simon."

"Simon was a monster."

"He was innocent! You killed him and then framed him. My boy wouldn't have hurt anyone. He was a sensitive soul."

"You deluded, foolish woman," he hissed. "Simon brutalised five, maybe more, young women. It started with the first girl who rejected him, Bridget Kane. He beat them, raped them, strangled them — not necessarily in that order. We found the trophies at his house, linked him to each killing."

"Utter rubbish," she sniffed. "All of it. You built a case on lies, manufactured to condemn an innocent man."

Rob shook his head. There was no reasoning with her. She'd made up her mind. He turned to Jamie, who stood hovering, his green eyes cold with menace.

"What about you? Enjoy killing?" Rob asked. "Doing Monica's dirty work?"

Jamie stepped forward, the dull light from the window catching his face, twisting his features into shadows. His strange green eyes gleamed with menace. "I have my own reasons for wanting to ruin you, Detective Chief Inspector." He spat the words with disdain.

Rob frowned. "What have I ever done to you?"

Jamie snorted. "You don't remember, do you?"

Rob searched his memory, but there was nothing — no reference to Jamie McNamara. He shook his head.

Jamie's eyes darkened. "My father. Patrick McNamara. You arrested him and sent him down for a bad investment decision. He was barely in two weeks when someone shanked him in the prison yard. He died alone, in that filthy place."

A flicker of a memory surfaced. "That was a long time ago."

"Seven years," Jamie corrected. "He was sixty-two."

"He robbed hundreds of elderly clients of their pensions." Rob looked from Jamie to Monica, realising both of them were equally delusional. "They lost everything. Some even took their own lives because of what he did. He deserved prison, Jamie. I'm sorry he died there, but that's not on me."

"He'd still be alive if it weren't for you," Jamie snarled, his composure slipping.

Rob let his head drop back onto the concrete. "So how'd you two meet? Some kind of forum for psychos with a grudge against the police?"

Jamie's eyes flashed. "Fate, actually." He glanced at Monica, who gave him a fond nod.

"I wanted justice for Simon, but I didn't know how to get it," Monica said, "until Jamie came to see me."

"The journalist, chasing a story?" Rob grimaced.

"I was looking into the circumstances around my father's arrest," Jamie said, his face swimming in front of him. His voice appeared disjointed, like it was reverberating around the room.

Rob closed his eyes.

"That led me to you. Then I read about the Surrey Stalker case — the one where you killed the suspect with your bare hands. Impressive, by the way. Also . . . disgraceful. Call yourself a law enforcement officer?" He scoffed. "You needed taking down. The evidence was flimsy, circumstantial, like Monica said. Nothing concrete."

"Except that I caught him trying to strangle my fiancée," Rob murmured. But Jamie wasn't listening, he was too absorbed in his own story.

"Monica and I talked, and it was obvious we could help each other," Jamie said.

"So you decided to bring the Surrey Stalker back." Rob looked at Monica. "If he was killing again, then your son must have been innocent all along?"

"Precisely." She gave a proud smile.

He shook his head in disgust. "You've read too many crime novels."

"Oh, I know." She chuckled. "I do love my books. They help me escape into worlds that make sense. Where real justice is served."

Rob exhaled, his mind racing. He was in serious trouble here. His team would know he was missing — it wouldn't take them long to come looking. Will would trace his phone . . . Jenny would figure it out.

"They'll find me," he said. "Just a matter of time."

Monica snorted. "That's where you're wrong, Detective. Your constable was already here, right above your head in my library, and he didn't suspect a thing."

"My car . . ." His jaw clenched. Of course they'd have moved it.

"It's in the Charing Cross Hospital long-stay car park. They won't find it for days."

His heart sank. "Seems you've thought of everything." But they didn't know his team. They were good. No, they were the best. They'd know he'd been taken. Just like—

"Where's Mayhew?" he muttered, fighting a wave of nausea.

"You'll find out soon enough," Monica said with a strange smile. Rob didn't like the sound of that. These two would have something planned — something slow, something brutal. If he could keep them talking, he might just buy his team the time they needed.

Jamie looked down at his phone, the screen casting his features in an eerie light.

"It's time," he said. "We need to move him."

"Time for what?" Rob demanded.

Neither answered.

Monica fixed him with a cold stare. "Goodbye, Detective. I hope you rot in hell for what you did to my son."

Rob watched as Jamie stepped forward, opening a rusted manhole cover in the floor. The cover scraped aside, releasing a foul stench that filled the room.

"This place was built right on top of a Victorian sewer tunnel," Jamie explained, pride in his voice. "Monica's idea. Brilliant, really."

A defunct sewer leading to the Thames. Mortlake and Barnes were riddled with them. Most weren't in use anymore, but they handled overflow when the river swelled.

Jamie seized Rob's arm, hauling him upright. Rob choked back bile as another wave of nausea hit. They were going to dump him in the sewer. Was that where Mayhew was too?

God . . . did that mean she was already dead?

"Don't throw up on me," Jamie snarled.

Rob swayed, his bound legs barely holding him, but Jamie's grip was solid. He dragged Rob to the edge of the manhole. He glanced down — it was a metre drop, no more, but the tunnel floor was already slick with water.

"High tide's at five," Jamie sneered. "You've got about an hour before the tunnel floods."

With a final shove, he sent Rob sprawling into the hole. Rob crashed onto his knees, then fell forward, just managing to keep his face above the filthy water.

"This is for my father, Patrick," Jamie said, slamming the cover shut.

CHAPTER 50

Trent didn't know what to do with his information, so he went to DCI Linden, who'd just got back from the raid at Thomas McNamara's place.

"I think I've found something, sir," he said, hesitantly.

"So have I." The DCI peeled off his protective vest, which Trent thought looked extremely badass.

The door opened, and they both turned.

"Any news on Rob?" Jo walked in, carrying her son, Jack, her face pinched with concern. With her were Jenny and Celeste. Will had obviously updated them.

"No, but there have been a few developments." Linden looked grave. He knew who Jo was, and didn't seem to have a problem with her being there.

"What developments?" Jo and Jenny asked in unison.

"We raided Thomas McNamara's place, and there are clear signs that Jamie McNamara has been staying there."

Jenny stared at him. "I had no idea Jamie had a brother. Why didn't we pick up on this?"

"Not enough time," grumbled Will. "We'd have got there eventually, but things moved pretty fast while you were out interviewing the flatmate."

Linden briefed them on his contact in the military. "Thomas is in Lebanon, submitting articles to the *Guardian* using his brother's byline, while Jamie is here, off the grid."

"Talk about an elaborate alibi," Harry muttered.

"It's a good one," Will admitted.

"What did you find?" Jo asked, positioning Jack on her hip. He was holding a small teddy bear and seemed content just to nuzzle her sleepily.

"An entire study full of information on the Surrey Stalker case," Linden said. "He had newspaper articles stuck to the walls, photographs of the victims, crime scenes — everything he could get his hands on." He lowered his voice. "There was also a video link to Mayhew's house. It looks like he's been watching her for some time."

There was an uncomfortable pause.

"Is that how he got her password?" Jenny whispered, shocked.

"Must be. The angle of the camera is towards her desk. It would be easy enough to see what she was typing."

"At least we know how he accessed our system," Will said, exhaling.

Jo just shook her head. "It's creepy that he's been watching her."

"For some time too," Will added. "He'd have set this up long before Lucy Andrews' murder. That's how he found out about the details of the original case."

"Where's the stuff?" asked Jenny.

"It'll be here soon." He paused. "Now, I believe PC Trent has some new information too?"

Trent felt everybody's eyes on him. "Yeah, uh, thanks. So I did some digging into the McNamara family, and it turns out DCI Miller arrested Patrick McNamara, Jamie and Thomas's father, for fraud and theft about seven years ago. He was running an investment scam — promised high returns to investors but skimmed off their money for himself. A lot of his victims were pensioners who ended up losing everything. He got eight years."

Jenny blinked in surprise. "He's in prison?"

"Not exactly. He was imprisoned, but after a couple of weeks inside he was knifed in the prison yard."

"Bloody hell," Jenny murmured.

Jo narrowed her gaze. "Is that why Jamie and Thomas are doing this? Is that why they're targeting Rob?"

"And trying to discredit the department," Will added.

"I don't think Thomas is in on it," Linden said slowly. "He claims he was doing his brother a favour because Jamie had a friend's funeral to attend and didn't want to risk losing his job."

"Actually—" Trent drew the attention back to himself — "I also found out Thomas McNamara is being investigated for benefit fraud by Wandsworth Council. He probably skipped the country to avoid prosecution."

"Now that is interesting," Will murmured.

"Like father, like son," said Celeste.

"How does this help us find Rob?" Jo asked, her eyes belying how worried she was.

"And Mayhew," Jenny added.

"I was thinking about that," Trent said hesitantly, "and I may be way off base here, but I can't help feeling something's not right with Monica Burridge."

"She's dying," Jenny said flatly. "There's a lot not right with her."

"What do you mean, Trent?" Jo turned towards him.

He bit his lip. "She was acting really strangely when I went there to look for DCI Miller."

"In what way?" Linden frowned.

"Well, about that wardrobe with the false back . . . When I commented on it, she said it had been installed by her husband because he wanted to forget about his son."

"Makes sense, I suppose," Celeste said.

"That's what I thought, but then I started wondering why you'd build a false back to a wardrobe in your own bedroom. That's hardly 'forgetting'. Why not box the stuff up and store it, or get rid of it entirely? Seems odd to keep it close, even if it's hidden away."

"True," Jenny mused.

"There's something else too. When I got there, the doors at the back of the house were open."

"You mean unlocked?" Linden asked.

"No, I mean *open*. When I told Mrs Burridge, she said one of the policemen must have left them like that, but DCI Miller was the last to leave."

"Rob would never have left the doors open," Jo said quickly.

"Da-da," gurgled Jack.

"Exactly." Trent looked at them. "Mrs Burridge said he left not long after the SOCO team."

"His car wasn't there, so that's likely true," Will said.

Trent nodded. "That's why I believed her."

"You think she was lying?" Linden asked.

"I don't know. I just got a really creepy feeling in that house."

"That doesn't mean she's involved," Jenny said. "It *is* a creepy house, and she rattles around in there all by herself."

Trent hesitated. "Then there's the fact that Jamie McNamara's car didn't get picked up by any of the ANPR cameras leaving Putney. He didn't cross the river, didn't go east towards Wandsworth, didn't go up Putney Hill to the A3, which means he must have stayed in the immediate area."

"What are you saying?" Jenny frowned.

Trent spread his arms and sighed. "I don't know, exactly. I mean, the only way the suspect wouldn't have been picked up by the cameras is if he went west towards Barnes or Mortlake. There are no cameras through the Common, or along the river."

"The same route he took that night we caught him on the boat club's CCTV," whispered Celeste.

Jenny sucked in a breath. "We know one person who lives down that way."

"Who?" Jo asked, urgently.

Trent met her gaze. "Mrs Burridge."

"Could Monica Burridge and Jamie McNamara be in this together?" Linden asked, looking around at them.

"He *was* pretending to be her physiotherapist," Will reminded them.

"That's a definite link." Jenny snapped her fingers.

"It would explain how he got Simon Burridge's DNA," Harry added. "We thought he'd done it under false pretences, but maybe she handed it over willingly."

"Then why the physio ruse?" Will asked.

Harry shrugged. "Could have been a way to visit her regularly without arousing suspicion. He's supposed to be out of the country, remember."

"It's possible, I suppose." Jenny bit her lip.

"Where does she live?" Jo glanced at Trent before shifting her gaze to DCI Linden. "Can we send a team around?"

Linden ran a hand through his hair, then took a decisive breath. "Okay, let's get a team to Monica Burridge's house. If they *are* in this together, there's a good chance they're holding DCI Miller and Superintendent Mayhew there."

Jenny sprang into action, reaching for her desk phone and placing the call.

Trent felt a heaviness in his chest. "That means DCI Miller was there when I went to look for him."

"You couldn't have known," Jo said.

"We don't know if any of this is true yet," Jenny said cautiously.

Except Trent knew he was right. He couldn't explain it. It was just a deep-seated feeling he couldn't shake — what DCI Miller would call listening to his gut.

CHAPTER 51

"Felicity, can you hear me?" Rob wriggled towards the prone figure of Superintendent Mayhew. She lay on her side, bound at both her wrists and ankles. No answer, and she didn't move. A cold dread began to take hold.

"Felicity," he said more urgently.

Was she even breathing?

It was dark in the tunnel, the only light coming from the grate at the end, where water was already washing in. He squinted at her abdomen, hoping to see some movement. He thought he did, but he couldn't be sure.

Wriggling closer, he laid his head on her side. Her body was warm, and he felt her take a breath. Weak and shallow, but she was alive.

Thank God.

"Felicity!"

There was chanting from above, and he realised they were lying beneath the towpath, where thousands of spectators were gathered to watch the boat race. A surge of hope made him shout, "Help! Can anybody hear me?"

Nothing.

Foolish to expect it, really, with the lapping of the current, the raucous shouts and the drunken chants of the spectators. He ground his jaw in frustration. All those people, barely a metre above them, oblivious to the fact they were trapped down there. If only he could get to the grate.

He wriggled past an unconscious Mayhew, feeling the cold air gust through the tunnel. The water was at least two inches deep now and rising quickly.

An hour, Jamie had said, before he'd shoved him in here. That meant it must be close to four o'clock. The men's race would be starting, the crew rowing with the incoming tide during the gruelling four-mile competition.

"Help!" he yelled again, spray hitting his face. "We're down here!"

No use. He didn't know exactly where the sewer was, but he thought it was below the high tide line, camouflaged by reeds and other riverbank foliage. The only creatures who'd see them were the ducks and swans drifting past.

He studied the grate. Rusty and covered in green gunge, it didn't look sturdy. Maybe if he kicked it, he could break it and get out that way.

With much effort, and several breaks to ease his aching head, he managed to swivel around. His legs were tied with zip ties, but he could still kick, so he lashed out as hard as he could.

After five minutes, he gave up. It wouldn't budge. Not the slightest movement. Exhausted, he dropped his head and got splashed in the face, realising the water was coming in faster now. He propped himself up against the side of the tunnel.

Mayhew made a spluttering sound. The water was reaching her mouth. If she didn't wake up soon, she'd drown.

He nudged her with his knees. "Felicity, wake up!"

A soft moan in response.

"Felicity!"

She stirred, and after a few blinks, managed to open her eyes.

"Rob? What—?" She stared at him, confusion across her face. "Where are we?"

"Jamie McNamara shoved us in an old sewer tunnel." His tone was grim. "The tide's rising, and if we don't find a way out soon, we're in trouble."

"Oh my God," she said as her memory came crashing back. "I'm so sorry. I went out for coffee, and . . . he followed me. I didn't mean for—"

"I know," Rob said. "He was one step ahead of us. I didn't expect him to move so fast either."

"I only went with him so you'd have a chance to catch him," she murmured. "I thought if I went along, I might be able to get proof of his involvement. I never imagined he'd get you too."

Rob grimaced. "That wasn't my plan either. Jamie ambushed me at Monica's place."

"Monica Burridge?" Mayhew managed to sit up, bracing against the opposite wall of the tunnel.

"Yeah, she's the mastermind behind the whole thing. Revenge for her son. Somehow, she convinced Jamie to do her dirty work."

"Jesus," Mayhew whispered. "But why?"

"It's a long story, but I put his father away seven years ago. He died in prison."

She raised an eyebrow. "Retaliation for him too?"

"Yeah, they're both delusional. Jamie blames me for his father's death, while Monica is still convinced her son was innocent."

Mayhew shook her head. They sat in silence, the only sound the water lapping through the grate.

"It stinks in here," she said, as cheering erupted above them.

"Yeah." He didn't want to think about what else was in the tunnel.

Mayhew glanced up. "What the hell was that?"

"They're standing above us. We're under the towpath."

"You're kidding?" She looked around at their cylindrical prison cell. "Have you tried the grate?"

"Yeah, it doesn't move. Welded on."

"I suppose they can't hear us?"

"No, I've tried shouting."

She gave a heartfelt sigh. "Well, this isn't how I pictured going out."

He had to admire her stoicism. They were trapped in a filthy sewer, less than an hour from drowning, and she was being sarcastic. She'd been more terrified of losing her job than of dying.

"Just for the record, I don't plan on dying here." He nodded to the ties around her ankles. "How many on your wrists?"

She wriggled her arms. "One, I think."

"You might be able to break it," he said, looking around.

"How?"

"Find something sharp. A jutting nail, rusty metal, anything that'll cut through it."

She wriggled against the side of the tunnel. "It's rusty, but there's nothing sharp."

"Keep trying." No way he'd cut through three zip ties. Mayhew was their only hope.

Eventually, she stopped wriggling. "There's nothing here. It's just stinking river sediment."

Rob sighed. It had been worth a shot. "Okay."

"I've read that you can break zip ties with your feet." She manoeuvred herself until she was nearly sitting on her hands. "Except, I can't get my body through without breaking my arms."

Rob leaned his head back against the cold wall. His head still throbbed from the concussion, though Mayhew seemed clearer. Maybe the fog was lifting.

A surge of water raised the level to their thighs, partially submerging them.

"Shit." Rob peered through the grate. "We don't have much time."

Mayhew shuffled towards the grate. "Maybe if we both shout?"

"We can try." He wasn't convinced it would help.

They shuffled up until their faces were at the grille, then yelled as loud as they could. Over and over, they cried for help.

Eventually, Mayhew fell back, spent. "It's no use," she croaked. "They can't hear us."

Rob's throat burned, his head pounding like a herd of stampeding elephants. "Our only hope is that the team will rescue us."

"How will they know where we are?"

"I'm hoping they'll figure it out. This house was the last place I was seen. Someone's bound to ask her what time I left."

"She'll just make something up."

"Maybe, but Officer Hunt from the SOCO team left before me. He'll tell them I was still there."

"It's down to whether they believe her or not," she said grimly. "And they've got no reason to doubt her."

"Except she's Simon Burridge's mother, and Jamie McNamara was pretending to be her physiotherapist. That ties them together."

She studied him. "You have a lot of faith in your team, Rob."

He gave a determined nod. "I do. If anyone can figure it out, it's them."

She sighed. "But will they make it in time?" The water line had already risen by a few inches.

"We could try blocking the grate," Rob said suddenly.

"With what? There's nothing in here."

"Apart from us? Might buy us extra time."

"Good idea." She shuffled back to the grille. "Let's lean against it, try to block it with our bodies."

Rob was already sliding into position. The water pushed at his lower back, cold and unyielding. He pressed himself against the grate as tightly as he could. It wasn't comfortable, but it beat drowning.

Mayhew did the same, though she wasn't as broad as he was. Water gushed between them, around the edges. "We need to be closer together," she muttered, shifting until they were side by side, hips touching.

"It's still coming through," he hissed.

"What's at the other end of the tunnel?" she asked, peering into the darkness.

"Nothing much. It's just a hollow that leads to another grate and disappears under the house."

"Can we kick that grate out?"

"Nope, same story. Welded firm."

"Shit." She pressed back against the grille. "This is it, then. Our only chance is to hold off the water until the tide turns."

"It'll cover the entrance," Rob said. "I don't think we can keep enough out to stop us from drowning."

There was a pause as his words sank in, then Mayhew said, "Well, I'm fecking going to try."

The water climbed higher, pushing harder against them. They blocked as much as they could, but streams still flowed in around the edges. Hopefully, it wouldn't be enough to flood the tunnel.

"The tide turns quickly," Rob said, trying to boost their spirits. His back was aching, and he knew Mayhew's must be too, though she hadn't complained once. "If we can hold it off, it might drop in time."

She nodded, teeth chattering. The cold wind and icy Thames water had dropped their core temperatures dangerously. Even pressed together, they couldn't keep warm.

"At least they'll bring in McNamara." Rob attempted to focus on something else. "He'll be outed as the copycat, and the world will see he was just a wannabe."

"If they can find him," Mayhew said.

"Oh, they will. I'm sure they'll make the connection with Monica too. It's only a matter of time."

"I don't know if the department will survive this," she said quietly. "Especially not after they find out I was the one leaking case details to the killer."

"We survived Tony Sanderson," he said.

"We nearly didn't." She dropped her head, then lifted it again quickly as water splashed over her neck. She squared her shoulders.

"How did you stop them shutting us down?" he asked.

She hesitated. "What the hell. I told Matthew Gray his wife would find out about his *extra-curricular* activities if he supported the Mayor's motion. I knew the Police Commissioner had a soft spot for me, so I schmoozed him and threw stats at him. Our closure rates are pretty high."

"There is that," he acknowledged with a faint smile. "Nice move with Gray. Couldn't believe he kept his job after the Debbie Morris thing."

"You know how it is. Old boys' network. But times are changing. The new generation won't stand for it."

"I hope you're right."

The pressure was intense now — the tide forced water through the grate faster than they could hold it back. Streams flowed in above their heads, making it hard to breathe. Mayhew spluttered, gasping for air. Rob found he had to lift his head, taking quick breaths to avoid the water.

The tunnel was two-thirds full, and this surge pushed it even higher. "They'd better find us fast!" Mayhew shouted.

Above them, a frantic roar broke out. It continued building in intensity until it reached a crescendo. The men's crews were rowing past the house. If he remembered correctly, the boat race was fifteen to twenty minutes long, which meant they had another forty minutes of this. Only then would it start to recede.

"Shit," he muttered. "The armada of boats follows the crews up the river. Any minute now, we're going to get hit by a monstrous wake."

Mayhew stared straight ahead, her chin raised to stay above the water. "How much time do we have, Rob?" There wasn't so much fear in her voice as regret.

He eyed the water level, now up to their chests and his jaw tightened. "Not long."

"Oh God."

"I'm sorry, Felicity," he said. "Sorry I couldn't solve this one."

She shook her head, gasping as water hit her face. When she'd caught her breath, she said, "This one's on all of us."

CHAPTER 52

Trent heard the roar of the crowd as he got out of the squad car. It was twenty past four and judging by the sustained applause, the race must have just ended.

SCO19 had been directed to Monica Burridge's house, and if he hadn't been so anxious about DCI Miller and the Superintendent, he would have got a kick out of watching them operate. Jo had wanted to come, but DCI Linden had been firm. She was to stay at the office and wait for news. Besides, there was nobody to look after her son.

They piled out of their van in full assault gear, equipped with Heckler & Koch L104A1 baton guns and lightweight Kevlar helmets, and made for the back doors, while Trent stood back with DCI Linden, Jenny and Harry, and waited for them to gain entry. Will and Celeste had stayed with Jo, and were going through the maps, articles and files from Thomas McNamara's flat.

As it turned out, they didn't need to break the lock or smash the glass — the sliding doors were open. Again.

Trent looked around, then tapped Linden on the arm and pointed to the end of the garden. The lone, frail figure of Monica Burridge, walking stick in hand, stood facing the river. She'd obviously been watching the race. She wore a brown scarf around her shoulders, almost camouflaged beside a weeping willow.

"Arrest her," Linden snapped, holding up a hand to signal the team to wait.

Trent and Harry marched up to her. She didn't turn around, didn't even acknowledge their presence.

"I wonder who won?" she murmured, her gaze fixed on the chaotic surface of the water. A huge armada of boats had just gone past.

Trent ignored the scene and the jubilant revelry of the spectators on the towpath just yards in front of them. "Mrs Burridge, I'm arresting you on suspicion of the kidnapping of DCI Miller and Superintendent Mayhew, and the murders of Lucy Andrews and Lena Jakubowski. You have the right to remain silent . . ." He recited the words he'd learned long ago when he'd joined the police force, as Harry secured her wrists with handcuffs. She didn't resist.

They led her back towards the house, supporting her now that she didn't have the use of her stick.

"Where are DCI Miller and Superintendent Mayhew?" Linden demanded, his dark eyes flashing. There was no time to take her to the custody suite, book her and interrogate her there.

"I don't know what you mean," she said, but Trent could see in her eyes she was lying.

"They're here, aren't they?" he blurted out, earning himself a sharp look from Linden.

"Of course not."

"Yes, they are. DCI Miller was here when I asked if you'd seen him, wasn't he? That's why the doors were open — because McNamara moved the Detective Chief Inspector's car and forgot to shut it."

She tilted her head to one side. "The doors were open?"

So, she was going to play the "forgetful old woman" card, was she? Trent sniffed. That wouldn't work with him. He had her all figured out, even if the others were unsure.

"You also said your husband built the false back to the cupboard, but I checked with him, and he didn't even know it was there. That was all you, wasn't it? You kept your son's things so you could plant his DNA at the crime scene to pretend it was the Surrey Stalker."

Her gaze narrowed, and he knew he was right. "You spoke to Gerald?"

"Yes. He told me you were obsessed with getting justice for Simon. You wouldn't let it go, so he couldn't move on. That's why he left you."

Linden studied Monica Burridge. "We analysed hair follicles from your son's shaving kit," he said slowly. "They match the DNA found at the original crime scenes. If you were trying to prove that he wasn't the Surrey Stalker, you failed. All you've proven is that your son was the killer all along."

Trent arched an eyebrow. He hadn't known the DNA results were back already. Linden must have fast-tracked them.

"He was framed," she spat. "You wanted to blame someone, so you pinned that DNA on him."

"No, madam," Linden said. "The evidence is irrefutable. That was your son's DNA. He killed those women, and you got Jamie McNamara to kill Lucy Andrews and Lena Jakubowski. We know that — we've already got him in custody."

Her head jerked up at that. "You can't have."

Trent stared at Linden. Was he bluffing? McNamara was in the wind. As far as he knew, his brother's flat had been found empty.

"He confessed to everything. We've also arrested his brother, Thomas, in Lebanon. He's admitted to posing as Jamie to provide an alibi." Linden shot her a hard look. If he was bluffing, he was damn good at it. Trent was impressed. "I'm afraid the game's up. You've lost."

An evil smile spread across her face. "Have I?"

Trent's heart skipped a beat. That didn't sound good.

She glanced back at the river, the water lapping over the towpath. "It's nearly high tide. I don't think so."

What did she mean?

Linden frowned, while Trent stared at the river, his mind racing. High tide. The towpath flooded at high tide. Why would that matter? Where could she be holding Rob and Mayhew so that the high tide would affect them?

He turned to Linden. "Was there anything in those maps and plans you found at Thomas's flat that mentioned the Thames or the tides?"

"I don't know. I didn't study them. We just collected the evidence and brought it back to the office for processing."

Trent turned away. "I need to make a call."

He rang Will, who answered immediately. "Any news?"

"Not yet. Hey, did you or Celeste see anything in those files from Thomas McNamara's place about tides or the river?"

Monica Burridge bent over, coughing. Without her walking stick, she nearly fell over. Harry gripped her upper arm, supporting her.

Trent walked further away, trying to block her out. He was wise to her tricks now. She might be dying, but she had a way of using it to her advantage. Every time he was onto something, or he asked a question she didn't like, she'd be wracked by a spasm.

"Yeah, actually, we did see something. Hang on, let me ask Celeste."

"Hurry," Trent urged, his pulse racing. The tide was coming in strongly now. He could hear the wash from the rowers and the cavalcade of boats following them lapping onto the path, and the shrieks from the spectators as they tried to avoid the surge.

"There are several maps of the Victorian sewage system in Mortlake."

Sewage system?

"Any particular section?" He scanned the garden and the edge of the car park. No grates or manholes were visible.

They could be hidden under the mess of vegetation in the garden.

Will spoke slowly, like he was studying the map as he was talking. "There's a circled area that looks like it could be under Monica's house."

"That's it!"

He turned back to Linden, heart pounding. "We need to get down into the basement. They're trapped in the sewers under the house."

"You're too late," Monica Burridge wheezed.

Trent shot Linden a pleading look, and the DCI gave the command.

In a heartbeat, the SCO19 team charged through the sliding doors and entered the house, Linden on their tail. Trent and Jenny followed, while Harry stayed outside with the suspect.

Down a set of dark, creaky stairs, through a rotting wooden door, and they were in the damp, smelly basement. Within seconds they'd located the manhole cover that Trent guessed led to the sewers.

"Take it off," ordered Linden.

Two men removed it, and they were hit by a foul smell as river water lapped just inches below.

"Bloody hell," muttered Linden. "We need to get someone down there."

"How? We don't have divers," said Travis, the SCO19 team leader.

Linden began stripping off his vest. "Someone has to go in and get them. If they are down there, they're running out of air."

"Are you sure, sir?" Trent's estimation of DCI Linden had shot up. He wanted to help, but he wasn't a strong swimmer. He'd probably be more of a hindrance than a help.

"No choice."

Linden kicked off his shoes and lowered himself into the hole. Trent and Jenny watched as he took a deep breath and disappeared into the murky water.

The SCO19 team leader swore under his breath and began stripping off as well. "He's going to need help." Dumping his rifle, vest and shoes in a pile, he followed Linden down the hole.

Trent's heart was thundering so hard he thought it might burst out of his chest.

Please let them be okay.

A short while later, a head appeared, followed by the broad shoulders of the SCO19 team leader. "Give us a hand!"

Trent and a couple of the SCO19 guys bent down and lifted an unconscious Mayhew out of the tunnel. Her body was limp and unresponsive, her head lolling forward like a ragdoll's.

The team leader followed, his chest heaving as he tried to get his breath back. "Is she alive?"

They laid Mayhew on the ground. Trent quickly pressed his fingers to her neck, feeling for any sign of life. "I've got a pulse," he announced, though it was faint. "But I don't think she's breathing."

"Oh, God," Travis muttered.

Jenny interlocked her hands, positioning them over Mayhew's chest, and began chest compressions — firm, rhythmic movements, just like they'd been trained.

Trent turned back to the manhole, where Linden had finally surfaced, gasping for breath.

Yes!

He had DCI Miller in his arms, but was struggling to keep the guvnor's head above water. Together, Trent and Travis grabbed hold of Rob and hauled him out. Miller collapsed on the ground, coughing violently, spewing water as he fought for air.

Jenny was still pumping Mayhew's chest, interspersed with breathing into her mouth.

"Come on," she hissed between breaths.

Finally, after several rounds, Mayhew's body jerked, her chest heaving as she made a wet, choking sound. Jenny swiftly turned her onto her side, supporting her as a torrent of river water spilled from her mouth, her breaths coming in ragged, shuddering gasps.

"That's it," Jenny murmured, rubbing Mayhew's back as she continued coughing.

Trent's legs finally gave out, and he sank to the ground, his heart pounding from the adrenaline and sheer relief.

Holy crap, that was close.

He ran a trembling hand over his face, staring at Mayhew as she continued to cough and gasp, her breaths slowly stabilising. Then at DCI Miller, who lay sprawled nearby, clutching at his chest, still fighting to catch his breath — but alive. They'd made it in the nick of time. Another few minutes and they'd both have drowned.

He couldn't stop shaking, even as he grinned up at Linden and Travis, both sitting heavily on the wet concrete, soaked and panting. They'd done it.

They'd figured it out and got to them in time. *He'd* figured it out. A surge of pride spread through him as he reached over and clapped Jenny on the back. She looked exhausted, but her eyes were sparkling.

Both DCI Miller and the Superintendent were alive.

CHAPTER 53

Felicity was staring at the wall when Rob walked into her hospital ward. She exhaled with relief. Thank God — she was going stir-crazy. "They won't let me go," she grumbled. "I told them I had a psychopath to catch, but they were having none of it."

Rob grinned. "My team's on it, don't worry. They want to keep you in overnight. You nearly drowned."

She groaned. "How come you get to go home?"

"I was conscious when they pulled me out of the sewer. They've pumped me full of antibiotics and sent me on my way."

She sighed. They'd given her the same cocktail. God only knew what was lurking down there in the sewers, and she'd swallowed more than her fair share of it.

"What's being done to catch McNamara?"

"We've launched a full-scale manhunt. Every law enforcement agency in the country's on alert. We're monitoring all the ports and airports, the train and bus stations. We're tracking his credit cards, his phone, CCTV. He won't get far."

She wrapped her arms around herself. "I hope you're right. Jenny told me about the camera. That bastard was watching me."

"Yeah, we've got the footage. The camera was attached to the light above your desk. That's how he hacked into HOLMES."

"Fucker," she whispered. A flash of anger at how easily she'd been manipulated surged through her. He'd used her loneliness to weasel his way into her life, into her house.

She shuddered. Never again.

"It's just a matter of time," he said confidently, though she sensed he was just trying to reassure her.

"You'll keep me updated?" It was strange — since they'd nearly died together, she felt closer to him than anyone else in her life. Yet they still seemed like strangers in many ways.

"Of course." Rob glanced toward the door. "I'd better get back. Get some rest, and I'll see you at the office in a day or two."

"If I still have a job to go back to." She sighed, a weary resignation in her voice. "They'll open an inquiry into the leaked files. Once the truth gets out, it'll be my head on the block." She made a chopping motion with her hand, but the gesture was tinged with real fear.

Rob's face hardened. "Leave it with me."

She looked at him, surprised. "You can't change what happened." The fact he'd offered to help moved her more than she'd expected.

"I'm not trying to change anything. You were a victim here. He approached you, and as soon as you realised you were being played, you took control. That was a brave move, and it helped us ID him as the killer."

"It also got me kidnapped." She gave him a rueful smile.

"You let him." Rob held her gaze. "You left us an important clue — your handprint. That's what led us to his vehicle. You caught him off guard."

She studied him, realising he was building a version of events that would protect her. "You know that's not exactly what happened."

He shrugged. "That's how it looked from where I'm standing."

She looked down, biting her lip. "But . . . the files?"

"McNamara hacked into your laptop. You suspected he might try, which is why you planted fake evidence in the database to draw him out."

"You did that," she whispered, understanding dawning.

"*We* did that." He met her gaze steadily.

Felicity fought back tears. "You know they're going to question you about all of this. They'll grill you about the files, about my involvement. You're really prepared to go through that for me?"

His voice was firm. "I'd do it for anyone in my team."

She blinked, her eyes misting. "Thank you," she whispered.

He turned and made for the door. "Get some rest. They're talking about making Galbraith Acting Superintendent, God help us."

She laughed, a sound that felt strange but welcome. As he walked out, she realised something had shifted between them — something that went beyond the chain of command, something forged in the darkest of places. And maybe, just maybe, they were finally on the same side.

CHAPTER 54

Two days later

There was a burst of applause as Superintendent Mayhew walked into the office, flanked by the Deputy Commissioner and the Mayor of London, Raza Ashraf.

"Good to have you back, ma'am," Rob said, keeping a straight face.

She met his gaze with a slight smile. "Good to be back, DCI Miller."

Ashraf cleared his throat, and the chatter died down. "I'd like to formally congratulate you on apprehending Monica Burridge and finding McNamara," he began, his voice gruff. "At least we can say the streets are safer tonight."

"I'll bet that hurt to say," Jenny whispered.

Yesterday, a joint operation with Merseyside Police had led to Jamie McNamara's arrest in Liverpool. Dishevelled and looking like he'd been living rough, McNamara had been trying to stay under the radar. He'd been spotted in a discount supermarket, buying bread and a tin of baked beans. It was clear he was down to his last few quid, avoiding using bank cards to evade tracking. The arresting officer suspected McNamara had been planning to catch the ferry to Northern Ireland, hoping to disappear from there into Europe. Liverpudlian officers were currently transporting him to HMP Wandsworth, where he'd be held until trial. Now, Rob's team faced the arduous task of collating evidence for the court case, with DCI Linden's team pitching in to help, as there was a lot to get through.

The Mayor gave a curt nod. "There are still some outstanding matters concerning the leaked files from the original Stalker case, but we'll handle those in due course. For now, just know that London is grateful for your hard work."

Rob glanced across the room, meeting Mayhew's gaze briefly before she looked away.

Assistant Commissioner Matthew Gray stepped forward. "I'd like to echo the Mayor's sentiments," he said, his voice carrying across the open-plan office. "You all showed remarkable dedication under pressure. You've served the people of this city well, and you should be very proud of yourselves."

"Self-serving prat," Harry muttered.

Mayhew thanked him, her tone measured, her eyes cold. Matthew Gray studiously avoided looking at her or Rob as he concluded his speech. They both knew he'd tried to interfere with their last investigation, and even though he'd escaped disciplinary action and had avoided losing his job, he still couldn't look them in the eye.

"Good," Rob thought. "Let him squirm."

Once the dignitaries had left, Mayhew made her way over to PC Trent. "I just wanted to thank you personally. I hear you were the one who pieced it all together."

Trent flushed. "Just doing my job, ma'am."

Rob was proud of his latest recruit. Trent had shown real promise, using initiative and following his gut to dig into Monica Burridge's past and the McNamara connection. The young officer had what it takes to be a good detective.

"You know," Rob said, "now that you've completed your probation period, there's a permanent spot for you on the team, if you want it. You'd have to do your detective's course, though."

"Really? I mean, thank you, sir." His face lit up, although his gaze flickered to Celeste's, who nodded encouragingly. Rob was glad to see the two of them getting on.

"I second that recommendation," Mayhew said with a nod.

"W-Well then," he stammered, blushing. "Yes, I'd love to."

The team broke into applause, and Mayhew gave a satisfied nod before heading to her office. Rob watched her go, glad things were settling back to some version of normal.

For now, anyway.

There were still storms ahead — the inquiry, for one — but he was confident they'd weather it. The trial would be taxing, but with the evidence they'd gathered, even the best defence lawyer in London wouldn't be able to save McNamara. Between the horror of the murders and the relentless media coverage, he was sure that both McNamara and Monica Burridge would be locked away for life.

"I've just heard from the hospital," Jenny said, turning to him. "Monica Burridge collapsed in police custody and was taken to Charing Cross. She's on a ventilator. They don't expect her to last the night."

He felt no pity. After what she and McNamara had done, they both deserved whatever fate had in store for them.

Rob glanced around the office. He was giving a press conference later, along with Mayhew, who was now on the phone, pacing up and down her office in her power suit. Business as usual.

It seemed they'd been given a reprieve. As he took in the scene, a rare feeling of satisfaction settled over him. His team had pulled off something extraordinary. Superheroes, the lot of them. He knew very well the dedication, long hours and resourcefulness that had gone into getting justice for Lucy Andrews and Lena Jakubowski, and to rescue Mayhew and him. Trent had come into his own, but it had been a team effort. He couldn't be prouder of them.

He was also grateful to DCI Linden for stepping in in his absence, and apprehending Thomas McNamara in Lebanon. A surge of something close to happiness rose in his chest as he sat down at his desk. He knew they were still skating on thin ice, but, for now at least, he felt like he could breathe. He grinned to himself. The best part was seeing that snake Ashraf having to say thank you.

He thought of Jo and their wedding. They hadn't set a date yet, but now that this investigation was over, it was time. He was looking forward to married life — hell, he was looking forward to life. When he'd been trapped in the sewer, all he could think about was how much he was going to miss out on, and how badly he'd wanted to live. He was convinced that's what got him through. That's what gave him the strength to lift his head a little higher, to fight a little longer. Tonight, they'd talk properly about setting a date. The future was calling, and he was more than ready to embrace it.

Rob was about to start writing his report when his desk phone rang. He recognised the number: Dispatch.

"Hello, DCI Miller?"

"Sir, we've had a report of a pensioner in Richmond who's been burgled and badly beaten. Can your team take it? Uniform is on the scene."

They hadn't even cleared the board from their last case, but this was the life of a detective. An endless stream of crimes, victims needing justice. Rob caught DCI Linden's eye across the room and signalled to him. His colleague nodded, understanding immediately.

"One moment, let me put you through to DCI Linden. His team can take this one."

At the desk beside him, Jenny raised an eyebrow. It wasn't like him to hand over cases, but for once, he was ready to let someone else take the reins. Today, he'd finish his report, give the press release and go home to the woman he loved.

They all deserved a break, even if it was brief. They'd be back in the fray soon enough. Of that, he had no doubt.

THE END

ACKNOWLEDGEMENTS

Firstly, I'd like to extend my heartfelt thanks to the wonderful team at Joffe Books for believing in the DCI Rob Miller series and for giving me the opportunity to keep doing what I love. I'm especially grateful to Kate Lyall Grant for her advice and support, and to my editors, Kate Ballard and Siân Heap, as well as Cat Phipps, who has worked on several Rob Miller books with me including the first one, *The Thames Path Killer*.

I also want to thank author and police consultant Graham Bartlett for his invaluable guidance. His insights and procedural expertise continue to shape the authenticity and realism of my work — and I'm happy to report this novel was far less taxing on him than some of the others have been!

The idea for *The Putney Bridge Killer* took root during a Sunday walk in Richmond Park with my partner, who planted the seed of a copycat killer in my mind. I couldn't stop thinking about it and a few months later, it had blossomed into a full novel, complete with chilling twists and an unexpected outcome.

In crafting the nail-biting final scenes of this novel, I drew on the rich history of the Victorian sewer networks of the Mortlake and Barnes areas. While these locations do indeed harbour old sewers and pipes, the specific entrances and locales I describe are born of my imagination. My thanks go to the Barnes and Mortlake History Society for pointing me in the right direction; from there, I took poetic licence to weave in the subterranean secrets of these locations for dramatic effect.

I'd like to thank my mother for her unstinting love and support, willingness to listen and be a sounding board for my (often wacky) ideas, and for the endless hours of reading to ensure my manuscripts are as good as I can get them.

Finally, and most importantly, I want to express my heartfelt thanks to my amazing beta readers, reviewers, and the wonderful readers and fans of DCI Rob Miller — some of whom have supported me from my very first book. Your unwavering support means the world to me.

THE JOFFE BOOKS STORY

We began in 2014 when Jasper agreed to publish his mum's much-rejected romance novel and it became a bestseller.

Since then we've grown into the largest independent publisher in the UK. We're extremely proud to publish some of the very best writers in the world, including Joy Ellis, Faith Martin, Caro Ramsay, Helen Forrester, Simon Brett and Robert Goddard. Everyone at Joffe Books loves reading and we never forget that it all begins with the magic of an author telling a story.

We are proud to publish talented first-time authors, as well as established writers whose books we love introducing to a new generation of readers.

We won Trade Publisher of the Year at the Independent Publishing Awards in 2023 and Best Publisher Award in 2024 at the People's Book Prize. We have been shortlisted for Independent Publisher of the Year at the British Book Awards for the last five years, and were shortlisted for the Diversity and Inclusivity Award at the 2022 Independent Publishing Awards. In 2023 we were shortlisted for Publisher of the Year at the RNA Industry Awards, and in 2024 we were shortlisted at the CWA Daggers for the Best Crime and Mystery Publisher.

We built this company with your help, and we love to hear from you, so please email us about absolutely anything bookish at feedback@joffebooks.com.

If you want to receive free books every Friday and hear about all our new releases, join our mailing list here: www.joffebooks.com/freebooks.

And when you tell your friends about us, just remember: it's pronounced Joffe as in coffee or toffee!